The Thr

Book 3
in the
Struggle for a Crown Series
By
Griff Hosker

Published by Sword Books Ltd 2019

Copyright ©Griff Hosker First Edition

The author has asserted their moral right under the Copyright, Designs and Patents Act, 1988, to be identified as the author of this work.
All Rights Reserved. No part of this publication may be reproduced, copied, stored in a retrieval system, or transmitted, in any form or by any means, without the prior written consent of the copyright holder, nor be otherwise circulated in any form of binding or cover other than that in which it is published and without a similar condition being imposed on the subsequent purchaser.
A CIP catalogue record for this title is available from the British Library.

Cover by Design for Writers

Historical Characters

- King Richard II of England and his wife Queen Anne of Bohemia
- Henry Bolingbroke, Earl of Northampton, Earl of Derby, Duke of Hereford
- Henry of Monmouth-son of Henry Bolingbroke
- John of Gaunt, Henry's father and uncle to the King: Pretender to the throne of Castile, Duke of Lancaster, Duke of Aquitaine
- Edmund of Langley, Duke of York, the King's uncle
- Edward, Earl of Rutland, son of Edmund Langley
- Henry Percy- Earl of Northumberland
- Sir Henry Percy- Harry Hotspur
- King Jogaila of Poland
- Thomas Mowbray- Earl of Nottingham, Duke of Norfolk
- Cathal mac Ruaidrí Ó Conchobair, King of Connaught
- Thomas of Woodstock, Duke of Gloucester, the King's uncle
- King Charles VI of France (Charles the Mad)
- Maelsechlainn Ó Cellaigh, King of Uí Maine

Part One
The Baltic Crusade

Chapter 1

I was now Sir William of Stony Stratford. When first given the manor I had been a gentleman but now I had been knighted. I had been elevated so much that I could scarce believe it. I had been an urchin, the child of a camp follower and a drunken warrior, who followed the Free Companies and now I was a knight. I knew none who had made this journey. Henry Bolingbroke, the Earl of Northampton and Derby, had been the one to dub me and he had promised me another manor but, as yet, I had not been told where it was. I did not mind. I was happy with my tiny manor for my wife, Eleanor, was a good manager of the land and we lived well. For my own part I was just pleased to be away from the struggle for power. I had had enough of living cheek by jowl with conspiracies and plots when I had lived at court. I had served both King Richard and his rival Henry Bolingbroke. I had never betrayed either man but I had trodden a difficult path to do so. I was just happy to have time with my children: Tom, Alice and Harry.

For King Richard the period after the Battle of Radcot Bridge was a humiliating time. Robert de Vere, the Duke of Oxford and a malignant influence on the King, had fled England and his close friend Sir Simon Burley had been executed. De La Pole, who had been his Chancellor and hated by all, had also fled to Europe. The King was alone except for his wife, Anne of Bohemia. Parliament had taken away some of the King's powers and was, effectively, ruled by those who sought to curb King Richard. Despite that, now that Robert de Vere was out of the way, King Richard became a better man and a better king. That was down to his wife, Anne. She was a good influence. He was happy with her and she understood the complicated man that was King Richard. He did not need me. Had he sent for me I would have gone to his side for I had sworn an oath to his father. He did not send for me and I stayed in my manor. I was no farmer and my wife did not expect me to be one. I had grown up with the Free Companies and I was a warrior.

For three years I had peace and I became a man of leisure. However, I had grown up a man of war and so, each day, I practised my art. I helped to make John, now my squire, into a warrior who might, one day, become a knight. I had learned how to do so with Sir Henry of Stratford. His grandfather had assumed I knew what was necessary. I just trained John as I had trained Henry. That was the way that Red Ralph and Old Tom had taught me to be a warrior when I had been in the Blue Company. I knew nothing of playing the rote or the laws of chivalry. Instead, I knew how to kill as quickly and efficiently as possible. I knew how to take treasure from a battlefield and I knew how to survive. King Richard had also been taught by me as had Henry Bolingbroke. The difference was that they also learned the courtly skills a knight needed. Perhaps that was why I was not invited to court or to dine with the lords of the County. I did not care that the local nobles ostracised me. Only Sir Henry invited me to dine and that was not above twice a year.

Thanks to the prosperity of the land and the skills of my wife we prospered. It meant I could continue to pay my handful of archers and men at arms. They were a luxury but so long as we prospered then I paid them and my wife did not mind. Sir Henry used us to keep the forests clear of bandits and there was pay for that. My wife's skills were such that she purchased another manor from Sir Henry at Whittlebury to the north west of us. The manor had been run down as the previous lord of the manor, Sir Roger, had drunk any profits which the manor produced. He died without an heir and Sir Henry, with King Richard's permission, sold it to us.

When my men and I were not hunting bandits, we were training my eldest son, Tom. He had the best of teachers; my men at arms and archers. I had never learned the bow but Tom did. He would, when he became a man, be bigger and stronger than me. When he grew, he would be a far better archer than I was and the equal of me as a swordsman. Life might have gone on that way for some time had not two things happened at the same time. The first was a bad summer producing a disastrous harvest. Secondly, the Earl of Northampton, Henry Bolingbroke, decided to go on crusade. He did not choose the Holy Land but he joined the Teutonic knights in their war against the pagans in Lithuania.

The poor harvest occurred first and my wife reacted quickly. "We have too many expenses, husband. Your men at arms and archers must do without pay and work the fields. And you must sell your war horses."

I shook my head, "Neither of those events will happen, my love. There is no war at the moment. Since the battle of Otterburn, the northern border has been quiet. If we sold the horses, we would not receive their true value. You would not wish us to lose money, would you?"

She set her jaw, "We have to cut costs somehow."

"Then let me try to find work for my men and I. There may be lords abroad who need swords for hire."

"You would leave me?"

I sighed. Arguing with women was an impossible task. They altered their defence before you had countered their first argument. "No, my love, I would save you expense and make money. If you do not have to pay my men will the family survive?"

She nodded, "Yes, but not in the manner to which we are accustomed."

"When I came back here you were a pauper and I was a sword for hire. Do not forget that." She took my hand and kissed it. It was the nearest she would come to an apology. "I will leave tomorrow and speak with Sir Henry."

"Very well." She shook here head. "This is your fault for you do not go to church often enough and God is punishing you!"

I did not point out that God was also punishing many people who did go to church. I merely nodded and said, "Yes dear."

I went to see my men. I was honest and explained the situation. I told them to prepare to leave within a sennight. Roger of Chester was my most senior man. "I think that we will have to travel abroad, lord. Since the troubles England is at peace. Castile again? John of Gaunt always needs men."

I nodded, "Aye we could, I suppose."

My squire, John, smiled, "You do not seem keen, lord."

"Nor am I. I do not think that it is a war that he can win."

Harold Four Fingers shrugged, "So long as we get to fight, lord, then there will be profit. None of us here care what happens in Castile. If it was England then we would worry."

While we prepared weapons, we spoke of the merits of fighting abroad compared with England. I was unique. I knew of no other knight who had come from such humble origins as I. It meant I could speak the language of my men. Unlike many knights I had no lofty ideals. I was a warrior. I fought for pay. If it was a good cause then that was something to be celebrated. I had been trained to be a good one. That was why I had been selected to train both King Richard and the Earl of Northampton.

Tom had been listening to all of this, "And do I get to come with you, father?" I was silent for I was conflicted. Part of me wished to take him but another part feared for his life. Campaign was not the place for someone as young as my son. My men and I had done much work with him but he was still not ready. "I have seen almost seven summers, father. When you were my age you were with the Free Companies in Gascony."

I saw my men grinning. They liked Tom and wanted him with me.

"The difference is, young Thomas of Stony Stratford, that I was born in a ditch and had endured three years of tramping behind the army when I was your age. I knew how to scavenge and how to catch, gut, skin and cook a rat. You just have to wait for one of the servants to bring you a platter of meat!"

He was not put off by my harsh comments, "Then this might be a good time to learn."

"The point is moot as we do not have an employer as yet and do not know who will hire our swords or where we shall go. Until then you can help us to prepare."

I had given him hope and he helped John to pack my armour in the chest. I wore more armour than the men of the Free Companies. Red Ralph and Old Tom had worn mail shirts with just a breastplate and a sallet on their heads. Even that was more than most sergeants at arms wore. I had mail on my forearms, legs, thighs and hands as well as my mail shirt and coif. I wore less mail than most knights. I preferred the freedom of movement. My helmet was an open bascinet. Most wore a helmet with a visor. So long as I had my skills and my flexibility, I would continue to wear the minimum of armour. I had a mail hood for my horse but I just used a caparison rather than a full mail coat. I had sold my best war horses in Castile. The ones I had were coursers. They were good warhorses but neither as expensive nor as aggressive as a destrier. A destrier could cost as much as a small farm and all the attendant animals. It was a waste for something that might be used once or twice every few years.

That evening, as we ate, Tom asked me again if he might come. He did so deliberately for he wanted his mother to hear the question. For a child my son was clever in a cunning sort of way. He hoped that she would forbid it and that would make me all the more determined to take him. Eleanor was also clever and she caught my eye and winked at me, "I am sure that your father does not want to be encumbered by someone who still needed his breeks changing not that long ago but if he wishes to nursemaid you then, of course, you may go. It would be one less mouth for me to feed here and, with the poor harvest, there will be less food for all of us. This way I can fatten up Alice, and Harry."

There was the inevitable sibling rivalry between all of my children and I saw Tom chew his lip. He remained silent as he pondered his next move.

After they had gone to bed I said, "Roger and my men wondered if we might seek an employer in Castile."

"You brought good treasure home the last time."

"The trouble is that involves expense. John of Gaunt is in Castile. We would have to pay passage on a ship and that is not cheap."

The thought of paying money out which would not be replaced for half a year did not appeal. "Why not see his son, the Earl of Northampton? He might put up the coin. Or Sir Henry?"

"Sir Henry has his own manors to run."

"Yet he is rich and he has a debt of honour to you. You risked all to save his grandparents."

"And in that I failed. Their deaths were upon me. His grandfather did not outlive his wife by much." I was a proud man and I would not seek coin from Sir Henry. I had been brought up to rely on myself and I would continue to do so. I would ask him if he knew of any lord who wished to hire us but I would not take his charity.

The next morning, we were just preparing to ride to Stratford when we heard hooves galloping down the cobbled track from the village. We stopped what we were doing. It was a pair of mounted men. They were cloaked and hooded. I had seen enough treachery in my time to be wary and so my hand slipped to my sword's hilt. When they reined in, I relaxed. I recognised the livery. They came from Henry Bolingbroke. It was one of his squires, Edward, and a servant. I had fought with Edward at the Battle of Radcot Bridge and I liked the squire. I was surprised that he had yet to attain his spurs. He bowed, "Sir William, I am asked to take you to Monmouth Castle."

"The Earl has need of me?"

"I believe so, lord. I was asked to fetch you forthwith."

I smiled, "That sounds like the Earl. Your master likes to command, does he not?"

Edward nodded and grinned, "Aye, Sir William. He does."

"And have you not yet been given your promised spurs?"

I saw the disappointment in his eyes. He shrugged, "When Richard was knighted, two years since, I had hopes but since Radcot Bridge there has been no need."

I nodded, "Then get inside. Tom, ask the servants to feed Master Edward and his servant. John, saddle horses for us and for our guests." We had good horses and the two which had just ridden in looked lathered.

"Aye lord,"

"Roger, I just need you and David of Welshpool to accompany me. Have Alan of the Wood take command of the rest. I think that this summons may provide us with work!" Stephen the Tracker had been the one who had formerly commanded my archers but Alan of the Wood had gradually taken over. Stephen enjoyed hunting in my woods. He was more of a solitary figure these days. Alan had a wife and seemed more assured. The two were great friends. They behaved differently to knights. I had seen knights advanced and those who had been the same rank resented them. That was not the way with the Free Companies. It was not my way. I had a few men but we lived together in harmony. I trusted them and they trusted me. There were many nobles who wished for such mutual loyalty.

When I went in to my hall to tell Eleanor of my plans Tom asked, "Can I come with you, father? This is not war and I should like to see the land beyond this tiny hamlet."

I looked at Eleanor who smiled, "For me you can, but it is your father who will have to worry about you falling from the back of a horse. He will have to mend your broken coxcomb."

I realised it would not hurt and it might take some of the sting from my refusal to take him to war with me. "Aye, but John will have to watch you. I cannot."

"I will go and prepare my mount!" He raced from my hall.

It was over ninety miles to Monmouth. We broke our journey in Tewkesbury. It was as we ate that I learned more about the Earl and his life since Radcot Bridge. Edward was guarded in his comments for he was loyal but I discovered that Henry Bolingbroke had spent the last years building political alliances and powerful friends. We were weary as we approached the western bastion of the Welsh Marches. I had never seen Monmouth Castle before but as we approached I realised that it was as big as Windsor. It was a fortress against the Welsh. They had been quiet for some time but even if they rose, I doubted that they had either the men or the siege engines to reduce it. The Earl was hunting when we arrived in the early afternoon. My men went to the stables with the horses and then they sought out the warrior hall. The steward had a chamber for myself, my squire and my son. For Tom this was an experience beyond his wildest dreams. He was surrounded by armed, mailed men and he was in a castle. He was so excited that he was speechless. For my part this was like a visit back to a former life. When I had commanded King Richard's guards this had been commonplace. John and I were seasoned campaigners. Even though we were in a castle we did as we would if we were in a tent or a hovel. We arranged our clothes so that they were ready to hand. We hung our swords and daggers. We washed and we changed from travelling clothes and then we prepared to descend to the Great Hall.

"Tom, you should just watch and listen. You are not even a page. You are here because you asked to come. You will be bored for we will be talking of matters which do not interest you. If you are tired then John will take you to bed. There will be no mother to tuck you in!" Even as I spoke to him, I realised this was a good thing. He had an idea that when I was not at home, I led an exciting life. I hoped that the boredom might make him reconsider his request to come to war with me.

Henry Bolingbroke was now a man grown with children. He had been given more manors by his cousin King Richard and that had ended, temporarily at least, the animosity and rivalry between them. I had spoken with Henry Bolingbroke during the campaign which led to the battle of Radcot Bridge. He still had ambitions to be King but so long as Richard had no children then that dream was still possible. Henry was a patient and calculating man. He believed that King Richard had flaws in his character which would bring about his own downfall and Henry was ready to pick up the pieces when that happened.

When he strode into his hall surrounded by his household knights, I saw a confident leader. He had been a youth when I had first met him and now, he had fought and won battles. He was assured and he was hungry for more. His face broke into a smile when he saw me and John. He had fought alongside us both. "William! You came! I hoped you would!"

That was a little disingenuous of him. He was, as the Earl of Northampton, my liege lord. When he requested, I obeyed. That was the system. "Of course, my lord."

He put his arm around me. He had grown so much that he was almost as big as I was. "What say you to a foreign war?"

"Castile, my lord?"

He shook his head, "My father has incompetent men around him and I would not have my name associated with failure. No, William, I sail to the Baltic. The Teutonic Knights have a holy crusade against the pagan Lithuanians." He pointed to a knight who wore a wine tunic with a black cross. "That is an emissary from the Grand Duke of Lithuania, Alexander Vitautus. He is Frederick von Plettenburg, a Teutonic knight. They are ridding that land of the last pagans in Europe. This is a chance for glory and to make a name for myself." Henry was a clever man and he knew how to read other's minds. "You need no glory and so, you ask yourself, why should you come?"

I smiled, "You are my liege lord."

"And this would involve more than forty days campaigning. I am no fool. You and your men are worth the extra payment to keep you six months. I would pay you and your men for their service. I would pay you two hundred English pounds. Half now and half when we return in six months."

That was a small fortune! I pictured my wife's face when I told her.

"Six months, lord?"

"I intend to make a name for myself. If I cannot do it in six months then I will never do it."

"And horses, lord?" Some lords expected men at arms and knights to bear the expense of a horse lost in war.

"I will make good any losses when we return to England."

"Then I am your man. When do we leave?"

"You have a month to ready your company and to bring them to Hart-le-pool. It is in Durham. We sail from there. It will be the shortest voyage and do the least harm to the horses." He nodded to the Teutonic knight, "Speak with him. You are the warrior. The knights who follow me are brave enough but they are young and you have a mind for the battlefield. Discover all that you can before we reach the north. You will find Sir Frederick an interesting man."

I sat next to Frederick von Plettenburg. There was no place for my squire or my son and they ate with the warriors. John did not mind but I thought Tom would burst into tears. In light of what the Teutonic knight later told me I was pleased that they were absent.

"The Lithuanian pagans are vile and abominable. If they capture a knight then they tie him to his horse and burn them both alive. They plant bodies on spears and do other things which are so despicable that they do not bear utterance."

Despite his own words, while we ate he gave me savage examples of the men we would be fighting. They seemed as fanatical as the followers of Islam. This crusade, however, looked as though it might stand a chance of success for the King of Poland, Jogaila, had joined forces with the Grand Duke of Lithuania. Both were sworn enemies but it appeared, from the knight's words, that they had put aside their differences to finally rid Lithuania of the last of the pagans. The cynic in me wondered what would happen when the pagans were eliminated. Would the two fight over the carcass that would be Lithuania? I did not worry about that for the money we would be paid was more than enough to stave off disaster. I would be able to give Eleanor ninety pounds immediately and the promise of the rest would ease her mind.

Henry Bolingbroke came over to me before he retired for the night. "I know you will leave early but come and speak with me before you do. You trained me well, Will Strongstaff, I too am an early riser." He waved a dismissive hand at his household knights all of whom were enjoying a good drink. "These young bloods will have thick heads and bleary eyes on the morrow."

Despite the lateness of the hour, Tom was still awake when I entered the chamber. John looked apologetic, "I tried to get him to sleep, lord, but…"

I smiled. Since I had been at home, I had experienced the difficulty of getting a child to sleep. Eleanor managed it easily but they knew how to manipulate me. "Never fear John, it is not your fault. You get to bed and I will deal with this rebel."

"I am no rebel father!"

"And this is no way to get me to take you to war." I had already decided that the pagans of Lithuania were too dangerous to risk my son. "You have to learn to obey all those above you and that includes John."

He lowered his voice, "But he is just a squire!"

I lowered my voice, "Aye and you are beneath him, Roger of Chester and all of my men at arms and archers." I rubbed my chin, "I suppose that Cedric the Swineherd might take orders from you, in the fullness of time, but… let us see. So, why did you want to wait up to see me?"

"Where are you going to fight?"

I was impressed by the speed of his mind. I was also aware that John was listening too, "I take my men on crusade to the Baltic. It is in the north and is a cold and inhospitable place."

"And I go too?"

I shook my head and kissed his forehead, "No, for you are too young. The work will be hard and I need John to watch my back and not wipe the snotty nose of my son!" I saw his disappointment. "Tom, I will be away for six months. While I am away you eat, you grow, you practise and when I return, if you have grown enough, then I will take you the next time I travel to war." I lifted his chin so that I could see his eyes, "Good enough?"

He gave me a wan smile, "Aye father and I will work!"

I rose early and while John and Tom packed our bags I went down to meet with Henry. He was speaking with the Teutonic knight. As I approached the Earl waved away the knight. "Sit, William. Von Plettengburg's words did not put fear in your heart?"

"If I thought these savages could capture me then I might be afeared. I have good men and we have mail. From what the knight told me these savages are fanatic but do not wear mail."

He smiled, "Good. It is why I have you here now and not my young bloods. They blanched when he told them. They will fight but they do not have your confidence. I hope that your experience will put steel in their backs."

"I will try."

"Will, do not put yourself down. You are a knight. I elevated you. None of my men are bannerets. All are equal. When we return, I hope to give you the manor I promised you and with it shall come a banner."

A banner meant a larger manor with more coin. However, I would not anticipate a quick reward. I had waited some time for the knighthood. Both King Richard and the Earl, his cousin, had promised me a knighthood but it had been as a lure to keep me loyal.

"I have a manor in mind, Weedon, not far from my castle at Northampton. There is no lord there yet for the village belongs to a monastery in Normandy." He smiled, "You will be pleased to know that I have spoken to my cousin, the King, about this and he is in agreement. Because there is no lord of the manor, we cannot use the men of the village to fight for us. We cannot tax them for they answer to the Abbot of Bec-Hellouin. As you can imagine that does not sit well with either myself or the King. We have a plan which should bring the manor back into English hands. The King has his clerks creating the legal documents so that when we return you will be able to build a hall there and we can take the coin that goes to France for our coffers."

"Will the Abbot not object?"

"They can object. They own the village and the properties but not the people. My cousin and his wife are clever. This plan was conceived by Queen Anne. We use our minds to take what should be ours. I benefit as does the King." He smiled at me. "You should be pleased. The two youths you trained are now working together."

"I am pleased, lord, but I am no farmer."

"He laughed, "Farming? I should think not! Any man can be a farmer. You are a warrior and you will take this village and make it ours once more. There are more than fifty houses and that means they have a hundred men, at the very least. You will train them so that in times of war we can use them. Up to now they have tilled their fields and enjoyed the peace of England. There is a price to peace and they must begin to pay it." He handed me a parchment. "This gives you the authority to build a manor house. The King does not wish a castle but you are allowed to make the hall defensible. When we return then the documents for you to tax the people will be in place. You will need a clerk and the King will find one for you. He will be in place at my castle when we return. Your star is rising William. The son of a sword for hire is destined for greatness and the King and I will be your sponsors!"

Chapter 2

When I gave Eleanor the ninety pounds and told her of Weedon I thought she would burst. "I have married the best of husbands! When all seems dark, he comes back with a golden goose!"

I held up my hand, "Let us not spend the money just yet. The King has to put the legal niceties in place first. I have, first, to go to war."

She nodded, "And it gives me six months to find a reeve who can run these farms here at Stony Stratford. I have a man in mind! "Husband," she embraced me, "we will build a hall so fine that the King and Queen themselves could stay with us!" From then, until the time we left, my wife was like a whirlwind. She was up before me and retired after me. She had had everything taken from her and she would not let that happen again. She saw, in this, the hand of God and she would not spurn his generosity.

I had much to do. It would take upwards of seven days to travel the two hundred miles to the port on the north east coast of England. I was honest with John and my men. I told them of the pagans and they were philosophical about the matter.

Stephen the Tracker spoke for them all, "We are doing God's work and he will give strength to our arms, lord. I fear no hairy arsed barbarian. With our arrows and your men at arms we will break their spirits and their bodies so that they will not get close enough to us to burn us on our horses!"

Roger and my men were all of the same opinion. They were Englishmen and it was the pagans who had to fear us. They busied themselves carefully packing their weapons. My archers made as many arrows as they could and bought spare bow strings. They carried spare heads and would fit them to the shaft when they saw our enemies. They had three main types. There was the heavy war bodkin, the needle bodkin and the swallowtail. If we were fighting men without mail then they would use the swallow tail. It made a terrible wound which would bleed. My men at arms all prepared the two or three weapons each of them would take. They chose the horses from my stable. I would take a palfrey, Blaze, as well as my courser, Jack. We had ten sumpters for our baggage. Henry Bolingbroke either had to have greater financial resources than I thought or he hoped that we would profit in the crusade for the cost of the ships would be exorbitant.

I planned our route carefully. We could pass by Northampton on the first day and that would enable me to pass through Weedon. It was but a slight detour north. We would spend our first night ay Medeltone Mowbray. I vaguely knew the lord of the manor there. He had been at the Battle of Radcot Bridge. Then we would push on to Ollerton. I knew no one there but the alternative was to take a deviation and head east to Lincoln and stay with Old Tom. I knew not what disruption we might find on the old Roman Road North and so I would forego that pleasure. Our next stop would be York. I hoped to see Peter the Priest. I hoped he still lived for he had, along with Red Ralph, made me the man I was. After that, I was in unknown territory. The Sherriff of York was a political man, Sir James Pickering was no friend of the King, for he had been Speaker of the House and participated in the persecution of the King's friends. He was, however, a friend of Henry Bolingbroke. I would be welcomed and I would be able to receive assistance to travel the last sixty odd miles to Hart-le-pool.

Tom ran off the day we left. He was angry that he would not be able to come. He had promised that he would work hard to become big enough but he was still a child. My decision not to take him was vindicated. "Fear not, husband. He will return and I will counsel him!" My wife was practical. From her there were no tears. She had much to do for we had a new manor and when I returned then she would move the family there. That needed preparation. She would deal with Tom in her own inimitable style.

Weedon was but a few hours from my home. It was a neat village. It looked to be a number of small holdings with a large garth which looked like a church farm. For a village it had a fine church with a bell tower. The house attached to the church was a grand one. It was bigger than the one at Stony Stratford and we would not need to build a hall. The road through the village was cobbled. It was prosperous. As we watered our horses at the trough the priest and his assistant came from the church to speak to me. One looked well fed to the point of corpulence while the other was lean and young.

The corpulent priest addressed me, "Can we help you, my lord?"

I smiled, "We serve the Earl of Northampton and we are travelling north on his business. We stopped to water our horses."

"This village belongs to the Abbey of Bec in Normandy, lord. It is not the Earl of Northampton's fief." The priest sounded almost indignant that we should be using his water. I noticed that he had a French accent.

I nodded amiably as Blaze slurped more water, "And yet this is English water come from a village in England. Do you deny us the right to water?"

I saw the first flicker of fear in the priest's eyes, "No, lord. You are more than welcome to the water. We are a Christian community. And, as you say, you are passing through." He made the sign of the cross, "Go with God."

"Thank you, father." I did not tell him our purpose. He was in for a rude shock when the King's edict reached him. His village was about to become part of England once more. We headed up the road for the long journey to York.

I did not know York well. We were admitted through the gates of the city and we headed towards the keep. It was on a high mound overlooking the river. The tower was a round donjon and it now looked old fashioned but the walls around the city were amongst the strongest I had ever seen. Henry Bolingbroke had given me a parchment with his seal and that of the Bishop of Hereford. It asked all churchmen and lords to grants us accommodation as we were doing the Lord's work. The Sherriff was in London and the castellan was happy to accommodate us. There were just eighteen of us for we had not brought servants.

As the horses were taken away, I said, "An old comrade of mine, Peter the Priest, came to York some twelve years since. Have you heard of him?"

He rubbed his chin, "The name Peter sounds familiar. There is a Peter who runs an alms house for maimed warriors. It is on this side of the river by the Lendel Bridge."

I left Roger to see to my men and took John up the river to the alms house. There were many alms houses in large cities and towns. Run by churches, they were for the poor and the old. They were not particularly pleasant places to live but the people who lived in them faced either starvation on the streets or a roof over their head and gruel twice a day. The alms house was not large. It was also close to the river. I knew that the Ouse flooded frequently. As we neared the door, it opened and I saw Peter the Priest. I recognised him straight away. He had aged and lost all of his hair but he still had the build of a warrior. He wore a simple brown shift. I watched as he emptied a bucket of what looked like night soil into the river.

He did not hear me approach, "The Peter the Priest I knew would have walked downstream to do that! How things have changed!"

He turned and put down the bucket. He wiped his hands on his shift, "Will!" I saw his eyes pass up and down me. He saw the spurs and bowed, "My lord!"

I walked up to him and embraced him, "None of that. I am still the same Will you trained to be a warrior!" I spread my arms, "I see you are now doing God's work."

He nodded, "I would invite you in but a man died yesterday and the smell of death still hangs on the air." He looked at John.

I said, "This is John, my squire. John, this is Peter the Priest, one of the best warriors with whom I ever fought."

"Those days are long gone."

The sun was setting, "Can you spare some time to talk to an old friend?"

He nodded, "Aye but first I must feed my charges. There is an ale house yonder, it is called 'The Saddle'. The landlord, Alf, is an old soldier. He serves good ale and hearty food."

"Then we will hie hither and wait you."

The landlord was, indeed, an old soldier. He had lost all of the fingers on his left hand in some long forgotten battle and the scar down his face ruined any looks he might have once had but he seemed happy enough and I chatted to him as we awaited Peter. I learned that Peter lived like a Celtic priest. He had spent all of his money from his days as a soldier to build the alms house and relied on the charity of locals to keep it going. Alf shook his head, "He gets nothing from the church or the city. It is a shame." He held up his maimed hand, "If I had lost my whole hand, I might need old Peter's help. I do what I can for him, my lord. It is little enough but any food which is left over goes to him and we give him the slops from the ale. I will fetch food when Peter arrives."

I pushed over some coins, "Here is for the food and the ale and a little more to keep him in ale for a while after I leave. When I return, I will fetch some more."

"Return, lord?"

I nodded, "We are bound on crusade to the Baltic."

He tried to push the coins back to me, "Then this will be free. You do God's work!"

I shook my head, "We are paid and I will take no man's charity. Take it Alf, lest you offend me."

"Aye, lord. You are a rarity. Most knights take what they can and then some more. I can see that Peter had an effect on you too."

Peter looked weary when he entered and I saw that, close up, he was a little thinner than he had once been. His face lit up in a smile as we toasted each other. The food was brought and he forced me to tell him of my life since we had parted. Every so often he would stop eating and clutch his cross. He would shake his head and say, "The Good Lord works in a mysterious way."

When I had finished and told him of my quest he nodded approvingly, "That is good. You do God's work and repay him for the bounty he has brought you."

"And you Peter, are you happy?"

He beamed, "Never more so. The men to whom I minister have all been warriors. Many were from the Free Companies. I have tended some alongside whom we fought. It is a rewarding life although hard at times."

I took out my purse. I had kept ten pounds for expenses. I counted out five of them, "Here, this is half my purse. Take it for your work."

He shook his head, "I cannot take such a princely sum, Will. This would pay for the alms house for six months!"

"We go to war and our food and such are taken care of by the Earl of Northampton, Henry Bolingbroke. There will be more and you know that we will profit from war."

He nodded and slid the purse over to his side of the table, "Aye, Will, you were made for war. I am just pleased that you fight for a good cause."

"Amen to that, old friend. And speaking of old friends. Do you see much of Red Ralph? He lives not far from here at Middleham."

"I saw him some years ago. He came to York with his wife, son and daughter. He has done well. He farms and raises horses."

"I know not the land. Is it far from our route?"

"If you wish to visit with him then it will add just a day to your journey."

I looked at John and he nodded, "We have not spent as much time as we thought, lord, on the journey thus far. We can visit your friend and still reach the muster two days early."

"Then it is decided. We will travel to Middleham."

It had been good to see Peter. When I spoke with the castellan, I pointed out the good work which my friend was doing. He shrugged, "If we fed all of the poor and cared for all the needy then we would impoverish ourselves. The Sherriff does what he can."

I resolved, as we headed north and west, to speak with the Queen. She had a kind heart and I was sure that she would wish us to do something for those who had nothing. If I did not see her then I would send coin to him.

Peter had given us good directions to my friend's farm. It was on the road north out of the village where his farm was found. He could see the standard on the castle of Middleham from his farm but no more. It was secluded. The road led us through the dales. There were woods but much of the land had been cleared as pasture for sheep, cattle and horses. Red Ralph had always enjoyed working with horses. I was pleased that he had found something to occupy him that was worthwhile.

We did not have to pass close to the castle but we saw it. I knew that Ralph Neville was not at home for no standard flew. His father had recently died and he was in London to settle the estate. The Nevilles, along with the Percys, were the powerful family here in the north east. I knew that the Percy family had ambitions and were viewed with suspicion by both the King and his cousin, Henry Bolingbroke. That had been the world I had left. I saw the horses in the pasture before I saw the farm. Ralph had cobbled his yard and when we clattered in it brought all from the small hall he had built. I do not think he recognised me at first for I wore my new livery and I saw him squinting into the sun. I dismounted and, in the shadow of Blaze, he recognised me.

"Will! Is it really you?" He saw my spurs, "And a knight! Has the world gone mad?"

I laughed, "Probably!" Sweeping a hand around I said, "And you have done well."

He nodded and, turning, shouted, "Wife we have guests. You will stay the night, will you not?"

"We are bound for Hart-le-pool where we take ship."

"Then the delay will not harm you. I will loan you some horses and I will come with you. With a change of animals, we can do the journey in one day. I have much to ask you!"

In truth, I wanted to speak with my mentor. He, along with Peter, had been the reason I became the warrior I was. "Very well. Roger, the men can sleep in the barn. See to the horses."

"Aye, lord!"

Ralph nodded at them as they passed us, "Your own company eh? Are they good men?"

"Old Tom had a hand in picking most of them. What do you think?"

"Then they will do! It is good to see you! Come!"

I saw a youth of about eleven summers hovering close by. I took it to be one of Ralph's children. He looked to be muscled for one so young and he had his father's look. Red Ralph himself had aged. He had retained his hair but it was thinner and it was white. He still had the walnut coloured skin of a man who spent his life outdoors."

"This is my wife, Mary. I am a lucky man." I saw that Mary was about my age. That made sense for he had children. Had he married someone his own age then that would have been unlikely. "Ralph, go and fetch your brothers and sisters. Let me introduce them to Sir William...?" He looked at me for my appellation.

"Strongstaff!"

"A good name and it suits you." He gestured to a seat. The room was plainly furnished but the table and chairs had been well made. The pot jug in the centre looked to have been locally produced and the beakers were home made of wood turned, no doubt, on a lathe which Ralph must have made. "Sit, and this is your squire?"

"Aye, John. He is a good squire."

Ralph gave John a serious and penetrating look. "Look after this knight, John. He is a real hero. He was a hero when he was even younger than my youngest son, Tom!"

"I will, sir."

Ralph laughed, "I am no sir but I thank you for the compliment." His son arrived with another boy and three girls. "This is Ralph my eldest. Tom my youngest son and the girls are Mary, Isabelle and Maud. Say hello, children, to Sir William Strongstaff. He is a knight and he is my friend!"

"Good day, Sir William," they chorused.

"Now go and help your mother." He poured me some ale and then raised his beaker. "To the Blue Company."

"The Blue Company."

"Now tell me all for your journey is so remarkable that I can scarcely believe I am awake."

His family had joined us and food had been served by the time I had finished. Even his youngest daughter, Maud, seemed rapt in the tale. The food was plain fare: a rabbit stew enriched with the animals' blood and filled with home grown vegetables but it was comforting food and I enjoyed it. As we finished both the stew and the tale John stood, "Thank you Mistress Mary, that food reminded me of the food my mother cooks but now I must go and see to our men. I will return when I have done."

Mistress Mary nodded, "I will keep your posset for you." She ladled out the pudding.

Red Ralph nodded towards him as he left, "Seems like a good lad."

"He is the son of one of the farmers in my manor. He did not wish to farm and I took him on. When first I did so I was just a gentleman with no prospect of knighthood. Now that I have attained the impossible, perhaps he can too." I saw Ralph exchange a meaningful look with his wife and eldest. "And now, as I enjoy this excellent posset, you can tell me your tale." As I sipped it, I wondered where they had managed to get the spices for it was more heavily spiced than I might have expected.

"When I came here, what was it, wife, twelve, thirteen years since?" She squeezed his hand. "I bought this farm. The hall and barn were as you see them but the land was devoid of animals and crops. I was lucky that I had money enough although this farm ate it all up very quickly. Mary came as a serving girl to me for her father farmed over at Richmond and his farm fared badly. Mary was my servant was one less mouth for her father to feed." He leaned over and kissed her cheek. They were as close as the King and the Queen. I was pleased for Ralph. "We soon realised that we got on and we wed. I used the last of my money to buy a pair of mares and a stallion. I was never afraid of hard work and we lived from the land. We grew vegetables and I hunted rabbits."

I gave him a sharp look, "The lord of the manor did not object?"

He laughed, "The Nevilles have great ambitions. Their eyes look further afield than this little backwater. They cared not in the beginning and when I began to breed palfreys which were sounder than the ones they had then I was given permission." He nodded towards my empty bowl of posset. "In the early days we could not have afforded the spice for your posset but fortune favoured me. Young Lord John Neville had a courser which was hurt in a raid on the Scots. They called for me to put the animal down. I saw that, while the animal could never be ridden to war again, it could be given a life." He smiled at me. "I like saving creatures which are close to death and giving them life. Perhaps I did that with Bill."

"Bill?"

"My courser for that was what I named him. We nursed him back from the brink of death and then began to breed from him. When I sold my first foal, back to the Nevilles, I made enough coin to buy more breeding mares. It may be that Bill wished to thank me or maybe the years of war gave him, as they gave me, an appetite for life for every mare he covers gives us young. I am the horse breeder whom all the knights of the Riding come to for animals. We live well and we have spare coin."

John returned, "The men are well and Roger has organised them."

"Good, then eat your posset." I turned to Ralph. "I am glad I came here, Ralph. When I go on crusade, I will be happy knowing that the last three of my shield brothers from the Blue Company have good lives and a retirement which fulfils them."

He nodded and poured some more ale. Mary brewed a good beer. "I have a boon to ask, Will, and you can say no. I will understand."

"I doubt that I shall say no but ask anyway. I owe you and the others all that I have."

"No, you do not. We saved you from your father but you took your own life and changed it. Your mother was the same. She started with nothing and now lives the life of a lady."

I shook my head, "She is a concubine but you are right. She has a better life than the one she was given."

"I have trained my son, Ralph, well. He would be a warrior." He put his arm around the son whom now I saw was almost identical to his father in looks. The red hair must have been the same colour as his father's when he was younger. "I thought to send him to Lincoln for Old Tom still knows men but your arrival here is fortuitous. You go on crusade for six months and I know that you would teach my son the right way to war. The experience would mean that he could find work elsewhere. It may be that six months of a campaign in the Baltic drives all desire to be a warrior from his mind and he would return here to the farm. His mother would like that but this is a chance for him." I hesitated and Red Ralph took that as a sign that I would refuse. "I will make it worth your while. I can give you four good horses."

I shook my head, "No, Ralph, you misunderstand me. I am more than happy to take your son but we both know that there is no guarantee he would return." Ralph nodded. "No, the hesitancy is just my musing on the paths we take and the way they intersect. I had not planned on visiting Middleham. Had we not had such a speedy journey and had I not spoken with Peter then I would not have seen you. Of course, he can come with us. We need a groom for the horses and a groom who can fight will be doubly useful."

I saw young Ralph's face fall, "You mean I get to watch the horses while you fight?"

His father laughed, "You have much to learn, my son. Sir William here used to watch over Old Tom's horse and scavenge for us. He learned to war that way. Do not think that the practice you have had with me is anything like a combat in a real battle. When we fought at the battle of the bridge in Spain Will defended Sir John Chandos from the French when they were trying to hack his body to pieces. I still know not how he survived."

"Your father is right, Ralph. I have archers and sergeants with me. I see from your chest that you have the skills of both. You will have an opportunity to choose which path you take and you will learn from the best. I do not include myself in that but my men, well, they are men like your father. They are honest warriors and they will show you how to soldier." I stood. "We have an early start. My bed calls. I thank you Mistress Mary for you have made John and I welcome." I kissed her hand, "We thank you."

Chapter 3

We left at dawn. Young Ralph wore his father's sword and carried the familiar helmet hanging from his cantle. He had a mail coif and a metal studded leather jerkin. He rode a good horse. In fact, only my horses were better. Tom, his youngest son, came with us and Ralph provided horses for my men so that we could change animals halfway to our destination. We would be able to travel faster. Young Ralph was, as I had expected, a good rider. We rode hard and rejoined the Great North Road. We crossed the Tees at Hurworth where we stopped to change our horses.

Red Ralph said, "We ride regularly to Hart-le-pool. The Nevilles often send their horses to Newcastle for they are related to the Percys. They send good horses by sea. There are still horse thieves north of here. I know many of the merchants in the port and it is from them that I am able to buy spices and the other things we cannot either grow or make. We have simple tastes. The pots and bowls you used last night may not be what you are used to but they serve us."

I laughed, "Then you do not know my wife. She is frugal. All the coin we make she uses to buy more land and farms. We also use wooden bowls and the reason we have goblets is that they were a gift from Sir Henry of Stratford. He was the knight I trained." That seemed to put Red Ralph's mind at rest. I think he feared I had grown airs and graces.

We spoke, on the last twenty odd miles to the port, of what the war might be like. Neither Ralph nor I had ever fought in a cold climate. It was for that reason that we had brought good oiled cloaks and extra blankets. "You will need furs, Will."

"I know but I have a feeling that they will be easier to acquire in the Baltic than they are here."

He laughed, "Will the Scavenger will find a way to get them. There was none better than you for finding food, lodgings, ale and coin. You will do well." He turned around to look at his son who was deep in conversation with John and Roger of Chester. "Bring him back alive, eh Will? His mother wept all night for she is loath to lose him and yet she knows this is right. She hopes that the six months away will show him that he wants to live in Middleham."

I nodded, "I will do all that I can but we both know that if the joy of battle is in his blood then he will be as his father was and only settle for a farm when the red of his hair turns to grey."

"Aye, you are wise and yet you go to war." He laughed.

"We did not know how well off we were in the Blue Company. There we had choice. If we needed coin we fought. I do not have that luxury. The Earl of Northampton shouts jump and I say 'how high, my lord?'"

"They say that Henry Bolingbroke has ambitions to be king. You swore an oath to protect King Richard. You are a man of honour. How will you reconcile the two?"

"I know not. I am a simple man. I did not fight against King Richard when all others sought to do so. I kept my honour but I confess I walk a narrow piece of rope."

"Then let us hope you do not fall from it for now you have risen you have further to fall."

Hart-le-pool was the most important port in this part of the world. King Edward had used it to take his army to defeat the Scots. With a solid wall around the port it was well defended but the icy wind which swept in from the east told you that the nearest neighbours lived in a cold land. It was a warning of what we might expect. The fleet to take us east was already in the port. The Bishop of Hereford had sent priests to organise the loading of the ships. A handful would come with us to give us spiritual sustenance but the ones who greeted us were clerks who knew how to tally. Our horses were placed in pens by the church of St. Hild and we were allocated a ship. It was the smallest of the ships that we saw moored. Her name was ***'Maid of Hart'***. She looked a well-found ship. Our men took our war gear aboard. The spears and the chests, along with our shields, were carefully stored for the voyage. It was one less task to worry about. We would not board until Henry Bolingbroke himself arrived. The clerks told us where he was. He was coming from the west for he had visited with the Cliffords. Robert de Clifford was lord of the Scottish Marches. Along with the Nevilles and the Percy family the three ruled the north. Henry Bolingbroke was making alliances for the future. Red Ralph's words had stuck in my mind. One day I would have to make a choice and it would not be an easy one.

Red Ralph's connections found him and his sons a bed for the night and we had good service at the ale house which was close to the harbour. This was a fishing port too and the fish we ate was amongst the finest I could remember. The Earl of Northampton had not arrived by the morning. Red Ralph had teased as we ate. "So how do you address the young would be king? Is he the Earl, my lord, your future majesty? Which is it?"

I had laughed, "It depends upon the company. The more elevated the company the nobler the title. When we are alone 'my lord' suffices. We do not mention his aspiration to be king. He and the King have an accord. The Queen keeps the King's temper in check but the Earl of Northampton does not tempt fate."

The following morning Red Ralph and Tom rose and left as soon as the town gates were opened. His parting from his son Ralph was formal but I could see that my old comrade would worry about Ralph while he was abroad. He, of all people, knew the inherent dangers of fighting on foreign soil. "I will fetch home your son on our way south."

"Aye Will and I am in your debt now."

Young Ralph looked a little lost when his father and brother had departed. I waved him towards me, "I am pleased that you have joined us but you should know that, once we reach Danczik, then we will be in a land where there is danger around each corner. None will be able to watch over you. For that reason, I say here, while we are still in England, that we do not expect you to risk your life. Your presence is unexpected. Your skill with horses will be invaluable. If you have to fight then there is no shame in your disengaging and fleeing if you must."

He shook his head, "I could not do that. My father told me how the Blue Company all stood together to fight."

"And they were warriors all. When I was your age, or perhaps a little younger, I did not stand in the fore."

"And yet you fought, my lord."

"Aye I did and that is why my advice is sage. Until Roger of Chester tells me that you are a warrior then you care for the horses and protect our backs and baggage. Six months is longer than you might think and you have time to learn."

We went to the horses to ensure that they had not suffered during the night. We had no remounts. Henry Bolingbroke had promised us that our horses would be replaced if they were lost but he did not say how. We would husband what we had. I went with John to the market to buy provisions which would keep. We would be fed by the Earl but a good soldier was prepared and we were good soldiers. We had just returned to the harbour when the Earl of Northampton and the bulk of his men arrived. My position was made quite clear when I was ignored as he rode in. He held a counsel of war with the senior knights who had already arrived. I was not invited. He was making a statement. The other knights had power and influence. I was the lowest ranked knight he took. I would be consulted but only when fighting was necessary. I heard, from one of the priest clerks, that the Percys and the Nevilles had been invited to crusade but they had refused the request to attend. Apparently, they still smarted over the lack of support from the rest of England when they had lost the Battle of Otterburn the previous year. Grievances were developing and it did not bode well for England in the future. Some of those we had spoken to in the alehouse suggested that many in the north favoured an England with a Percy or Neville ruler. The fact that they had very little claim to the throne seemed irrelevant.

Geoffrey, one of the Earl's squires, sought me out on the evening, "Sir William, the Earl wishes you to board your horses and then your men. The fleet will sail on the last tide of the day. He wishes you to be the vanguard when we land in Danczik." He handed me a standard. I unrolled it and saw that it was the standard of the house of Lancaster and the Earldom of Northampton.

I knew Geoffrey and so I asked him the reason that I would carry the banner and be the vanguard, "Why do we carry the standard and why is the smallest ship in the van?"

He looked embarrassed but I continued to stare at him, "My lord, we have been invited by the Teutonic Knights but the Polish King, who is an ally, is not happy about our participation. He fears England's ambitions and the Earl is related to the King." He pointed to the standard which bore the quartered colours of the royal family, "And the standard is that of England."

I saw then the reason. I smiled, "Ah, we are expendable. Thank you for that honesty, Geoffrey. Fear not I will not mention it to the Earl. In my time I have stepped into hotter places than Danczik." I laughed, "I suppose anywhere will be hotter than Danczik! Besides, it suits us. It allows us to get decent accommodation!"

He looked relieved, "Thank you, Sir William. You are less prickly than most of the knights." He pointed to the standard he had given me. "He asks you to display the standard on your ship so that our allies know whence you come."

I remembered when we had been in Galicia. We had not been the first to land but we had been early enough to find a good house which we could rent. I did not think that we would be in Danczik very long for the Earl only planned on a six-month campaign.

We began to have the horses loaded. Ralph paid for his passage during that two-hour process. He led each horse on board. His own horse was first followed by Blaze and then Jack. He sang to them as they were loaded and we had no problems. That contrasted with the next ship down where some of the horses became quite agitated and had to be led away. We were loaded the quickest and our captain was ready to sail the moment the tide turned.

As we waited to leave, I told my men of the Earl's plan and my reaction. Roger of Chester was an old campaigner. He knew the Earl well. "Why does he wish a campaign, lord? I cannot see what he will gain. If these are pagans then there will be little coin to be had."

I liked to be honest with my men. I hid nothing from them and, I liked to think, they were as honest with me. "Roger, we all know that he has ambitions. A crusade to the Baltic involves a shorter journey than one to Jerusalem and yet still gives the Earl the acclamation of the Pope and the church. King Richard said he would go on crusade and has not done so. A crusade is the mark of a pious king. Do you not remember Castile? We spent barely six months there. It was enough time to garner the glory of our victory and yet, not enough to lose too many men and animals nor to be tarnished with defeat. We will leave when defeat looms on the horizon." I know I sounded cynical but this was the way the great and good carried on. They played chess thinking five moves ahead. I could barely plan my next move when I played.

We set sail in the dark and while many of the other ships gathered in the harbour were still being loaded. The Captain, a local man called Peter Northgate, for his family lived close by the north gate of Hart-le-pool, rubbed his hands as we left the narrow harbour entrance. "I tell you, my lord, that this is a most unexpected occurrence. I know not why the Earl wants you and your men to land first but it suits me. We do not need to worry about fouling another ship in the night and we do not have to tack back and forth waiting to leave the harbour."

"Aye but what happens when we land at Danczik? We know not the language."

He grinned, his teeth shining in the moonlight, "But we do. My first mate was one of those whose family lived in the city before the knights took it over. They escaped the massacre and his family came to live in our port. He speaks their language fluently and he knows the locals. We trade regularly with them."

"The locals?"

"Aye the Teutonic Knights massacred ten thousand so they say and then brought in their own settlers but there are still many of the people who lived there, the Kashubians. Piotr is of those people." He gestured behind him with his thumb. "Many of those captains will find themselves cheated or even robbed but we will not." He pointed to the bow. "There is a cabin for you and your squires there, my lord, but I am fraid that your men will have to share the hold with the horses."

"How long will the voyage take, Captain Peter?"

"God willing and we keep this wind then six days or more. The Skagerrak is the most difficult part and there are still pirates in those waters. You and your men may be called upon to defend my ship. It is a rare occurrence these days but we have to be prepared."

I nodded, "Do not worry about my men. We know how to fight!"

John and I went to bed almost as soon as we had left the harbour. The small ship bobbed up and down on the waves for the wind and the sea were both fresh. Ralph was too excited and he stayed on deck with my men. When dawn broke, I left the cabin to a grey day with ominous clouds on the horizon. I made water and then walked to the hold. I descended into the Stygian dark. The horses seemed calm enough and I spied Ralph asleep in the hay close to them.

Simon the Traveller came over to speak with me. "He was so excited we could not get him below deck and then he became green and brought up most of his supper. He has slept ever since."

"And the horses?"

"They are fine although they have produced so much piss and dung already that I fear young Ralph will struggle to keep anything in his stomach."

I nodded, "It is part of the process he has to learn."

The weather was no better over the next few days as we headed across the seas to the northern coast of Denmark. We kept a good watch for it was not only Baltic pirates we had to worry about. There were Scottish and English ones too. Perhaps that was another reason we had been sent out ahead, as bait to draw out any pirates. We saw none and, as we approached the Skagerrak our journey was almost over. We had sailed the dangerous part. Captain Peter had told us that the Baltic was a gentler sea than the one we were crossing. Apart from keeping a good watch we all had to take a hand in keeping the ship clean. The Captain had ensured that we had plenty of hay and straw. Each day we would hurl the spoiled material astern and lay down fresh. Ralph soon recovered from his sea sickness. In fact, mucking out the horses helped him as it was something with which he was familiar. In the odd moments of rest, he questioned the men at arms and archers constantly about what he could expect on campaign. My men were patient. They had done the same for John and, I had no doubt, when Tom came to war with me, he would be just as inquisitive. I had not asked questions when I was Ralph's age for it was all around me and I lived it.

We were passing between Gotland and the islands to the south when the pirates came for us. We had sharp eyed lookouts but it was Simon the Traveller who first spotted them. As his name suggested Simon had travelled the world with his bow. He recognised the low lean ships propelled by oars which were packed with warriors. Their ancestors had done the same. As Vikings they had raided England and France. They were not the force they once were but they were still a threat.

"Three pirate ships coming to cut us off!"

Captain Peter did not panic. He sent his crew to give his little ship every piece of sail they could. I shouted. "Arm yourselves. Alan of the Wood, half the archers to the bow castle and, Stephen the Tracker, take the other half to the stern. Roger of Chester, have the men at arms gather close to the mast."

John handed me my helmet, coif and sword. He held my shield and I shook my head, "I will use a dagger instead. Ralph, take your bow and go to the stern. Today is your first lesson in becoming a warrior."

I pulled on my coif and donned my helmet. I drew my sword and dagger and I walked to the mainmast. I had never fought at sea and I hoped I would not have to now. The deck pitched and rolled around. We were in a worse position than the pirates for they had no sail and no mast. Their ship pitched around less. They were like lean greyhounds and we were like a milk cow! Seamanship was the Captain's domain. Slaughtering pirates as they tried to board was mine. I had on my mail hauberk but no armour. If I fell overboard then I was dead. John just had his leather hauberk. I watched the three ships as they came towards us like wolves hunting a sheep. Two were coming for our steerboard side and the other, the largest, for our larboard. I was no sailor but I guessed that the larger was the leader. "Natty and Geoffrey, stay on the steerboard side. Keep watch on those two pirates and tell me if they close with us. The rest of you to the larboard. I want us in a double line. John, you will be in the second. We attack any who manage to board."

I watched the crew pick up hand axes and wickedly curved short swords. They would sell their lives dearly. The pirates had chosen a narrow stretch of water from which to launch their attack. For more than half a mile the Captain had no sea room. I estimated that the leading pirate would hit us almost as we reached the passage to the open sea. Looking aft I saw that the Captain did not look concerned. He shouted something to one of his sailors and a sheet was tightened. Glancing at the mast head pennant I saw that the wind was coming from our steerboard quarter. We began to move faster. The leading pirate also benefitted from the wind even though she had no sail. She began to not only keep pace with us but also to close. Her two consorts on the other side, both smaller boats, were merely keeping pace with us.

I watched as Alan of the Wood released an arrow which arced high in the air. He was aiming at one of the smaller boats. It was a ranging arrow. It plunged into the wooden prow of the leading one. He was our best archer and it told him that they were out of range for he had the greatest range. He turned and shouted, "Aim at the ship to larboard!" He knew that the leader was in range for they were closer. With just a few bows he would have to keep up a regular rate to whittle down the numbers who might try to board.

The nine bows of my men rose high and their arrows dived like vengeful birds into the belly of the pirate. I heard, across the water, the shouts and cries as the swallow tail arrows found flesh. Another flight soared and there were more cries. Our captain was keeping us to the north side of the channel. I suspect it was the safest channel. It meant we were converging with the pirate. The oars of the pirate were more ragged now for men had been hit. The boat began to slew around as the oars on the far side of the ship seemed to suffer less. We were higher in the water and I could see the ship below us. I looked down its length. There had been upward of forty men aboard. There were less now for I saw bloody bodies and men nursing wounds. A voice shouted from the centre of the boat and four men rose, as the bows came towards our centre. Even as the four grappling hooks were thrown and gripped into our gunwale, I saw the helmsman and the pirate next to him fall. As he died his body pushed the pirate to parallel our course. The bow would not ram us but the movement laid it alongside us.

"They will try to board us. Single line. Natty and Geoffrey, join us!"

We stepped to the side of the ship and began to hack through the ropes. More hooks snaked over towards our gunwale. Natty and Geoffrey ran directly to them and began to cut them. The arrows still thinned the ranks of the pirates. I think they were just trying to delay us until the other two ships could join them. Men began to climb up the side of our ship. They swarmed up the ropes. These were strong men who rowed great distances. Pulling themselves up a rope was child's play for them. However, they could not pull themselves up and carry a weapon. I saw that each of them had a small hand weapon gripped in their mouths. Most had a knife or a dagger while the first pirate whose face appeared before me had a small hatchet. As he pulled himself up our ship lurched a little and the movement made us step back while it allowed the pirates to gain the deck. It was a fluke of the wind but it stopped me from completing the swing I had begun. As he gained the deck, the pirate grabbed the hatchet with his left hand while he began to draw his sword with his right. This time I had my feet firmly planted and I brought my sword from on high to hack deep into his shoulder close to his neck. The hatchet fell from his fingers but he was a tough man. I saw the anger in his eyes as he tried to force his dying body to swing the sword. I punched him in the face with my left hand and he tumbled over the side. As he did so he crashed into the next man who was clambering up. It slowed the flow of pirates.

My men were despatching the handful who had made the deck. I shouted, "John, use the hatchet to sever the lines!" I swung my sword, blindly, down the side of our ship and it connected with the skull of the Danish pirate who was pulling himself up. A second was thrown into the well of the ship as John severed a line. Nine arrows struck the handful of men who were preparing to join their comrades and then the last line was severed with a twang. The pirate suddenly drifted away and, being freed, *'Maid'* leapt forward like a stallion of the sea. I turned and ran to the steerboard side. The two pirates were less than five lengths from us but, even as Alan and my archers loosed arrows at them, we burst into the open waters of the Baltic. We were freed!

Sheathing my sword, I left my men to strip the dead and throw them overboard. Had they landed in numbers they might have caused some damage but man for man we were better armed, mailed and trained. Captain Peter had a huge grin on his face, "My short cut almost cost us there my lord! But for you and your men things might have gone ill. I am in your debt."

"Short cut?"

"Aye, we are shallower draughted than most and the passage we have taken can save almost half a day. The wind was with us and…" He made the sign of the cross, "God smiled on us and I have learned a lesson. Still, all is done and we now have clear water to Danczik. We will be there by dawn!"

Chapter 4

Danczik was a revelation. The Teutonic Knights had taken the town almost half a generation ago and they had tried to impose their will upon the town. The result was that it looked like a mixture of two cultures. Some older parts looked almost exotic while the newer structures showed that the Teutonic Knights had an eye for defence. The Teutonic Knights liked to build their castles and defences in red brick. They made for a distinctive looking castle. They liked regular concentric lines; higher one closer to the keep, were surrounded by low outer walls. The one at Danczik had a keep with a bailey in the centre. It appeared to be like a monastic cloister. I had never seen the like.

As we made our way through the myriad of small traders which plied the waters, I wondered why the Earl had not sent the Teutonic Knight with us. Von Plettenburg could have translated. I hoped that Piotr knew his business. I looked up at the fluttering standard. The quartered three lions and fleur de lys were overlaid with five points ermine. I wondered if those ashore knew what that meant. I had been slightly honoured that the standard flew from our ship but also a little apprehensive.

Captain Northgate made for a section of the quay which had been left clear. The black crosses on the white standards fluttering along the quay which marked that section told me that they belonged to the Teutonic Knights. As we edged towards our berth, under reefed sails, I saw a small party leave the red brick gatehouse which lay close by and walk towards us. I saw that one wore spurs and was a knight while the other four were sergeants.

I turned to Ralph, "You had better get ready to fetch the horses ashore. The sooner we give them their legs back the sooner they can be ridden." Ralph had never seen the effects of a voyage on horses. I had. It had not been as long as the voyage to Spain but it would still take a couple of days for them to recover. I had no doubt that Henry Bolingbroke had sent us ahead so that we could be used as we had in Spain. We would scout out the land for him.

Lines were thrown and we were tied to the shore. The gangplank was put in place and the captain said, "I will send my mate to translate when all is secured, my lord, but feel free to go ashore until we have secured the ship."

I nodded, "John, come with me. The rest of you, help Ralph to fetch the horses and our war gear."

We strode down the gangplank. I knew that when my feet walked on the cobbles they would feel as though they did not belong to me. I concentrated on placing my feet on the flat part of the gangplank. Walking in spurs was never easy. The last thing I needed was to pitch forward before the Teutonic Knight. I was so relieved when I planted my feet on the stone that I smiled. The Teutonic Knight thought the smile was for him and he smiled back.

He held out his hand and I saw that he was younger than I was. For some reason I had expected older men to be in the ranks of the Teutonic Knights. He spoke English. It was accented but it was English and that surprised me too.

"I am Bengt Birgersson. In my previous life, before I found God, I was a jarl. We are all brothers in the order but if you wish to give me a title then I am happy for it to be 'sir', as I have been knighted by the King of Sweden."

"Thank you, Sir Bengt."

"I assume you are from the Earl of Northampton?"

"I am. We were sent ahead. I am Sir William Strongstaff. Your English is good and I am relieved that I do not need my translator. Did you live in England?"

He shook his head, "My family come from Sweden and one of my ancestors, Jarl Birger Persson, fought in the Holy Land with an English knight who came to fight for us against the Estonians. Some of his men remained in our land. Our family has a tradition of speaking your language. It is a useful skill. I went on crusade to the Holy Land and met many Englishmen there. My language aided me."

Just then Jack was led from the ship. "John, take Jack from Ralph and walk him along the quay to get his legs."

"Aye lord."

"A fine horse but not a destrier."

I shook my head, "I prefer a courser and I believe we will not be fighting knights."

He gestured with his arm to lead me towards the gate into the tower. It allowed more room for the horses to be exercised. "There will be knights but you are right. We fight savages. I fought the Seljuk Turk and they are almost saintly compared with the Lithuanians. The Pope was quite right to demand a crusade to rid the world of these pagans. They are the last remnant of a savage past." I hid my smile. Sir Bengt was a true zealot. I could see why he had joined the order. "Come with me, I will take you to meet the Komtur."

"Komtur?"

"Our commander." He turned and rattled off commands to his sergeants. "I have asked them to take your men and horses to the barracks. It is good that you arrived first. We have accommodation for the ten knights the Earl brings with him but we can only provide beds for forty of the men at arms and archers."

We headed through the tower gate and into the city. The castle and keep dominated the town and we headed towards it. As we walked, I told him of the encounter with the pirates. He nodded, "They are the bane of the Baltic. One day we will eliminate them. They are the Victual Brothers and are like a curse on the Baltic. Your ship was small enough to tempt them. If your Earl keeps all of his ships together then there should be no danger. We must first subdue the pagans before we can bring order to this sea."

"Your order has grand plans then?"

"Aye we are not like the Templars. We do not forget our purpose. They spent too much time accruing money and forgot why they began the order. We understand the need for discipline."

As we walked into the castle, I could not help but notice that the order's surcoats and cloaks were all pure white. I knew from the state of my blue and red surcoat and blue cloak that they showed stains really quickly. I guessed that the order had an army of servants washing them to keep them so white. The armour and weapons were all of the highest quality. They wore the shorter surcoat which covered their hauberk. They had cuisse and poleyn for their legs. Their elbows and arms were well protected. Their helmets were all the open-faced bascinet. These were warriors. If the stories I had heard of the Lithuanians were true then they needed to be. If they were captured there would be no ransom.

We entered the keep and went up a narrow stairway to the office of the Komtur. The interior of the square keep showed that it had been well designed. There was a sentry outside the office. He stood aside when Sir Bengt approached. The Komtur was a grizzled grey-haired knight. His face showed that he had fought. Ludolf von Feuchtwangen reminded me of Old Tom. I did not know him long but I liked him. He did not suffer fools gladly and he knew his business. For a warrior that is the best kind of leader. Had he been in command of the siege of Vilnius then events might have turned out differently.

He nodded, "Ah, the English knights have begun to arrive." He too spoke English. I guessed that many had been on crusade to the Holy Land where there were still many who spoke English.

Sir Bengt said, "This is Sir William Strongstaff."

The Komtur leaned back and smiled, "Well, Sir Bengt, the ten knights the Earl brings should make all the difference eh? I expect the Lithuanians are shitting themselves." There was mockery in his voice. He looked at me, "Shitting themselves is the right word is it not?"

I smiled, "It is and your English is also excellent, my lord. I am guessing that you did not learn it at court."

He shook his head, "I served in the east and learned it from the sergeants of the Hospitallers. They were good warriors. So, what is your story, Sir William? Are you a young lord who wishes to kill a few savages and go back to England to woo the women with your tales of heroics?" He nodded to a seat, "Sit, please. Sir Bengt, see to Sir William's war gear. I would talk with him."

He poured me some wine and I raised the goblet to him. "I am a warrior, Komtur. I was one of the Free Companies in Gascony. I was made a gentleman and then knighted. I served as a bodyguard to King Richard. The Black Prince was my lord."

His face changed, "I am sorry, Sir William. I misjudged you. You have a fine pedigree. If you served with Edward the Black Prince and have been raised to a knighthood then that speaks well of you. We have time and I am interested. Tell me your tale."

There were things I could not tell any for they bordered on the treasonous but I told him the truth. I spoke of the victories and the disasters. I told him of de Vere and the attempts to destroy King Richard's power.

At the end he nodded, "Then I have higher hopes than before I spoke to you. When the Grand Master, Konrad von Jungingen, asked for help from Europe, I think he hoped for more than ten knights."

"Komtur, it is my belief that the strength of English warriors lies not in their knights, for although they are brave enough and well-armed, it is the archers and sergeants who are the reason for our success on the battlefield. The English and Welsh archers decide battles and then we knights claim the glory."

He laughed and slapped his hand against the table, "Honesty! How refreshing! And does your Earl Henry share your belief?"

I decided to be honest, "I doubt it but he knows the worth of our archers. There will be fifty that we bring and they are fifty who will be mounted. My liege lord could have brought five hundred more men but they would not have been mounted. I know not the land over which we fight but I am guessing that it involves travelling over great distances and horses will make the journey easier?"

"Aye you are right and I had not thought of that. The King of France could have sent many men and by horse for they could have travelled over land. He sent us his good wishes instead of men. It is no wonder they call him mad. I forget that you are an island." He rose and held his arm out, "I look forward to the reports of your conduct. Sir Bengt will be travelling with you as well as von Plettenburg. Your Earl will have to leave almost as soon as he arrives."

As we walked down to the inner bailey the sentries snapped to attention This was a world I had not yet met. This was a world with order and discipline. It felt more like a monastery. Sir Bengt met us at the gate. John and Ralph had my chest between them. The Komtur nodded to me, "I will speak further this evening when we eat. Bring your squire. Here we use our squires and pages to serve us rather than servants."

"Thank you, Komtur."

Ralph's eyes were wide. He had seen York of course but this was something totally different. The white Teutonic robes and the martial air were the difference. The white against the red brick seemed a stark contrast. This was a frontier castle. Sir Bengt said, "The Komtur is a great warrior. He was rewarded with the title of Komtur for his bravery in defeating the pagans. I am proud to be one of his knights."

Our chamber was cosy enough for John and myself but I sensed that Ralph also wished to stay with us rather than in the barracks. John confirmed it, "My lord, Ralph would be as a page to you and stay in our chamber."

The boy had none of the skills needed to be a page but I saw the pleading in his eyes. "There is no bed, Ralph, you will have to sleep on the floor."

He grinned, "My father trained me to sleep on the ground so that I could be close at hand when the mares foaled. I do not mind, my lord, and I will learn all that is necessary to be a page. I am raw clay but John has promised he will help me."

"To be a warrior you do not need such skills you know. Your father did not have them."

He nodded, "Before I left my father said I was to emulate you and not him. You have risen above your station and I would too. It will be a long journey but I am content. All journeys start with a man putting one foot in front of the other. I am not yet a man but my foot is heading in the right direction!"

"Then welcome to our chamber."

We took out the only decent surcoat and tunic I had brought with me. After almost twelve days in the chest they both needed airing.

When we had washed and bathed in the basin in the chamber John had to trim and comb Ralph's unruly hair. If he was to wait upon me then he had to look a little less wild. John loaned him one of his surcoats and it did not look too big upon him. While I walked the walls of the castle John taught Ralph the rudimentary role he would have to play.

I saw that the castle walls overlooked all of the city walls. As I wandered the fighting platform, I saw chests of crossbows. I did not see any bows. The Teutonic Knights would see a difference between the two weapons when our fifty archers were used. None of the sergeants I passed spoke English and I could see that they were less than happy with my presence on their fighting platform, but the fact that they had all seen me speaking with the Komtur seemed to make me acceptable. As the sun began to set, I headed down to the chamber. There was no sign of the other ships in our fleet but that was not surprising. Captain Peter had deliberately taken a short cut and he was travelling alone.

I had not eaten in what was, to all intents and purposes, a monastery. This was a religious order and there were no women to be seen. There were no minstrels. The King and the Earl always had minstrels and musicians playing their instruments. This was an austere room. The knights entered in silence. The squires stood at attention behind the chairs. As guest of honour, I was seated to the right of the Komtur. The Komtur and all of the knights bowed their heads and a priest began to speak in Latin. I understood not a word. The prayer seemed to go on forever. I kept my eyes open as I did not want to be stood by myself when all the rest were seated. As soon as the priest took his seat the knights sat.

Sir Bengt was seated to my right. He smiled, "My squire speaks English. He will explain to your squires what they must do."

When the food arrived, it was plain. The food was almost grey and it was hard to tell what we were eating. The cooks seemed to have cooked any taste out of it. The Earl enjoyed his food and I knew that he would be disappointed if this was the staple diet. The Komtur saw my face and he laughed, "We are an austere order. We are dedicated to God. We suffer no distractions. The wine is watered, the food is bland and there are no women. We reserve all of our energy to destroy God's enemies. When you are on campaign then you will cook for yourselves." He saw the relief on my face and laughed again. "You English like your food. For us it is unimportant."

With bland food and watered wine, I found I was able to concentrate on the words of the Komtur. He and Sir Bengt explained to me the problems we would face. The Polish allies had only recently converted to Christianity and the alliance was not a firm one. The Komtur was honest. They did not trust the Poles and the Poles did not trust the Knights. It was not a marriage made in heaven. He told me that they had been besieging Vilnius for some months. The Hochmeister, the Order's Grand Master, had decided to ravage the countryside around Vilnius to help bring the city to its knees. I gathered that would be our role. The Poles would continue the siege with the help of the order while the bulk of the order and the crusaders from England, Sweden and Denmark would, in effect, conduct a major chevauchée. It was a type of warfare I understood. The meal ended earlier than it would have done in England and we were abed sooner than we had expected. Ralph and John were both bemused and fascinated by the whole experience. I confess that, for me, it was a new experience. I was used to having meals with lords who plotted and planned. Some would be boorish drunks and others would be quietly plotting. The knights with whom we had eaten were dedicated to God and their order. Nothing else mattered.

Being abed early meant I rose early. The Teutonic Knights were up earlier and had been at their services. I wondered how they would fare when they were on campaign. Perhaps they took priests with them. The Bishop of Hereford had sent priests to help the Earl. I broke my fast in the refectory and then I went to visit with my men. I spoke with Alan and Roger. "You were treated well?"

"Aye we were lord but the food was not to our taste."

Natty nodded, "And we didn't understand a word they spoke but the ale was good."

"I have a feeling that we will not have better food on campaign. Let us go to the market and buy what we can, while we can. I will speak with Captain Peter." I turned to Ralph, "You and John had better exercise the horses." They looked disappointed but they had enjoyed the evening with the Knights and knew this was the price that they had to pay.

I gave coins to Alan and Roger and left them to buy what they could. I went to the *'Maid of Hart'*. I smiled as I saw that they were still cleaning the hold of the detritus of the horses. Captain Peter gave me a wry smile as I approached. "It will be some time before we have rid the ship of the stench of horses. It is a good job we were well paid by the Earl. Now if this had been King Richard there would have been a set rate and not as profitable."

"Will it be you that take us home again?"

"Perhaps. I am afraid that the sea is a cruel mistress. We have been chartered to return in six months but storms, pirates and the worm can upset plans. We often travel here for they have good timber and wheat." He pointed to piles of timber and sacks of wheat which were being readied prior to loading. "We already have a cargo to take to Newcastle. Why do you ask, my lord?"

"Because I have sailed with other captains. Some were good and some less so. I can trust you and would rather put my men's lives in your hands than another."

That seemed to please him. "Then we shall do our best to survive for you, lord."

Just then one of his seamen shouted, "Captain, looks like the fleet is on the horizon."

The Captain nodded, "Aye, well I shall soon be in a fleet again. At least the pirates will have to give us a wide berth!"

Sir Bengt arrived with his sergeants when the leading ship, the Earl's, headed through the harbour entrance. "We had a messenger from the Hochmeister. He is anxious for your Earl to join him."

"That may be difficult. It takes some days for horses to acclimatise to the land after so many days at sea."

He shrugged, "Your Earl's contingent is the last to land. The other foreign allies are all with the Hochmeister. I do not think your Earl would wish to be on the periphery of the action."

He was right of course. The whole purpose of this crusade was to get Henry's name noticed. When he returned to England, he would be able to use the crusade to garner favours from the church and to hold the moral high ground. I watched the Earl's ship dock close to the *'Maid'*. It dwarfed the tiny carvel. The Earl, his closest knights and his squires were waiting for the gangplank to be lowered and they strode off the ship as soon as it was secured. The Earl, Geoffrey and Edward had done this before. Sir Richard had done it before but Sir Hugo d'Avranches had not and his legs buckled as soon as he stepped onto the ground. The sailors and those on the quay laughed. The knight tried to get to his feet quickly. I heard the Earl say, "Take it steady, Sir Hugo. You are embarrassing me." Sir Bengt and I strode over to him. The Earl smiled, "All is in order?"

I nodded, "It is, my lord. Your knights, priests and squires will be accommodated in the castle. There is room for thirty archers and men at arms. The rest will need to find rooms elsewhere."

"And my minstrels?"

I shook my head, "I am not certain that the Komtur would approve my lord. This is a religious order." I gestured to Sir Bengt. "This is Sir Bengt Birgersson. He has been sent to smooth our passage. The Grand Master is anxious for us to join him."

Henry shook his head, "We need a week at least to get over the voyage."

Sir Bengt and I exchanged looks. The Swedish knight said, "The army is assembled, my lord, save for you and the men who will ride with us from this castle."

Henry Bolingbroke smiled. He was used to getting his own way. "Then they will have to wait!"

In the end we stayed but an extra two days in Danczik. The horses recovered quicker and the food was not to the taste of any of the men, especially the lords. In addition, we had a warning of winter when snow began to fall. It did not lay on the ground. We headed south and east. The siege of Vilnius needed more men and we were going to end the siege which had already lasted longer than the Hochmeister had expected.

Chapter 5

There were just two hundred and fifty of us in the column. The English archers were the only missile armed men who accompanied us. There were no crossbowmen with the Teutonic Knights. The commander of the column was a Hauskomtur, Siegfried von Plauen. His uncle was a powerful Komtur. It was said he had ambitions to be Grand Master. He was not impressed by the Earl's titles nor his royal blood. To him we were swords. As we rode down the muddy tracks which passed for roads, I saw the Earl of Northampton changing. Hitherto he had been a powerful magnate and other lords took heed of his actions and his words. Here we rode behind the white cloaked Teutonic Order. None knew his name nor his heritage. He was here to kill pagans and that was all. He was not happy with his relegation to a sword for hire. He took some strange pleasure in the fact that their white cloaks soon became bespattered with mud. Our translator, Sir Bengt, also rode with his brother knights. Our priests and the minstrels were the unhappiest. None were horsemen and the sumpters they rode did not give the easiest of rides. I wondered if the Earl regretted bringing minstrels with him. Their horses could have been used for remounts. He had not really understood the nature of a crusade.

I did not mind either the exclusion nor the weather. We would be paid handsomely for six months work. Thus far we had seen little danger. The attack from the pirates had not hurt us and my men had managed to acquire coins and a couple of weapons from the dead. They had all shared in the small bounty. Even Ralph had been given coins. If we continued in the same manner then we would return to England a little richer. Hopefully we would have had a better harvest and my wife would be happier.

We had a journey of over three hundred miles. Even with horses this would take more than a week. There was a shorter route but that would have involved us passing through lands which were, as yet, unconquered. We stayed each night in towns and villages. The people who lived there were not thrilled to have over two hundred men and horses take over their homes. This was not the Holy Land. There the pagans, the followers of Islam, could be identified by the colour of their skin. Here, the pagans and the Christians looked identical. We had little idea of the religion of those who lived in the houses through which we passed. I made certain that we kept a good watch each night. The sergeants of the order patrolled but my men did so also.

We were halfway to Vilnius when trouble struck. I had no idea of the names of the places through which we passed and as Sir Bengt was not near us then there was no one to ask. All we knew was the land was largely flat and there were still many forests which looked to be virgin. Many areas that we had passed through had been cleared to grow wheat which, along with timber, appeared to be the major products upon which the people depended. They kept a few pigs and cows but they were not kept in large numbers. As we headed to Vilnius the civilized land was replaced by forests and woods. It was as we entered yet another one that my senses began to tingle. We were towards the back. Teutonic sergeants guarded the baggage behind us. I could not explain my sixth sense. Perhaps it had developed when I had anticipated a clout from my father and ducked out of the way. It may have been from the times I scavenged, often on my own. All I knew was that I had learned to trust my sixth sense.

I turned to Roger and Alan, who rode together behind me, "I am uneasy. String your bows and ready your weapons. Keep a watch on the trees."

Neither man questioned me. They had followed me long enough to trust my senses. I heard John say to Ralph, "Don your helmet and be ready to draw your sword. Tie Jack's reins to your cantle and it will free up your hand."

"But I see nothing!"

"Sir William smells trouble. Trust his nose, Ralph."

This was not England and we did not travel on Roman roads. As far as I knew the Romans had never reached this part of the world and the roads over which we rode were made of mud. It meant that our horses did not clop. They were almost silent for the mud was soft and deadened the sound. That helped me to hear. I did not look for if there were attackers then they would be hidden. Their clothes would blend into the brown of the land. It was an absence of birds which alerted me. The birds close to the track had been silent in each of the forests through which we had passed but I had heard them in the distance. Here they were silent even in the depths. That meant there were predators in the woods. I wondered if we might be too powerful a force to tackle. Alan of the Wood had been an outlaw but his band had numbered less than twenty at its height.

For the past two days the Earl had ridden surrounded by his household knights and priests. Our conversation had lasted but one day and then he had tired of me. I did not speak politics. I did not plot. I was a warrior who could fight and protect the Earl. Henry Bolingbroke had elevated me but that did not mean he liked me. He did not dismiss me but, gradually, he became surrounded by the ambitious young knights who would be given manors and estates as the Earl increased his power. We were behind the squires and the priests but ahead of his sergeants and archers. My men had closed ranks around me forcing the Earl's men closer to the horses.

The attack, when it came, appeared to be at the head of the column. We heard shouts and the sound of horses whinnying. The trumpet sounded, ordering us to stand to. We drew weapons. My warning meant that Alan and his archers had their bows strung and arrows nocked before the notes had died away. I pulled up my coif and drew my sword. I raised up my shield. Turning around I saw that my men had done as I had but the Earl's men simply stared around. They appeared bemused for there was nothing to be seen.

I shouted, "Don your helmets and draw your weapons. Archers, nock an arrow! Guard the baggage!" My words stirred them and they had just obeyed my order when a shower of arrows and stones descended from the forest. We were close to the baggage and that was the target. "Archers dismount. Roger prepare to follow me." I held up my shield as I wheeled Blaze around. Arrows and stones cracked into it. I saw one of the Earl's archers felled by a stone and a man at arms clutch his arm. Two of the Earl's priests ahead of us were thrown from their horses by arrows. The pagans would target priests! They were seen as Christ's wizards by the pagans.

Alan of the Wood and his archers used their horses to protect themselves and they began to choose targets. They had good eyes for the terrain and the arrows which flew from the woods identified where attackers lurked.

"Ralph, dismount and stay here. Watch the archers' horses. Roger, John, let us root out these savages."

I spurred Blaze and headed into the forest. I held my sword below and behind me. My shield was held over Blaze's head. Almost as soon as I entered the forest, I found myself in a dark and gloomy world. The trees were huge and ancient. That meant there was little undergrowth and men had to hide behind trees. When they sent an arrow at the column, they had to expose themselves. An arrow came from nowhere and skittered off my shield while another hit my chest. It stuck there, caught in my surcoat and mail. When it did not penetrate then I knew they were using hunting arrows and not war arrows. That gave me confidence. I had seen the movement of the arrow and I pulled Blaze to the side and rode towards the hidden archer. He must have thought that he was invisible for I saw him nock another arrow. Blaze was fast and, even as he drew back the string, my sword swept across his chest. It tore open his body and, bleeding heavily, he fell to the ground. The archers and the slingers had now lost their advantage. We were so close to them that they had no time to react to charging horses ridden by mailed men. I wheeled Blaze to the left and rode at a bowman who was oblivious to my presence. He sent an arrow towards the column and only sensed me at the last moment. The last thing he saw was my sword sweeping towards his head. I sliced off the top of his skull. It was a quick death. My men and I were few in number but the archers and the slingers could do us little damage. They began to flee.

This was where my men's training paid off. I shouted, "Wheel! Ride to the other side of the woods!" The attack had come from two sides of the trail. We had eliminated the threat closest to us. I had no doubts that the knights of the order would be hunting down men at the front but the pagans were after the horses and the baggage. As we neared the trail, I saw that men with swords and axes were attacking the baggage guards. Two sergeants were hauled from their horses and butchered. The other side of the road would have to wait.

"Wheel left!" I used my sword to direct my nine men.

The pagans fought half-naked. They had no helmets but their long axes, spears and double handed swords were biting into horses and sergeants alike. There were almost forty of them close to the train. I saw younger warriors leading off horses. The horses had tents and weapons on them. To us they were more valuable than gold! The first Lithuanian I slew knew nothing about it for my sword hacked into the side of his head even as he swung his pike at one of the Earl's archers. I switched my sword to strike over Blaze's head at the next Lithuanian. He saw the blow coming but my horse's snapping teeth and my shield distracted him. I split his skull in two.

Then I was spotted. Perhaps he was a chief, I know not but he wore a metal ring around his neck. He was a huge warrior with an axe and he shouted something. Five men turned to face us. He swung his axe in apparently lazy circles. This was where Blaze's training would pay off. John was to my left and Roger of Chester to my right. I could ignore the other men and I rode at the chief. They had no shields and were in a loose line. The chief's swings meant that none were close to him. An axeman has to choose his moment to strike. Perhaps this chicf had never faced a horse. I hoped so for, as he decided that my horse was in range, he swung harder. I jerked Blaze to the left. The axe struck fresh air and I saw resignation on his face as my sword swept down and across his face. He was a large warrior and a brave warrior but my sword ripped open his face and he was dead before I had withdrawn my weapon. There were cracks and cries from behind me as my men rode through and over the five men who had turned with the chief to face us.

We swept around the mass of men trying to get at the horses. The Earl's men and the Teutonic sergeants had organised themselves and they began to drive against the barbarians. A horn sounded from the woods and the barbarians fled. We did not allow them to leave unmolested and we hacked, slashed and stabbed at all who tried to pass us. Some of the Earl's men looked to follow them. I shouted, "Hold! Reform for there may be a second attack!" Thankfully they obeyed.

There were dead and there were wounded amongst our men. Only two priests had survived. Some of the pagans had almost deliberately sacrificed themselves to attempt to hack the priests to death. Horses had died as well as sergeants and, crucially, three irreplaceable archers. I went with my men to finish off the wounded and to collect the weapons and their valuables. When I reached the chief, I took the torc. It was a gold alloy. I handed it to John to put in his satchel.

The Earl himself rode down our line. I saw him speak with his sergeants and examine the bodies of the dead Teutonic priests. He looked shocked. I walked over to him and he dismounted. He shook his head, "Savages! Savages!"

"Now we know the type of man we fight, my lord." I think that the Earl had expected a slightly easier opponent. After all, they wore no mail and did not use horses. How could they stand against knights?

He nodded to me, "My men said that you took charge and it was because of that we did not lose more. Thank you. You have justified your selection."

"Aye, but we lost three archers, lord. That should not have happened."

"How could we have stopped it?"

"You need the archers under one commander. We should use them as a block of bowmen."

"And who would lead them? You?"

I shook my head, "Alan of the Wood. He could command."

"But he was an outlaw."

"And he was pardoned." I pointed. Alan and my archers were walking through the woods retrieving usable arrows. "That is the mark of a bowman. Your men stand around just grateful to be alive. They are good archers but they need a leader."

"You are right. Make it so."

After collecting the horses which the pagans had tried to take, we rode just four more miles to camp at a small village. It was deserted, which led me to believe that it was pagan and they had been part of the attack. Our dead were buried in the village. Their bodies would be dug up and despoiled once we left but I had no say in the matter. Siegfried von Plauen was commander and he made the decision. I spoke to Sir Bengt and told him my thoughts.

"You may be right but what else could we do?"

"You could have buried them in the huts and then burned the huts. Their graves would have been hidden. It is done now. Tell me, Sir Bengt, why do you not use scouts?"

"We cannot trust the locals and we have none ourselves. I fear this will happen again."

"I have an idea how to deter the enemy. Come with me to the Earl and then we will see the Hauskomtur."

The Earl was still in a state of shock. Two of his minstrels had also died and it had shaken him. He agreed and we went to the Hauskomtur. Sir Bengt translated my words. The Teuton nodded and spoke. Sir Bengt said, "He thanks you for suggesting that we use your archers to watch the flanks and the woods but he fears that they will just be sacrificed."

"Tell him that I am confident that they will not."

He finally agreed and I was vindicated. Over the next four days the pagans tried to attack us three more times. Each attack was spotted early by the archers. Warning was given and a wall of spears and shields greeted the attackers. The pagans were brave but without the element of surprise they could not harm us. My archers slew forty of them. The Earl himself managed to kill one who broke through our cordon to close with him. His colourful livery marked him as important.

We knew we were getting close to Vilnius when we spied the camps. The outer camps were the ones who served the Teutonic Knights, the Polish King and their allies. As we neared the siege works, we saw the camps of the white robed Teutonic Knights. The blue and gold of the Swedish contingent could also be spied as well as the red and white of the Danes. Sir Bengt pointed to a small and empty space close to the Swedish camp. "That is your camp, Earl Henry. I will visit with the Hochmeister and then return. I am to camp with you.

The Earl's face fell. We were on the periphery. It showed his lack of importance. He was a symbol. He represented England. His livery was that of the Plantagenet royal family. He gave legitimacy to the Teutonic Order's attempt to increase its territory. I let his men organise the camp for Roger had already picked out a place for us. I studied the walls of the mighty city. They were high walls. I saw ladders and towers. Men were attacking but not around the whole of the city. They had three towers and just two ladders attacking one section of the wall. This would not succeed. The pagans could just put their best men on the wall that was being attacked. Attacking walls was never a choice a man at arms would willingly make. You climbed a ladder holding on with one hand using your shield to protect yourself. You could not fight until you reached the top and there would be two men trying to kill you. Even as I watched I heard a trumpet and the attackers fell back. They had been beaten. Pulling back the towers brought more casualties and the ladders were left in place. They were lost to us. Each defeat made the next attack even harder. I dreaded the order for us to attack. I had with me just eight men at arms and if we had to scale the walls then I might not have any to take home.

We had one tent for us. My archers would make hovels. They wandered off to the wood we had passed three miles down the road. They would gather wood and, I had no doubt, hunt for game. We knew how to campaign. Ralph had grown during the time we had been in Lithuania. He had seen men die. He had witnessed horses being hacked to pieces by barbarians. The youth was learning to be a warrior. He found some timber and began to build a pen for the horses. Roger had chosen a site which was well away from any danger. We would have a long march to reach the siege lines but that was a price worth paying for security. The danger would be locals trying to steal our horses. Our run in with the barbarians in the forest had alerted us to the possibility of an attack in the night. Roger came to me when the hovels were erected. "Alan and I will have two men on guard at all times in the night, my lord. I wouldn't trust some of these others as far as I could throw them. We found some wild blackberry bushes. We have cut them down and we will use them to protect the horses."

"I know what you mean. The Teutonic Knights are the only ones who are trustworthy. As for the rest…" I suppose it was the same with all crusading armies. There were those who came for the right motives and there were those who were out to get whatever they could. We had not chosen to be here. We had been chosen. I think that the Earl realised that we had paid for our passage already. But for us more of his men and priests would lie dead.

Our archers had returned and we were cooking the game they had brought when Geoffrey summoned me to the Earl's tent. The young knights who had appeared so dismissive of me and my men when we had arrived now displayed a different attitude. Sir Bengt was seated with them and his squire. The Earl was not there. Sir Bengt said, "The

Hochmeister wished conference with the Earl. I believe he wishes to use you and your men in a display to make the barbarians think that the English army is coming to join us."

"Hochmeister?"

"Grand Master of the Order!"

Even barbarians knew the three golden lions and the fleur de lys. King Henry had created an Empire which had astounded the world. His sons might have lost most of it but the legend still remained. The knights gathered around me. Sir Robert d'Aubigny asked, "Sir William, where did you learn to fight against barbarians like that? When I saw you lead your men into the forest, I felt sure we had seen the last of you but you and your men slew twenty or thirty of them. How?"

"I have never been in a tourney, Sir Robert. I suspect I would do badly in one because I was not taught to fight properly. I learned as did my men by fighting as a sword for hire."

"I am sorry, Sir William, you were never taught, you say you learned? I do not understand."

"All of you, my lords, were taught to fight when you were squires. You learned to parry, to sweep, to thrust. You were shown how to fight from the back of a horse. When you fought in tourneys then you fought against men who were taught the same way. We learned in battle. We learned with men not trying to unhorse us or disarm us but men who would kill us unless we killed them first." I looked at their earnest faces, "I will offer some free advice. You do not need to take it but here it is. When you are in battle try to kill with the first blow. Forget ransom. Forget making a beautiful stroke. Use an ugly one if you have to. Take your dagger and saw a man's head off. Disembowel him from beneath. Do all that you can for if you do not then he will do that to you.".

Sir Robert nodded, "You make war sound as though it is something which is dark and dangerous. Before the forest attack, I would not have believed you but now I can see that it is so. I envisaged charging our enemies with lance and shield. I saw us sweeping our foes from before us and watching them sue for peace. They are barbarians!"

Sir Bengt Persson nodded his head in agreement, "Sir William is right. My ancestor learned to fight barbarians and he was taught by an English crusader and his men. The Lithuanians do not wish to be Christian. They want to cling to their old ways and if that means dying then they are happy to do so."

I looked into their faces, "Are you willing to die here in Lithuania?" I saw, in their eyes, that they were not. They did not answer me. "Then stay alive. Watch the sergeants at arms. They fight for pay and they kill efficiently They may not have the armour you wear but they protect themselves. Most will carry a dagger in their left hand behind their shield. When you sweep your enemy's sword away you stab him with the dagger. You all have good helmets. When you are close to the enemy and cannot use your sword then head butt him. You all wear poleyn. A sharp knee to the groin will hurt your enemies and then you can stab them in the neck. Survive, my lords, survive!" My speech was interrupted by the return of the Earl and his squire, Edward.

The Earl looked flushed with excitement. "We have been given the honour of leading the attack from one of the towers the day after tomorrow."

The Hochmeister had appealed to Henry's vanity and it had worked. He had never had to assault a castle and did not know the dangers. My words of warning had had an effect on the young knights who sat watching the Earl. They did not respond the way he expected. They did not look happy.

I asked, "Just our men in a tower, my lord?"

"We will have twenty Teutonic Knights and their twenty sergeants with us."

"And how many other towers will be attacking?"

"Two others."

I did not say so but we were doomed to failure. The Earl looked disappointed. "I know it will be hard but we are fresh, that is what the Hochmeister said. We are not tainted with failure. This just needs English courage."

The towers had been used in the attack and had been withdrawn from the city walls. They were guarded by the Polish sergeants. "Do we know which tower we shall use?"

He looked at me, "No. Why, is it important?"

"All have been in battle. Some will have suffered damage. I know a little something about siege warfare." I looked at Sir Bengt, "I would like to choose the one we use. Could that be arranged?"

"I do not see why not. Come, Sir William, let us go and inspect them. If the Hochmeister wishes the English to lead an attack then the least he can do is to let them choose their tower."

Walking across the ground with John and Roger of Chester allowed me to see at first hand the problems we would face. The ground before the walls was badly churned up already. That could only get worse. Perhaps a sudden freeze might make the ground hard but the skies looked too cloudy for that. Men who had fled the towers had discarded equipment. It would be another obstacle. The Poles who guarded the towers seemed totally disinterested by our presence. They ignored us and went back to cooking their meal. From the look and the smell, it was some rats they had trapped. On a battlefield there were always plenty of rats.

All three war machines had been damaged. I saw that one had been set alight and, although the fire had not damaged it too badly, I ignored that one. The second looked a little more solid but the logs which had been used to roll the machine towards the wall were not as thick as the ones on the first one. It would move more slowly towards the wall and that increased the likelihood of damage. The third one had better rollers but, when we ascended it, I saw that top had been attacked with axes. It would need to be repaired. The four of us stood on the top and looked at the walls of Vilnius, four hundred paces away.

"What do you think, Roger of Chester?"

"I think we should make our own, my lord. The three of them are as poorly made towers as I have ever seen."

"As we attack the day after tomorrow that cannot happen. I think we use this one and improve it."

Sir Bengt asked, "How?"

"We fit new timber to the top. We add spears fixed around the top."

Roger nodded, "There were many broken ones we passed on our way here. That will deter those on the walls from getting too close."

I pointed to the first, burned tower, "They will try to fire it, I want soaked hides and cloaks covering the front. We need to soak the wood so that it will not burn." I pointed upwards, And a better roof."

Roger nodded, "I will get the men to source the timber, hide and cloaks tonight and we will start in the morning."

Sir Bengt said, "And I will go and tell the Hauskomtur. He will not object."

As the three of us walked back to our camp I said, "We will need to drill the men. There are two ladders for each floor. Those ladders can each only bear three men at a time. John, I will put you in charge of loading the men in the tower. Once we are at the wall then you let the men up. You will do so six at a time; three on each ladder. When they have ascended then you send six more."

"Aye, lord. Will the other men at arms and knights obey me?"

I said, "You make sure that they do. I will speak with the Earl this night. If he seeks my advice then he had better support my decisions."

The food had been cooked and Ralph had platters of it for John and me. Roger was looked after by his men. The Earl had eaten and he looked at me expectantly, "Well?"

"There is one which might suffice but we will need the men at arms to repair it tomorrow. I have asked John to regulate the movement of men in the tower."

"Regulate? Command knights? He is but a squire and not a noble one at that."

"My lord, a wooden tower is not like a castle tower. It has ladders to ascend the floors. Too many men can break the ladders. Too many men on the top floors can make it unstable and it can topple. We need someone to regulate the flow of men. John can do that. It will be hard enough as it is."

"Very well. How many men can fight from the top at any one time?"

"No more than six."

"That does not seem many."

"It isn't and it explains why the attacks have failed. You need at least ten towers attacking along a wall. They will just bring twenty or thirty men to oppose each tower. We are protected until we raise the ramp and then their cross bows will tear into us. The range will be so close that they cannot miss and the power at such close range will penetrate plate armour. They will use fire to burn us. If we manage to get men on to their fighting platform then that is all that we could hope for."

"The Hochmeister made it sound easy."

I said, flatly, "He would, lord, for he will not be scaling the walls."

My words cast a damper on the mood of the Earl.

Chapter 6

The next day, while some men collected broken and discarded swords, daggers and spears from the battlefield, others went to find timber. A third group scoured the camp and surrounding area for hides and old cloaks. We soaked them in the river. While the broken weapons were fixed to the face of the tower, we had buckets of water poured from the top of the tower to completely soak the timber. It was late in the afternoon when we finished repairing the structure. Roger and my men at arms volunteered to sleep in the tower. After all our work we did not trust the Poles to watch it well enough. I spoke with Alan of the Wood before I ate with the knights and the Earl.

"You will need to support us from the side of the tower. You will be exposed to their crossbows."

"Aye lord. I had the men make pavise. We will make it hard for them but you know we cannot clear the walls completely."

"I do not expect miracles. Arrows raining down will suffice."

As he turned to go to his archers, he said, "You do not think that this attack will succeed, lord."

I said, "I have a better chance of becoming Pope than this attack has of success. For me the success will be that all the men I bring are safe and sound at the end of the attack."

I went over the plan with the Earl. Sir Bengt had identified eight knights who were fanatical enough to want to be the first to attack the walls. We would allow them to do so. The second group would be led by the Earl and myself. Sir Walter, Roger of Chester and the Earl's squire. Edward and three of the Earl's sergeants would be the second group. After that there would be another group of knights and the last group would be men at arms.

The other two towers would be manned by allies too. The Poles would take the slightly burned one and the Swedes the one which was hard to roll. All of us were in position hours before dawn. The three war machines had to be rolled into place and that took time. We just had Edward, the Earl's squire, on the top of the tower. The rest would both push and pull it into place. We had ropes at the front. There forty of our men, half pulling and half using their shields for protection, would haul the tower into place. There were bars which slotted into the side and other men would push from there. Finally, men would push from the rear. They were the ones who would not need protection.

Even though it was dark when we began, we knew that the pagans would hear us coming. A rolling war machine creaked and groaned like an old man rising from his bed. They would try to hurt us before we closed. The Hochmeister himself came, on his white horse, to order the attack to begin. I was with the men at the front. I had the Earl at the rear. John was with the Earl and I had my men at arms with me. My archers would scurry around like ants ready to loose at any crossbowman that they saw. Our tower was the only one thus protected. The rest had crossbowmen and their arrows had a flat trajectory. They could not be sent high into the air as could our arrows. They had little chance of hitting flesh. Alan's missiles could fall from on high!

I was at the front and the rope was tied around my waist. My men held the rope behind me. Teutonic Knights held the other seven ropes. With a rope tied around my waist I could protect myself with my shield. The word was passed and I strained against the rope. All of us heaved. I wondered if the tower was stuck for it seemed reluctant to move. It creaked and complained and then it moved. I found I could place one foot before the other. The ground over which we moved had been flattened when the tower had been moved before. Once we began it moved a little easier. The creaking of the timbers and the sound of men grunting alerted the sentries. We had not attacked for a couple of days. They were expecting something. Horns were sounded and I heard men racing along the fighting platform. I concentrated on using my body weight and my legs to drive us forward. We, in the front row, had the most dangerous of tasks but it was easier for us to walk. The ones behind had to copy our stride and avoid tripping up.

I had my shield angled slightly. The first bolt which struck it bounced up and over. I heard it thud into the tower. There were cracks along the shields as bolts hit us. They were sending them blindly for they could not pick out individual targets. It was as though to be hit was a judgement of God. The nearer we came to the wall the more the bolts struck shields. I heard cries from the other two towers as men were hit but we seemed to bear a charmed life. The ditch before the wall had been filled months ago during the first attacks. The men behind us carried further timbers which they would drop as they crossed. The weight of the tower compacted the wood already in the ditch with each attack.

When I reached the wall I, along with the Teutonic Knights, turned my back to the stone wall and raised my shield. Stones began to clatter down on it. When Roger reached me, he sheltered under my shield while he undid the towing rope. We would be tightly packed until the tower reached its final position. The bridge which would be lowered would span the gap. I saw the wood of the tower was close enough now to the wall and I said, "Move!" This would be the trickiest time. We had to run around to the shelter of the tower. I slipped my shield over my back and I ran. It was not a noble act but my legs carried me quickly around. As I did so I saw that the Poles had theirs in position but not the Swedes. They were still labouring up to the wall. That would delay the attack and allow the defenders to heat oil and to create fire. Already I knew that the attack would not succeed.

I saw the relief on John's face when we arrived. Sir Bengt, too, looked happy to see me. The Earl looked distracted. Glancing behind I saw why. There were bodies marking our passage. "It is time to climb, my lord!"

I entered the Stygian gloom of the tower. I nodded to John as I passed him. I climbed one ladder and the Earl climbed the other. There were another two ladders to climb. In mail it was not easy and I was already tired from the march to the wall. I reached the top and saw Edward. He was peering through a slit. He looked at the Duke. "They have lit fires, lord. They are waiting."

He nodded and remained silent. Sir Bengt arrived and he began to pass orders to the other knights. It was crowded at the top. Roger and Edgar of Derby untied the ropes which held the bridge. I swung my shield around and drew my sword. The bolts had ceased to rattle into the tower but I knew that the crossbows would be waiting. They would be aimed at head height and when the bridge was lowered, we would have to endure a storm. The bridge could carry four knights at a time. Sir Bengt and I, along with Edward and David of Welshpool stood behind the bridge with our shields. We would bear the brunt of the bolts and then step away to allow the knights to run across the bridge and on to the walls.

"Ready, my lord?"

"Aye, Roger! For God!"

The Teutonic knights also shouted something and then the bridge was lowered. I had just my eyes above the shield which was held tightly to my body. At first, we were protected by the lowering bridge but as soon as it came close to the crenulations then the bolts cracked into our shields. The four shields formed a barrier. One was driven so hard that its tip made the inside of my shield bulge. As soon as the thunder of the bolts had ceased I shouted, "Back!" We had a few moment's respite while they reloaded. We stepped away and the Teutonic Knights, in two rows of four, hurtled across. Even as they did so we stepped back to the entrance and the Earl, Sir Walter and Roger of Chester joined us. More heads appeared below us as the next men joined those who were about to attack.

Standing there I saw that two of the Teutonic Knights had already been slain but the other six had managed to gain a foothold. I stepped forward and even as I watched the crossbowman take aim at me, he was plucked from the walls by a red fletched arrow. That was one of my men. It gave me confidence and I hurried across the gap. We could not risk more than eight men on the bridge at any one time. Roger of Chester had strengthened it but the weight of mailed men would inevitably weaken it. Another knight was hacked in the side by a Lithuanian knight wielding an axe. Another knight was bleeding heavily from wounds. I was swinging my sword as I jumped to the fighting platform blocking the axe of the Lithuanian. He was about to butcher the wounded knight. I caught the axe's haft on my shield and the axe head was stopped. I punched him in the side of the helmet with the hilt of my sword. As he reeled, I punched with my shield. There were still bolts sticking from the shield and one found his eye hole. As the feathered bolt tore into the orb he screamed. His hands went to his eyes and I found that I had enough space to bring my sword up and under his raised arm. My blade came out of the other side of his neck and his falling body fell from my sword as he tumbled to the ground below.

We had our bridgehead but more men, armed with pikes and spears, were racing towards us. Worse they had heated oil ready. There were stone gullies which would bring it to the tower. We had made the tower damp but heated oil could kill mailed men "Roger! With me!"

We ran to the men who were kneeling with levers beneath the smoking cauldron. Two Lithuanians, not wearing mail, came towards us. Without breaking stride, I brought my sword over to hack into his shoulder. He turned and reeled. God smiled on us that day for, as he fell, he hit the cauldron hard. The burning liquid splashed up and into the face of the two men who were trying to lever it. The man behind was holding the torch with which he would ignite the oil. Instead it ignited the two men. Their faces and hair erupted in fire. The man holding the torch stepped back into nothing and fell to the town below. In their panic they ran towards a second man with a second torch. The torch fell on the fighting platform and the three of them tumbled, screaming and burning, to the town below. The torch was still burning. I shouted, "Roger! The levers!"

We grabbed the two levers and, placing them under the cauldron, we heaved. Even as I did so I saw that the Swedish tower had still to reach the walls and the Polish tower was burning. We heaved and the cauldron suddenly toppled over. The oil swam down the fighting platform. It hit the torch and a wall of flame leapt into the air. The defenders who were advancing towards us were either burned or forced back. Just then I heard a horn. It sounded as though it was in the distance.

Roger's voice was urgent, "Sir William, that is the recall. Come, this fire will soon reach our tower."

As I stepped backwards, I realised that five of the knights who had attacked lay dead and Edward and the Earl were pulling Sir Walter's body back into the tower. As we stepped into the tower the bridge was pulled up. While we descended, I thought of how close we had come to success. The accident with the cauldron might have allowed us to secure the wall but the failure of the other two towers had doomed us.

By the time we reached the exit of the tower, men were already pulling on the ropes to drag the tower back to safety. There were no bolts coming our way for a pall of smoke was blowing from the pyre that was the Polish tower and the fighting platform. We could hear orders being shouted as men who should have been fighting us were fighting the fire. The Earl did not pull on a rope but I did. I had been raised by Old Tom to work and not to shirk. The Earl had grown up as a pampered prince. The Swedish tower reached our lines first. I saw the Swedish commander kick the rollers. It had not been a lack of courage which had prevented the Swedes from attacking it was faulty war machines. My choice had been vindicated.

In the time it took us to return to our lines the fire on the fighting platform had been doused. The walls would need some repairs and I suspected that they would have to renew the fighting platform but it made no matter. With just two towers remaining to us we could not assault the weakened wall. By the time we had rebuilt a tower then the wall would have been repaired. The attack was a failure. The priests hurried forward to tend to our wounded. Edward had a gashed leg. He had been luckier than the Teutons who had died on the wall. Even as we looked back to the walls, we saw their heads displayed from pikes.

I had John and Ralph take my armour from me and I stripped off my mail. I smelled of fire and blood as well as sweat. I turned to Roger, "Well done Roger. That was bravely done."

He laughed, "No braver than you, lord. A man will follow a knight into hell so long as the knight leads." I saw the Earl and Sir Robert turn. They were listening.

My archers returned and I thanked them for their efforts. They had saved us losses. The burning Polish tower had taken half of the men within it to their deaths. The rest would be broken men. Some would be burned and others would have had the horror of seeing comrades ignited like candles.

My men and I were a tight band of brothers and we set to organizing food. We had worked hard. We had lost none and we were hungry. The Earl and his knights, none of whom had fought, sought solace in a jug of wine. They had been shaken by what they had seen. They had lost a knight and they saw their own mortality. I was glad that I had forewarned them.

Sir Bengt came to join us. He shook his head, "That was a bloody business. Do towers ever work? As far as I can see the advantage remains with the defenders."

"They do work, Sir Bengt, but they need to be coordinated with attacks up ladders and there should be at least ten of them to spread out the defenders. The army needs more archers. I am guessing that we lost fewer men than the others because we had archers supporting us."

"Perhaps. And now I must report to the Hochmeister. This was not the result he expected." He left us, followed by his squire. His squire's cloak had been blackened by the smoke from the burning walls. He had been lucky. We had all been lucky. Had the cauldron fallen the other way then we would now be burned as would our tower.

Ralph brought me a bowl of food and sat next to John as we ate. "Is every battle like that, lord?"

"Thankfully not. When we ride horses to war there is more control. We can use our skills. On the walls of a town or castle there is little room and skill does not count. It is the desire to live and to kill which is the difference. Do not worry, Ralph, you will not be risked on the walls. Your father wants you to learn how to be a warrior. He does not want me to return him a corpse!"

Sir Bengt did not come back to us that night. We set our guards and retired. The Earl had been in reflective mood. Even his remaining minstrels could not rouse him from his stupor. I had said nothing to him for there was nothing to say. We had naught to feel good about. Each of us would look inwards. This would either make or mar the man who would be king.

When I woke, the next morning, I wondered if we would be ordered to attack again. I had told the Earl's knights that it was unlikely but I did not know our new masters. After I had eaten and while we waited for the Earl to rise, I went, with Ralph and John, to the horses. They had now fully recovered from the voyage and the three-hundred-mile ride here. If we were not needed, I decided that we would take my men and ride forth.

Ralph had groomed both Jack and Blaze the day before. He knew horses, "These are good mounts, lord, and you have schooled them well."

"I take that as a compliment coming from the son of one whose father is now a horse master. I learned my craft in Spain where I looked after the horses of your father's company. The land there is not like England. It consumes horses. If you did not look after your mounts you went afoot and few afoot would survive."

Geoffrey, the Earl's youngest squire came running towards us. "My lord, you are needed. The Grand Master approaches."

My heart sank as we hurried back. This did not bode well. Where we to be berated for our failure or were we required to attack again? I saw that the Hauskomtur and his lieutenants were approaching our camp as well as representatives of the Swedes and the Poles. It looked like a delegation. "Ralph keep out of the way. This is the high and mighty we meet."

The Earl had been warned of the arrival and he had donned a fresh surcoat. With Edward wounded it was Geoffrey and Henry who tended to his needs. They waited in close attendance. The Hochmeister spoke English but I suspected the others did not and so Sir Bengt translated. He directed all of his comments at Henry Bolingbroke.

"Earl Henry, the Hochmeister is here to thank you personally for the valiant way you prosecuted the attack yesterday. The fact that we nearly ended the siege of Vilnius is down to you and the Teutonic Knights who followed you."

The Earl beamed. He loved compliments. The fact that he had not actually led mattered not, he had achieved that for which he came to Lithuania. He had made a name. He was seen as successful.

"Thank the Hochmeister. We all serve God and I am just sorry that we did not succeed. I pray you tell the Polish representatives that I am sorry that they lost so many knights."

It was the right thing to say and it met with the approval of all.

The Grand Master spoke at length. Sir Bengt nodded and began, "We are going to have four more towers built. This will take time. Before winter descends, we would have all of our knights ride forth and chastise the heathens. They will either be converted or they will be taken as slaves. The men will be slaughtered and the women sent to Königsberg to be shown the error of their beliefs. Earl Henry, the Grand Master asks you to ride north and ravage the lands around Ukmergė. It was thought that the town had converted to Christianity but priests were found murdered and the Hochmeister and King Jogaila wish you to be the instrument of their punishment."

"I am pleased that we can serve both the King and the Order."

Wine was brought and the great and the good celebrated as though we had won a victory. I was cynical enough to see why. The previous day had been a disaster. They were now turning it into a kind of victory. With winter coming I did not think that the towers would be built in time and they could not be used before the spring. We were being used to punish Ukmergė so that neither the Teutonic Order nor the Poles were tainted with its destruction. The other knights stayed with the Earl enjoying the wine. I left, with John, to tell my men of our next task. They were gathered around a fire. The archers had recovered some arrows and were fletching them. The sergeants had also recovered weapons from the field and were repairing them. One dagger and an extra short sword were useful additions to any warrior's armoury but my men liked as many weapons as they could get. John Bowland had a double scabbard over his back and had two swords he could use. The extra weight was minimal and, as he said, his back had extra protection.

I told them the news. "We raid." They nodded and waited. "It is to the north and we are going to destroy a town. It was thought they had converted but, apparently, it was merely a trick. We are to take the women and children captive for conversion and kill the men."

My men did not mind fighting men but women and children were something different. Roger of Chester looked at the other men and archers, "Hurting women and children does not sit well with us, my lord."

I nodded, "I know and we will not. We came here to convert the heathens. These have had one chance to do so in their own land. We will take them and others will transport them to a town where they will be schooled and taught to love God."

That seemed to satisfy my men. Alan of the Wood asked, "How far away is this town, my lord?"

"I confess that I do not know. I know that it is north of here and I got the impression that it is not far away."

"I only ask for we will need to forage. The Earl's men are hardy enough fighters but none have campaigned abroad. They seem to expect for food to fall like manna from heaven."

"There will be food in Ukmergė. We are supposed to destroy it but I would want to be in a town when winter comes. From what I have learned winter is harsh here. We are ill prepared to be out of doors when it begins to bite. I know not when we leave but I trust you all to be ready to do so."

They nodded and Harold Four Fingers grinned and said, cheerfully, "By my reckoning, lord, we have served more than a month and a half already. That means just over four months until we set sail again and return to England! Hopefully we will all bring booty and treasure back from this town I cannot pronounce!"

I laughed, "And I think that the Earl will share your sentiments. He has achieved that which he wished. Ukmergė may be just the gesture we need to have served our purpose and for us to leave here with honour."

Roger asked, "Honour lord?"

I smiled, "Not ours, the Earl's!"

Chapter 7

By the time I returned the delegation had left and Sir Bengt and the Earl were talking. The Earl frowned, "Where did you go, William? The Hochmeister wished to speak to the knight who began the fire. I told him it was you."

"The victory was yours, lord. I went to speak with my men. They need to prepare for this raid."

He waved a hand, "There is no need. We have a whole seven days to prepare."

"Is that not seven days for the people of Ukmergė to prepare their defences, lord? They must know they will be punished for slaughtering priests."

"Perhaps, but there are no city walls. The town merely has an old hillfort as a refuge. What can they do?"

A week later as we approached the town of Ukmergė, in the late afternoon, we saw what they could do. They had built a palisade around their town. They had dug a ditch. They were prepared. They had been warned of our advance. Although Alan and his archers killed four scouts, as we moved towards the town, there were others that they had not seen. They knew we were coming. My men had done their best but this was not their land. As we neared it, we saw that they had men behind the palisade. The hill fort had been manned and they had built a tower and a gatehouse. None of the defences were daunting but we would still have to take them. This time I was determined not to offer suggestions to the Earl. He would never become his own man if he relied upon me and my ideas His delay in starting out had already cost us.

He turned to me, "Well, William, what do you think?"

"I think that we have delayed too long and now we will have to assault prepared defences. We will lose men."

His eyes narrowed. He pointed to the wooden palisade, "That is not a stone wall. It is a series of small trees driven into the ground."

"And that, my lord, can still stop us. We have to clamber over it. They can use spears, axes, stones, swords, daggers and all manner of objects to strike us while we clamber over." I gestured with my right hand towards the wall. "Every part of the wall is manned. They may not have mail but they are willing to fight and I am guessing that there will be two men waiting to take the place of each one which falls."

He turned to look again at the town. When he looked back at us, I saw that he had seen the truth of the matter. "Then let us make camp here before their gates and hold a counsel of war. I am certain that we can devise a plan which will take it."

He was learning, albeit slowly.

We had horses and we did not need to surround the town. Our horsemen could stop any who tried to leave. We were not going to besiege it. Our purpose was to destroy it and its men. However, as a precaution against us being surprised, I had my men dig a ditch and line it with sharpened stakes. It would not stop an attack but it would deter one. I called Alan of the Wood over. "Alan, could our arrows harm the men on the palisade?"

"Aye, lord. It would be expensive in terms of arrows but we could clear it."

"Good. Hopefully we will find another way to attack for I hate waste but better we waste arrows than lives."

"Amen to that, lord."

"Have fire arrows prepared. Did we bring any?"

"We have twenty cage type arrows and we could make bag and resin ones."

"When time allows make some."

We lit fires closer to the enemy walls so that any foray into our camp would be spotted. I joined the knights with the Earl. He had not yet learned to include his captains of archers and sergeants at arms.

Of all of his knights, Sir Robert had changed the most. He and Sir Walter had been close. His friend had died and it had been a warning. Sir Robert had been the one to listen to my words. It was he who spoke. "It would be reckless, my lord, to risk our horses."

"That goes without saying, Robert." There was a hint of impatience in the Earl's words. He would have to learn to curb it or his men would not make suggestions.

"My point is, my lord, that means attacking on foot and, as Sir William has pointed out, they have the walls manned all around."

"And?"

"And that means that our best opportunity would be to advance and attack on foot and do so at night. They are used to fighting knights who wear white tunics and cloaks. We do not. We will be harder to see. They will have crossbows but sending a bolt at a shadow in the dark may not yield results." He pointed to me. "Sir William showed us that in conditions of poor light we have an advantage when fighting crossbows. We use our shields to cover us when we advance. We hack a hole in the palisade and pour our men through."

I liked the plan for it was well thought out. I saw the Earl mulling over the idea. "We cannot attack tonight."

I smiled, "And when we do not, they will think that we intend to siege. If we have men cut down a couple of trees tomorrow it will add to the illusion that we are going to build war engines."

"What do the rest of you think?"

Sir Richard smiled. He was the youngest of the knights. "We are all fighting a war for which we are ill equipped, lord. We have been trained to fight from horses against knights. Any idea which is suggested will be better than the empty void in my head. I think Robert's plan might well succeed and it is worth a try."

And so it was decided. We made a camp which gave the illusion of a siege but, during the day, while men cut down trees, we rested ready for the assault. I advised against attacking the gate. It was where they would expect an attack. Instead we chose a place four hundred paces to the east of the gate. The Earl decided to use half of the archers to send fire into the town while the other half covered us. We all knew that fire arrows were erratic but they caused fear when they were falling on homes. I had had the foresight to have Alan ready arrows. The Earl did not think about logistics. If he thought it then it would happen! The attack on the wall by the men with axes would be noisy and so the flaming arrows would, we hoped, draw men to the opposite side. Alan of the Wood was confident that, in the dark, they could outrange the hunting bows, slings and crude crossbows of the town. The caged arrows were good but Alan was able to use resin from the pine trees to make bag fire arrows which were slightly more reliable.

My men and I slung our shields across our backs. Ralph had wanted to attack with us but I asked him to join the archers covering our attack. He seemed happy about that. Edward, the Earl's squire, took charge of the fifteen men who would guard the camp. It included priests, pages, minstrels and the warriors who had been wounded in the attack on Vilnius. As darkness fell, we gathered. We were in three groups. I led my men, Sir Bengt, his squire and his two sergeants. The Earl led the knights and half of the men at arms. Geoffrey led the remaining men at arms. With less than seventy men it was not a huge number to attack a town with over four hundred men inside. However, they were townsfolk and we were warriors. If we could not defeat untrained farmers then we ought to have stayed in England. Behind us came three groups of archers: eight in each group. They would hit any who moved on the walls.

Alan led the fire archers. He would be on the far side, well away from us. I trusted his judgement. We crept to within a hundred paces of the walls. Sir Bengt had borrowed Edward's cloak and surcoat. His squires and sergeants had also borrowed darker clothes. We would be invisible. When I could not see the Earl, who was fifty paces from me, I led my men forward. The ditch had been dug and seeded with lillia, sharpened stakes. Had we been rushing then there might have been a danger of injury. Going as slowly and carefully as we did, we were able to see and avoid them. Suddenly the sky to the west of us flared with light as the fire arrows were launched. A bell sounded and men began to move. I heard the twang of arrows as the archers who were with us hit the men on the walls. We made our way through the sharpened stakes and clambered up to the wooden wall. Geoffrey of Gisburn and John Bowland took their axes and began to hack at the timbers which held the palisade together. The Lithuanians had failed to seal the gaps for they had erected it in haste, and the axes began to gouge holes in the wood. A body crashed to the ground just a couple of paces from me. He had an arrow in his chest. I swung my shield around for it would not be long until the timber defence was breached. The fire arrows had sown confusion. Those inside knew not whence the real attack would come. When the two pieces of wood on either side of the wooden timber we had hacked were broken Edgar and Wilfred pulled at the wood and wrenched it free. There was a gap and I stepped through. John and Natty followed me. We had a foothold.

Amazingly, some of the fire arrows had worked and I saw flames licking the roof of a building to the west. John and Geoffrey enlarged the hole so that all of my men were able to step through. The eight archers who had covered us joined us. It was bizarre. On our section of the wall we had cleared the fighting platform. There was no one above us. Others were closer to the gate trying to get at the Earl while the majority fought the fire and prepared for an attack on the western wall.

I pointed to the fighting platform and my archers, including Ralph, began to send arrows into the backs of the men who were trying to stop the Earl gaining entry. I led my nine men towards the townsfolk who had seen us and were rallying to stop us. None, except for the one who led them, had either a shield or a helmet but some of the weapons looked terrifying. They had improvised pole weapons using cleavers, axe heads and even a scythe "We keep together! Use our shields for mutual protection."

It was a mob of men who ran at us. They outnumbered us by more than ten to one. The leader had a long two-handed sword. He must have been a warrior at some time but he had a grey beard. He roared and screamed as he approached. His cries were infectious and the pagans joined in. They had lost all reason and all they saw was a handful of men standing before them. As the long two-handed sword came down, I blocked it with my shield and raked my sword across the leader's middle. I ripped him open and, even as he tried to hold back the flood of blood and entrails, I pushed him from me and thrust at the man just behind him. I skewered him in the throat. A spear came at my face. I had to trust my helmet as I had seen it too late for my shield to be of any use. It scraped off the side and I punched my shield forward into the man's hand. I hit him in the face with my sword hilt. I had accounted for three of the mob and my men had done the same. More importantly, our archers had cleared the walls and the Earl and his men suddenly poured into the side of the mob we were fighting. The Earl had more men than I did. The effect was astounding. They hacked chopped and butchered the defenders and within a few strokes most were dead while the rest turned and ran. When the last of our men entered the town, we were able to organise ourselves.

For once the Earl took charge. "Archers to the fighting platform and clear them. Harold of Derby, take four men and begin to set fire to the buildings behind us. The wind is from the west. We burn this half and work towards the other side."

One of his sergeants said, "What about booty, my lord?"

He snapped, "Forget booty! These are pagans. The Hochmeister wants this town destroying! Destroy it!"

He was showing a ruthless side which he would need if he was to lead men against barbarians.

"Yes, my lord."

"The knights and squires to the fore. Let us show them what English nobility can do."

We moved forward through the town. We found few men before we reached the gate. The main street led from the gate to the square and the small hillfort with the hurriedly erected wooden tower. The fire started by Alan's archers had been largely contained. It would flare up again now that men had stopped fighting it but we would have time to defeat the defenders. As we marched up the street Lithuanian defenders threw themselves at us in an attempt to slow us down. It was fruitless for their weapons struck shields or, at best, armour. The Earl kept up a steady pace for he was aware of the need to provide a solid front. The result was that we saw the fire begin to eat the buildings to our left. It would destroy that half of the town and the wall but, in addition, it would drive folk who had hidden in those homes towards us.

The dawn was beginning to break as we approached the hillfort in the centre of the town. I confess I had never seen anything like it. It was just a mass of mounds and ditches which had grassed over. It looked ancient. If it was not for the wooden tower they had built then it would have looked just like a hill. There were hundreds of men before it. Behind them I saw the women and children. The whole of the town had gathered. They were sheltering behind the mounds and in the ditches. I spied some shields and, on the top of the tower, I saw a few crossbowmen. There were too few for us to worry about.

The numbers were so huge that the Earl halted. He took off his helmet. "There are more men than the Hochmeister expected."

Sir Bengt said, "It may well be that they fled here from other towns. The massacre of the priests would be seen, by these people, as something of a sign."

I wondered if the Hochmeister had known that. Were we being sacrificed? Was he hoping that the death of a member of the English royal family might force the English to join the crusade? If so, he was mistaken. King Richard might go on crusade but it would be a crusade of his choosing.

The lightening sky showed our archers on the fighting platform. The Earl shouted, "Alan of the Wood, bring your archers. Let us use the one weapon they do not have." He turned to me and Sir Bengt, "We will form up a hundred and fifty paces from them and then let our archers rain death upon them. They have sealed themselves in their own prison. They cannot retreat."

Sir Bengt said, "They will attack."

"And our blades will hew them. Sir Robert, I want us in a solid line from building to building. See to it."

"Aye lord."

Henry Bolingbroke was making all the right decisions. This would be neither pleasant nor pretty but it would be effective. The sun had risen by the time the archers had gathered and the Earl had told them what he needed from them. The priest who had come with us blessed us as we prayed to God. He carried the holy banner which had been given by the Bishop of Hereford himself. The pagans seemed to be infuriated by the priest. A crossbow bolt was sent from the tower. It fell forty paces short. Then the priest joined the archers behind our shiclds. We donned our helmets and we marched towards the waiting warriors. They did not know how effective our archers were and I saw them bracing themselves as they sang themselves into a blood lust. They expected us to charge into their serried ranks.

We had two full ranks and a half rank of mailed men with helmets and shields. The Earl stopped us at the point where the bolt had landed. He raised his sword and I heard Alan shout, "Nock!" I could see the faces of the Lithuanian warriors. Some looked at each other wondering what our stopping meant. "Draw!" I heard the creak of bows. "Release!" Then there was the sound of more than ninety arrows hissing over our heads. "Nock! Draw! Release!" The commands were repeated twice more before the first of the arrows plunged down. The second and third flights added to the devastation of the first. Not a shield was raised until the fourth flights landed and by then the damage had been done. More than a hundred and fifty men, at least, had perished. Many had been the ones with shields. I saw one chief falling with an arrow sticking through his helmet and into his head. It took ten flights of arrows before it evoked a reaction. In those ten flights almost half of the men who had been facing us were struck by arrows.

I said, "They are coming, lord!"

The Earl shouted, "Brace!" He was just in time. It was as though a dam had burst and they poured from the hill towards the metal beast which stood before them. Our archers' arrows continued to strike bodies as the Lithuanians were so tightly packed as to be almost a single entity.

Ironically the closer they came to our swords the safer they were from our arrows for Alan and his archers did not risk them hitting us. The Earl was the first to slay one of the barbarians. The standard held by Geoffrey marked him as a leader and the helmeted warrior threw himself at Henry Bolingbroke, Earl of Northampton. He was now a man grown and a powerful one at that. The sword struck his shield but the Earl did not move. He pulled back his arm and swung the sword from over his right shoulder. It bit so deeply into the man's neck that his head almost fell off. It was held only by muscle and sinew. Then we were all in the fight. The Lithuanians lacked skill but they made up for it in sheer anger. Even when I stabbed one of them in the stomach he still tried to bite and gouge me as his body slid down to the ground. There were so many of them that my helmet was struck many times over as well as the armour I wore on my arms and my gauntlets but they were well made pieces and they held. The flesh we struck did not. Metal tore through arms and broke bones. Our swords gutted them and took heads. I tired of the slaughter but we could not stop killing for they would not stop fighting. As the last youth was slain by Sir Robert, the women began to keen and wail. We had won. We stood in weary silence as the last of the men we had hit moaned away to whatever passed for their heaven. The ground was covered in bloody bodies and parts of bodies. In places there were so many as to be almost as a wall. The Grand Master had demanded the death of every man and we had achieved that. We now had to burn the town and deliver the captives to the Hochmeister.

Even the Earl was wearied and dismayed by the bloodshed. He sent his men at arms to surround the women, children and the old. They would soon be captives. I turned to look at my men. David of Welshpool had had his helmet split by a club and his face was bleeding. Other than that, we seemed to be intact. Alan led my archers, including Ralph, towards us. When he saw the piles of the dead Ralph doubled over and began to retch.

Alan shook his head, sadly, "He should not have seen this, lord. Was it necessary?"

I nodded, "They were unbelievers and they killed priests. I did not enjoy doing it but had we not then more Christians might have died. We can save those souls, at least." I pointed to the women and children.

Stephen the Tracker said, "I will take some men and search the houses in case any are still hiding there. If the wind changes then the fire will do our work for us."

The Earl sent Sir Bengt's sergeants back to Vilnius to let them know that we had achieved our objective and to ask for priests. We had brought just one and he did not speak their words. If they converted then we would have fewer to march back to Vilnius. I did not relish that march for late autumn rains had begun to fall almost as soon as dawn arrived. They damped down the fires. While the relief from the smoke was welcome, I knew we would have the task of destroying the town and damp wood was hard to fire.

"While they are on the hill fort mounds they are contained. During the time we wait for the priests, we will encircle them with a new camp. Sir William, have the horses fetched. Sir Bengt, see if you can speak with them. Tell them that they will not be harmed."

"Aye, lord and food?"

"Food?"

"Yes, my lord, they and we will need to eat. I would suggest you have some men collect food."

Sir Robert said, "And the bodies of their dead, lord, the sight of them might inflame and anger the women. Sir Bengt, what are the funeral customs?"

Sir Bengt said, "Sometimes they bury and sometimes they burn."

The Earl shook his head, "We have not the manpower to bury them. We will carry them to the side of the town which was burned. It may be that our sergeants can re-ignite the fire but the bodies will be out of sight. That was a good suggestion, Sir Robert. I thank you."

Already the bond between leader and lieutenants was being strengthened. I went, with John and my men at arms, back to the camp. John looked pale and moved as though he was drugged. "Were you hurt?"

"No, lord. The mail I wore protected me but I confess that I was afeared for they were fierce and feared no death. I struck one a mortal blow and yet he continued to fight."

"He was fighting for his beliefs. I suppose we might fight as hard for ours. Remember, John, this came about because they said they had converted and then murdered priests." Even as I said it, I wondered at the true motives of the Polish King and the Hochmeister. Was religion merely the excuse to grab a country and make it their own? I had been told that Lithuania was the largest country in Europe. If that was true then whoever controlled it had a mighty prize.

Edward rose as we approached. Ralph was with him as well as the Earl's priest. "It is over. We have destroyed their men and captured their women. The Earl would have us camp within the town." Just at that moment the rain stopped. It had been growing lighter as we had walked to the camp and now a single shaft of sun shone down. I saw the priests make the sign of the cross. They took it as a sign that God smiled on our venture. I was just relieved for the earthen roads we had travelled would have become a muddy morass had the rain not stopped. "Come Ralph, John, I will help you fetch our horses. Roger, take down the tents and put them on the Earl's horses."

While Ralph strung our horses in one long line, I surveyed the town. The western half was blackened. The palisade had gone. On the eastern side of the town there were patches of black where the arrows had begun fires. Tendrils of smoke still rose. Overhead carrion birds were gathering. Unless we burned the bodies soon there would be an invasion, during the night, of rats, foxes and other creatures eager to devour the results of the slaughter. It was getting on to evening by the time we re-entered the town. Most of the bodies had been moved. The captives were a little quieter and I could smell food being cooked.

Harold Four Fingers found us, "My lord, Roger of Chester has made a camp on the western side of the hill fort. The Earl allocated our dispositions. He has spread his knights equally around it. Sir Bengt has found someone with whom he can speak. There were ladies who were married to the lords of the land and two speak Swedish. The Earl's priest found ten women and their families who said they were Christian." I gave him a sideways look. "He shrugged, "Who knows what is in someone's heart, lord? They were given the task of cooking. One of the Earls sergeants, William of Bolsover, watches them to see that there is no mischief." He lowered his voice. "We found treasure. Roger told the Earl who said he would rely on you to divide it equitably."

"Treasure?"

"Chests buried in the floors of the houses. There were some larger halls which looked to have belonged to lords. There will be enough to give coin to all the men." He pointed over to a line of twenty bodies. "We were lucky, lord, there are twenty sergeants who will remain in this heathen land."

I would have said that we had been lucky but I knew that was not the case. I had chosen well and my men and I had been together so long that we fought as one. The Earl and his knights had taken sergeants who they barely knew. They came from their lands but they did not share their hall. That was the difference. I might have had the smallest number of men but they were the best.

The stink from the captives began to grow in the middle of the night watch. The Earl had thought of everything save the needs of nature. I was on watch and I began to smell it. Added to the smell of the bodies it was a nauseating and pungent aroma. I also heard the noise of scavenging animals. I roused Sir Robert, who had the next watch, and Sir Bengt. "I do not like to wake you but I think we ought to burn the bodies in the dark. The smell of the smoke and fire will dissipate the smell of dung and piss."

"Aye, lord, for it had disturbed my sleep."

Leaving Roger and my men to watch we sought oil and pig fat. As I had expected they had laid in stores to be used against war machines. The three of us carried pails to the bodies. The Earl had had them placed on the burned timbers but omitted to have them burned. It was an oversight. As we approached it was as though the bodies were moving. It was the carrion fleeing before us. We poured the oil and fat all over the bodies and then we each picked up a brand. A circle of them had been laid around the bodies. We hurled them in. The clothes on the bodies and the hair of the men burned first and there were small flames. As the fire took hold and grew so the flames rose higher. It was almost hypnotic to watch.

The Earl's voice from behind me made me start I was so entranced, "I should have done this last evening."

"You had much to think on, my lord, and the rain had only recently stopped, lord. This is good. I thought to drive away the smell of the captives."

"This may be God's work but it is hardly glorious work. I intend to set off back to Vilnius in the morning. Marching on foot and with women and children it will take two days."

Sir Robert said, "When we passed through the unburned parts of the town, I saw wagons. There are a few horses. Perhaps the older ones could travel in the wagons. It would make for a speedier journey."

"Good, Robert."

I nodded, "But I fear that some of them will flee on the journey." The Earl looked at me, "It is something that will happen, lord, and you need to decide what you will do. Will you hunt them down or let them go?"

He looked at the bodies, "I will let them go. This is not the crusade I envisaged back in England."

Chapter 8

Even with wagons we did not reach Vilnius until late in the afternoon two days later. We fired the town before we left. It was a good site for a town but it would have to be completely rebuilt. Only the ancient hillfort had survived the flames. You cannot burn a hill. The rest was a huge blackened scar. The priests who returned with the sergeants had catechised some of the captives but I think they still believed that their god, whoever he was, would send help to them. The sight of the siege works around their capital made all but a hundred and fifty of them decide that Christianity and the attendant freedom was a price worth paying. They chose to convert. Teutonic Knights guarded the captives which included the wives, daughters and sons of the chiefs of Ukmergė. They were taken close to the tents of the King of the Poles and the Grand Master. Our tents lay just a little way away from them. We were further from the siege works but we saw the women as they gathered, each day, before the huts which had been built for them. They were housed and well-guarded as they were a symbol of what would happen to all pagans. They would convert or they would be prisoners.

The rains had come on the way back to Vilnius and, as the days passed, they became increasingly wintery. Sleet mixed with the rain and, as the days passed, snow mixed with the sleet. Some of the treasure we had taken in Ukmergė had been furs and winter clothing. They had been stored in the houses of the great and the good. As the rain turned to sleet and then snow, the hovels our men had built were improved and the furs and seal skins used to protect us from the weather. All of my men had a fur and most had a seal skin cape. However, after a month of such weather, all of our spirits were laid low.

The Earl was summoned to a counsel of war. When he returned, he appeared for the first time since our return from Ukmergė to be optimistic. "The Grand Master believes that the resolve of the defenders is weakening. Tomorrow he and the King will go, under flag of truce, and show some of the captives to those within Vilnius' walls. He has discovered that two are related to the besieged leaders."

I was not sure of the efficacy of the strategy but I was a mere sword for hire. What did I know? The Earl and his knights were invited to witness the meeting. They declined for the Earl had developed a cough and he stayed close by the fire, wrapped in his furs. Although they marched under a flag of truce, the two leaders had bodyguards as well as the Bishop and four priests. They were all armed. Four women, better dressed than the rest, were taken to within two hundred paces of the walls. Horns sounded and we saw faces appear above the gate. All wore armour. These were not common men. They were their lords, their leaders and their priests. We could not hear the words. We heard nothing. The intermittent sleet and snow had stopped and a wind wailed across the ground. It was obvious that there was a conversation going on for I saw hand gestures from those on the wall and before the wall. Suddenly one of the women broke free from her guards and bared her breasts. A crossbow bolt flew from the walls and struck her in the centre of her chest. All hell broke loose. A priest and a Polish warrior were struck by bolts as was a Teutonic sergeant. The Grand Master drew his sword and, in three strikes, decapitated the remaining three women. With shields protecting them the party hurried back. More of the Teutonic Knights and Poles ran to help their leaders.

The Earl turned to Sir Bengt, "Go and find out what happened. I am sure this was not planned."

It took hours for us to discover what had happened. Sir Bengt looked shocked when he returned. "It seems, my lord, that their plan did not go the way they expected. King Jogaila tried to use the women as hostages. The wife of the lord of Ukmergė broke free and begged her cousin to kill her and the other women for they did not wish to be the cause of the ending of the siege. He obeyed her wishes and we saw the rest. The Grand Master and the Bishop had to persuade the King not to slaughter all of the captives. The Poles now guard the captives but the Hauskomtur is also present. I am afraid this has created dissension. The Poles were already smarting from their losses in the burned tower."

The Earl nodded, "And the new towers appear to be no further forward. We did what we were expected to and yet we are no closer to ending this siege." Just at that moment the sleet turned to real snow. Great white lumps fell from the sky and the Earl shook his head. "And now winter arrives!"

We returned to our tent. Our men had already built up the fire. Each day, since our return, Alan and his men had ridden the few miles to the nearest wood to cut down timber for firewood and to collect dead wood. We had hoped to dry it out before the snows came but that would not happen now. I had managed to find a seal skin cape in the town of Ukmergė and that, along with the bear fur I had found, meant I was as warm as I was likely to be. Ralph and John also had furs. Our archers had hunted most days and we had rabbit and hare skins made into hats and mittens. We would find it hard to fight but we were relatively dry and as warm as we could be. I saw my men at arms using the falling snow to pack around their hovels. When it froze it would keep the wind out. With cloaks soaked in water for their doors then the hovels would probably be warmer and cosier than our tents.

When Alan and his men returned, they had managed to catch and kill a couple of mink and a polecat. When skinned we would enjoy a stew and the furs we could also use. They had their horses laden with kindling and wood. Alan shook his head, "The snow is thicker to the north and west of us, lord. I know not how the people who live here move in it. Already it is difficult to walk." He waved his hand at the snow. There is not a problem here yet but," he pointed to the black clouds, "soon it will be."

"I will speak with Bengt and see how the Swedes cope with this type of weather."

I went alone to speak to the knight. He was with the Earl and they were drinking. "Come and join us William, Sir Bengt has brought this distilled liquor which warms from within."

I shook my head, "I came for information, lord. Sir Bengt, how do your people move when the snow lies so thickly on the ground?"

The Earl laughed, "This is not thick!"

"It will be, lord. Is there some sort of trick?"

Sir Bengt shook his head. "We do not use wagons, we use sledges and we have wooden planks for our feet. We call them skis. When the snow freezes you will find it easier. It is when it is wet that it is more difficult to move. The next few days will see the snow become deeper. When it stops and the skies clear then it will become ice. We stud our shoes with nails and that stops us sliding around. Horses become less effective when there is ice."

The Earl looked appalled, "What a God forsaken land!"

I smiled, "I think, my lord, that is the reason we are here. God has not forsaken it. He has sent us to save it!"

I told my men the dire news. Camping in winter in a snow-covered land was not to be undertaken lightly but they were philosophical about it. Harold Four Fingers said, "Well, lord, if we cannot move then neither can those in Vilnius."

John shook his head, "I am not sure that is true, Harold Four Fingers." He pointed to the pile of snow which covered the bodies of the four women. "They have not yet been moved. That must have an effect on those within the walls of Vilnius. They are a symbol."

Harold looked at the snow and then nodded towards John, "Your squire has a clever mind, lord. The King and the Grand Master left the bodies of those women outside to rot. You can see people viewing them from the walls. If they thought to hurt those inside it is not working. Wilfred of Loidis here reckons that they are barbarians and will not sit idly by and endure the insult."

I looked at Wilfred who shrugged, "I was on duty close to the walls and I saw the looks on the faces of those on the walls. They were not happy faces."

My squire, John, said, "I am not a lord and not of noble blood. If my mother and her sisters were treated as the captives were then my father and I would try to do something about it. We would not sit and do nothing. I know these kinds of people, lord. There are no pagans in our village but we all lived simply. Family is all to us. The woman was the cousin of the lord of Vilnius. This will eat away at him. I think God sent the snow to keep them within the walls. Let us pray he does not turn it to ice."

The storm raged for four days. The land became a sea of white with little lumps which marked the hovels. Ralph and my men spent each day clearing the snow from around our horses. They piled it up to make wind brakes. Finding forage was hard. Now we had to find food and kindling for us and for our horses. It sapped our energy and the mood of our camp was depressed. Then the snow stopped. The nights became so cold that some horses and sentries died. Sir Walter's horse died. His squire was distraught and blamed himself. Our snow walls, built to keep the wind from our horses now became solid walls of ice. John's warnings prompted me to seek the Earl. Sir Bengt had been right. It was easier walking on ice than through snow. It was also dangerous. I fell over twice on the short journey to the Earl's tent.

"My lord, I came to warn you that those within Vilnius may use the ice to come and cause mischief."

"What makes you think so?"

I did not quote John for he would be dismissed as a squire who knew nothing. Instead I gave his theory as my own. Surprisingly, he did not think it a ridiculous one and Sir Bengt agreed. "I will go to speak with the Hauskomtur."

When Sir Bengt had left us, the Earl pulled his fur a little tighter around his shoulders. "The work has stopped on the towers. Food is scarce and there is no prospect of a surrender. Why did I come, William?"

I did not say it was for the glory instead I gave him the answer he wished to hear, "God sent you here, lord, and, alone out of all the men who are here, our men have saved some souls for God."

He brightened, "You are right. I would go home now but our ships will not be here for three months at least." The other raiding parties had not found enough pagans to capture. They had slaughtered all that they found.

I shook my head, "The Baltic might well be frozen. Sir Bengt told us that sometimes happens."

His shoulders slumped. "Then we are stuck here, even longer! What is happening in England while we are trapped in this sea of ice?"

When the Swedish jarl returned, he brought with him no comfort. "The Hauskomtur does not believe there will be an attack but he thanks you for your concern."

I stood, "I, for one, will have my men keep watch this night. We can sleep during what passes for the day in these parts. If nothing else it will give the men something to do."

"And I will watch with you, Sir William." The Teutonic Knight and his squire would be a useful addition to my men.

I told my men to sleep while there was daylight. Ralph was happy to do so. He was worried about the horses. He had managed to find some discarded and torn cloaks. Using a needle, he had repaired them and all of our horses had a winter coat. He had also managed to acquire some old apples. I suspect he stole them. He might have even brought them from Ukmergė. The result was that our horses were in better condition than the other English horses. I slept too. As darkness fell, we rose and we ate. The other English archers now emulated mine and we were all fed better than the Poles and the Teutons. We went, in the dark, to guard the perimeter of our camp. We were armed and mailed although we did not use helmets. Instead we wore our fur hats instead of comforters beneath our mail coifs.

As I stood with Alan, Roger and John I confessed that I did not know what exactly we were waiting for. Roger just nodded towards John, "I think Master John has it right. Those women were brave 'uns all right. They were willing to die. The lads inside the town, well, they destroyed a tower and they sent us packing but they have not done anything as brave as those lasses. I reckon that they will come tonight. They will have been building themselves up while the snow fell and will be ready about now. This ice makes it easier to move. If I was the one in charge of those inside the town, I would try to rescue the captives." He pointed, "They are close to the King of the Poles and I am betting they would like to have his head. There will be the hard lads just waiting to come out and do what they have been desperate to do for a while, kill Christians."

Roger's simple assessment of the situation made sense to me and we waited. We watched the gate, although I did not think for one moment that they would use that way to come. There had to be sally ports or they could simply clamber down a rope. I stared up at the moon and the stars. It was so clear that it felt as though we could reach up and pluck the moon from the sky. And it was cold. The rabbit skin hat I wore was a better defence against the freezing cold than my coif.

Stephen the Tracker was the one who spotted the Lithuanians or their shadows, at least. They were close to the two remaining war towers. He told me and I was about to shout the alarm when a cry ripped the night. The Polish sentries on the towers had been slain and one, in his dying, had given the alarm.

"Stand to!"

Bengt shouted the same in German and Polish! We drew our weapons and our archers strung their bows. Flames suddenly leapt up the two towers. Men began to rush towards the burning towers. Bengt shouted, "Let us go and help!"

I shook my head, "Wait. There are more than enough for that. I think it is a diversion." Earl Henry and his knights emerged from their tents and I pointed to the burning towers. "It is a distraction, lord. Arm!" The Earl and his knights would waste precious time donning mail. My men and I were ready.

Alan pointed to the tents of the Polish King and the Grand Master. Shadows were moving towards them and the captives' camp. As I watched I saw four of the sentries butchered. The sentries guarding the tents and the night guard were all racing towards the burning towers. The rest of the camp was waking up. "Follow me!"

I raised my sword and ran towards the captives' camp. I heard the clash of steel from the tents of the commanders and their bodyguards. Alan and his archers stopped and began to send their arrows towards any who looked like a Lithuanian. A Teutonic halb-bruder, a sergeant, was hacked down by a mailed warrior. The Lithuanian was surrounded by ten other men. "Alan, go and see that the King and the Hochmeister are protected."

The captives' camp had a gate. The Lithuanians were busy tearing it down and we were able to close to within twenty paces before they saw us. These were warriors for they immediately went into a defensive formation. Bengt stood at one side of me and Roger of Chester and Harold Four Fingers on the other. We had our shields. We did not run across the slippery ice. We moved steadily as though we were one being. The Lithuanians were more confident. I think they had better footwear.

Their leader was not only mailed, he also had a war axe. It was a long-handled weapon with a small head and a beak like extension. It could break armour and bones. The reverse side had a spike which could be used to smash into a helmet. He was not an opponent with whom I could take chances. He moved easily on the ice. His round shield was much smaller than mine. I braced myself for his first blow. I led my men but I could not watch them. I had to watch out for myself. As the war axe came towards me, I followed its line, watching it come effortlessly closer. The sharp night and the clear skies aided me. He had angled the blade so that it would strike down on my shield. I turned my hand over so that my palm was uppermost and the axe head slid down the face of the shield without damaging it. It missed my poleyn by the width of a finger. As the war axe slid towards the ground, I took my chance. I brought my sword from on high. I was aiming at his shoulder and he brought up his shield. It was too small to fully stop my strike and, although it blocked my blow, the sharpened blade of my weapon gouged a hole in the edge. As I pulled my blade out it exposed him a little while he was pulling back his right arm for another blow. My shield was still horizontal and I rammed it towards his neck. I hit it hard and he began to gag. Instinctively he pulled up his shield and so I swept my sword across his thigh. He wore no mail there as he had on a short hauberk. He reeled as blood spurted. He had to step back on his good leg, his right one, and that unbalanced him. Instead of hitting me with his axe he had to use his right arm to keep his balance.

Behind me I could hear my men and the Teutonic sergeants. They were fighting and slaying the other Lithuanians. Some of the captives had managed to escape from their camp and they were running towards Vilnius' walls. I could do nothing about them for I still had a dangerous opponent to fight. He was far from finished. He roared and swung his axe from behind him. This time I could not angle my shield. I would have to block the blow square on and my shield would be destroyed. I had no choice. I used the ice. I turned to my right to spin away from the blow. I could have fallen but God was watching me and I did not. As I came skidding around, I brought my sword hard into his side. He was wearing mail but my sword broke links and then broke ribs. His roar was like that of a wounded animal. He flicked his axe at me. My hands were fast enough to block the blow which had no force behind it. His wounded left leg was bleeding badly. The cold was congealing the blood but the wound had to hurt. I balanced myself and then swayed from side to side. He knew the blow was coming but not from which direction. My moves had shown him that I was fast and he had to react.

His war axe was now a liability. It had no edge. He could not spar with me. He had to make a decisive blow.

He was cunning. He pulled back his right arm and then smashed at my face with his small shield. Although not the best weapon to defend against a sword the shield was perfect for punching and he hit me square on. I saw stars and then started to tumble. He stepped forward on his good leg and raised his axe to slay me. I was groggy and dazed but I had just enough wit to let go of my shield and I threw it towards his feet. He stepped onto the shield with his good leg but the ice beneath it made him slip. His right leg could not support him and he tumbled to the ground. In one motion I rose to my feet and drew my dagger. I launched myself at him. My sword drove into his side but it was my dagger which killed him. It drove up under his chin and into his skull.

I heard cries and shouts coming from the tents. I saw that Wilfred and Natty had both been wounded and that Ralph had his sword in his hand and was helping John despatch the last of the Lithuanians. The remainder of my men were rushing to help the beleaguered King of Poland and the Hochmeister. Sir Bengt was already there with his squire and sergeants and they had a protective ring around the Hochmeister who lay in a pool of blood. I picked up my shield and ran at the Lithuanians. My sword had a tip and I rammed it through the back of the warrior who was about to stab Sir Bengt in his back. When Ralph and John ran to add their swords to the battle then the tide was turned in our favour. I saw Earl Henry leading his knights and men into the fray. We now had numbers.

King Jogaila was the one who slew the last of the raiders. The King was bloodied but alive. Around the two leaders lay the bodies of half-dressed warriors who had died defending them. Sir Bengt shouted, "Healers! We need healers!"

I saw that my archers had empty quivers, "Go and watch the captives."

"Some escaped the camp, lord, but they were slain before they could reach the walls of Vilnius."

I shook my head. What a waste. I saw that the two towers had been destroyed but they were surrounded by a pile of bodies. More men ran to us and they formed circles around the two leaders. The King looked at me and said, "Thank you!" I bowed and saw a frown on the face of Earl Henry. I wondered if he saw this as his chance for glory and a name which would be honoured by other Christian princes. It could have been his but he had not recognised the danger.

My two men were not badly wounded but they would be in no condition to fight for some time. The Hochmeister had a bad wound but he would recover. As dawn broke the Earl and I were sent for.

Sir Bengt translated, "The King and the Hochmeister wish to thank our English brothers for their timely arrival. We should have heeded your words, William Strongstaff." Sir Bengt picked up a small chest. "This is for you and your men who saved the King of Poland."

I bowed, "Thank the King but I was just doing my duty."

When the words were translated the King came over and put two arms around my shoulders. He said something and Sir Bengt smiled and said, "The King says if all men did their duty as you did then this siege would be over already."

I stepped back. I was desperate to see what the chest contained but that would have been churlish of me.

Sir Bengt turned to the Earl. He handed him a similar sized chest, "This is for you. Earl Henry, the King asks that you take the captives to Königsberg. There they will be taught to love God. Their presence here will merely encourage more attacks such as this one. An assault on the walls will not be possible until the towers are rebuilt and he gives you permission to go home to England. You and your men have done your duty. In the chest is a letter authorising you to commandeer ships to take you home."

"I thank the King but know that we are more than happy to continue to serve God here."

The Earl did not mean it but the King nodded his thanks. We were going home. We were heading back to England.

Chapter 9

There were just forty women and thirty children to be taken to Königsberg. Some had died of the cold, some had been killed during the attack and some had managed to flee into the snow. We had fewer to guard but it was not a short journey. It was almost two hundred miles. Sir Bengt and his men took wheels from the wagons and fitted runners so that they could be used as sleds. Even so, the journey would take almost nine days. We bade farewell to a siege which was doomed to failure.

It soon became obvious that our horses were the best in the column. As a result, the Earl had us at the fore. Bengt had to be with us for he knew the route we would take. His expertise helped us almost within hours of setting off. Instead of heading due west as we had expected, we headed north and west. I asked why and he pointed to the frozen river ahead. "The sleds will find the going much easier on the frozen ice. True, we will have further to travel but we will travel twice as quickly. The only danger is that the Lithuanian rebels use them too. We will need to be alert but as there are no leaves on the trees and the rivers are wide and open, we should see our enemies when they are far away."

It made sense and when we actually reached the ice, I was amazed at the speeds we managed. We managed thirty miles that first day. He told us, as we made camp the next day, that we would be leaving the river to head due west and travel over a series of lakes.

We had no grass for the horses but we had taken wheat from the town of Ukmergė. Some had been spoiled by the fires but it served to feed the horses. I had feared that the captives would try to escape but, as we made our camp, we heard wolves howling. We were in a land devoid of towns. If they left us then they would die. The ones who had tried to flee to Vilnius had been the brave ones. These were just resigned to their fate.

The next day we left the river to head across country. Here the going was harder. We went up inclines. We passed over what would have been steep slopes if they had not been softened by falls of snow. It was there where we had an accident. My men were kindly men at heart. Ferocious in a fight they were sentimental about children. Harold Four Fingers was just such a man. He was at the rear of our column riding before the first sled. A small child, no more than two years old, was not listening to his mother and as we went over a bump the child slid from the back of the sled. Had we been on the flat then there would not have been a problem but it was a steep twisting path up a slope which passed between trees and the ground fell away to the south. I guessed that when there was no snow it would have been a rocky crag. The child rolled down the slope and then toppled and slid over the edge. He was saved halfway down by a fork in the branches of a tree. He was lodged but in a precarious position. He screamed, I guessed for help. The mother, a thin young thing herself, wailed. Harold was the closest warrior to the bairn and he did not pause. He threw himself from the back of his horse and took off his sword and belt. He reached the edge of the snowy crag and did not hesitate.

We dismounted and ran to see if we could help but it looked hopeless for the child was a good ten feet from the top. He had landed in the fork of the tree and was held there by two thinner branches. Had the tree not been there then the child would have fallen to his death. Harold began to climb down the icy cliff. The snow had frozen and Harold used the frozen irregularities to make his way to the child. It was only thirty or so feet high but the child was lodged twenty feet, at least, from the bottom. There were ice covered rocks there and the child would have died if he slipped. I think the child was terrified and frozen with fear. That saved him. Harold took off his mittens and continued his climb. It was an almost suicidal journey. The tree was beneath an overhang of frozen snow. The child had stopped wailing and was now calling, it sounded like, 'mama' which made the woman cry even louder. I saw the Earl, as he and the knights who were riding up as the rear guard, look over with a bemused expression on his face.

Harold was making good progress and he was just four feet or so from the child when he slipped. His good hand was his right one and, by some miracle, he managed to grab the branch closest to the child. I heard a crack. The forked branch was breaking. Roger and Natty had been the two who reacted the quickest. They grabbed a rope and ran to the cliff edge. Roger tied it around the cantle of Harold's saddle and Natty fed it over, "Grab the end Harold and we will pull you up!"

"Not without the bairn."

"Don't be daft, man! The branch is breaking! You have done your best but the child is doomed!"

Ignoring them we heard Harold as he spoke gently to the boy, "Now don't you worry. Uncle Harold will get you," He began to swing from his good hand. He reached the branch with the child and gripped it with his four fingered hand. He was now stuck. He could not grab the child for he hung on to two branches. The rope snaked behind him but he could not grab that either. I heard another crack. The weight of the child, Harold and the ice were breaking the branch. "Right little man. Climb on Uncle Harold's back and I will give you a ride." It was ridiculous. The child could not understand him and yet, miraculously, the child put a hand out to reach Harold's arm. "Good lad!" The touch seemed to give the child confidence and he launched himself at Harold. It was too much for the branch which broke. Harold's arm flailed as he tried to keep steady on the one remaining fork of the branch. The boy clung on to Harold's arm. I saw Harold gesturing with his head, "Come on son. Arms round my neck eh? Come on. You can do it!" The boy threw his arms around Harold's neck. He gripped so tightly I was sure that he would strangle him. Harold just grinned and he flapped his now released left arm. He grabbed the rope and shouted, "Have you got me Natty? I will have to let go of the branch."

Roger of Chester shouted, "We both have you and the rope is tied to your horse. Let go and we will pull you up!"

I saw Harold close his eyes in a silent prayer and then he let go of the branch and grabbed the rope with his good hand. It held and Harold's hand gripped the rope tightly for two lives depended upon it. All of the men at arms and archers cheered. Roger shouted to Harold's horse, "Back up Bucky, back up!" The horse walked away from the cliff and gradually the two fish were hauled from what had seemed certain death just moments earlier.

As we pulled the two of them to the top the mother broke free from the arms of those who had been restraining her and hurled herself at Harold and the child. She squeezed the boy tightly and then, holding him away from her began such a tirade that the boy burst into tears.

Harold wagged a finger at her, "Now then, lady, I didn't risk my life so that you could terrify the poor little soul." He stroked the boy's head. The child turned and seeing Harold threw his arms around his neck and hugged him. Harold Four Fingers was a terrible man in battle but I saw his face crease and tears welled up in his eyes. The woman reached up and kissed Harold. She began a flood of words.

Sir Bengt smiled, "She says she owes Harold more than she can pay. Whatever he wants from her is his."

Harold looked embarrassed. He shook his head and handed the boy back to his mother, "Just doing what any Christian would do." He turned to the Earl, "Sorry for delaying us, my lord, but I couldn't let a little one die like that could I?"

The Earl shook his head and smiled, "No, Harold Four Fingers, and I think that your kind act has ensured that there will be no trouble from these captives on the way home." All of the captives were applauding Harold.

Sir Bengt translated all of the words and the Earl was right for we had smiles instead of scowls from then on. The Poles and the Teutonic Knights might be their enemies but the English were seen as saviours.

As we set off, I said, "Harold, you had better ride by the sled. I think it will make it better for the child and his mother if he can see you." He nodded, "That was bravely done and I am proud of you."

We stopped when we reached the lakes. We made camp and fed the horses. We lit fires and we set sentries. "Harold you have done enough this day. You need not stand a watch."

"Thank you, lord. I will just go and see how the bairn is. "

Roger gave him a knowing smile, "And the bairn's bonnie mother has nothing to do with it?"

"Of course not."

It took some days to cross the lakes. Harold and the woman, we learned her name was Magda, became closer. I think that Roger was correct. Harold was smitten but he was smitten by them both. The child clinging to his neck had bonded them. It made our journey easier for the women actually helped us to cook the food and the smiles from the captives made life easier.

When we left the lakes and the rivers then the going became harder. The sleds moved slower but Sir Bengt assured us that we were making good time. I suppose we were but I had the itchy scalp which always boded badly for us. We were descending a welcome slope on what was, in summer, a road. Now it was a flatter piece of ice. Stephen the Tracker was at the fore and when he pulled back the reins then I knew there was trouble. As soon as he nocked an arrow I shouted, "Ware the fore! Enemies!"

The Earl galloped up to me, "I see no enemy!"

"Nor do I but Stephen has nocked an arrow and I am guessing that he has!" I saw Alan organising my archers.

We stopped and the Earl waved ten of his men at arms to guard the rear. My archers spread out before us and the other archers, now used to obeying Alan, rode their horses closer to him. We now had our forty-eight archers as a thin line before us. I nudged my horse forward and joined Stephen and Alan. Stephen the Tracker did not turn as he spoke. "I am sorry, lord, but this does not feel right. There is a wood ahead and when my men and I rode along the ice the clatter of our hooves should have made the birds flutter off. None did. There are no birds there and I wonder why. I think that there are men in the woods waiting to ambush us."

I could not see a way around the wood. We would have to trip the trap. "What do you suggest?"

"I will take ten archers and move to within bow range. I will leave Simon the Traveller here with the rest of the archers. If I can make them follow us then you and Roger of Chester can deal with them."

I nodded, "Then let us do this."

I turned my horse and rode back to the others. "Alan and I think that there is an ambush ahead."

The Earl looked sceptical but Sir Bengt said, "This area is known for its pagan beliefs. We have tried to drive them hence many times and we have failed. You may be right."

The Earl looked resigned, "What do we do?"

"You wait here with the knights, squires, priests and minstrels. There are men guarding the rear. I take the others and if Alan can make them attack us then we will deal with them."

Sir Bengt shook his head, "You make it sound easy."

"Not easy but it is what we do. We are comfortable with such attacks." I nudged Blaze forward, "Ready when you are, Alan of the Wood."

My archers rode towards the woods. They were not horse archers that is to say they could not ride and release arrows while mounted. They could, however, stop and by turning their bodies draw back their bows. The long bow was too long for a horse. When they stopped the rest of the archers began to move as Stephen the Tracker waved them down the slope.

I said, to the men at arms with me, "Forward, but slowly."

The ten archers with Alan all drew. I guessed they could see what we could not. He had chosen woodsmen all. I saw the arrows descend. Nothing happened. A second and third flight followed. The third flight did it. The Lithuanian rebels raced from the woods. Clad in furs they looked like animals and not men. Stephen the Tracker halted his archers and I heard him shout, "Nock! Draw! Release!"

I drew my sword as we moved down the slope. I could feel Blaze's hooves sliding on the slope. Perhaps that was what the Lithuanians were counting on. Certainly, the sleds would have been hard to control if we were descending and under attack. Alan and his archers rode through Lol and his men. Stephen the Tracker's archers' arrows fell amongst the Lithuanians. Although they struck, they did less damage than I might have hoped. I saw fifteen bodies close to the wood but there were more than a hundred of them and they had spread out across the ground. Our archers had a more difficult time. As they closed with us, I saw why our arrows had done less damage. These men had shields. They were not large ones but the arrows had not come as a flight of forty and the Lithuanians had seen the arrows coming. They had raised them to protect themselves.

"Archers fall back and support us. Sergeants at arms, Sir Bengt, let us do God's work!"

The pagans who advanced outnumbered us. However, by spreading themselves out they had given us a chance. We rode in a tighter block and headed for their centre. I only had thirty men with me. Some sergeants had been killed and wounded and others were driving the sleds. The thirty men I led were aided by four Teutonic Order warriors. I was confident.

I pulled up my shield. Roger on one side of me and Sir Bengt on the other did the same. The Lithuanians we had fought thus far had, generally, been smaller than other warriors. They were squat and broad. I held my sword below me and I was ready to lean to the right. Blaze was a clever horse. He would avoid, if he could, any attack from my left. A group of Lithuanians saw our intent and they closed together to give each other support. It was not a shield wall for they allowed each other the room to swing their weapons. I chose the man I would kill. He wore a simple round helmet and he held a pike. His weapon would reach me before I could strike him. Rather than swinging he thrust at me and, as the head came towards Blaze's neck, I swung my sword up. My blade severed the shaft below the head. As I passed, I flicked the sword at his head. The tip scored a long line down his neck. It did not kill him but it was a bad wound for it bled.

I brought my sword down again and hauled back on the reins. I did not want to get ahead of the others. We had broken through their first warriors but there were more. As I pulled back to swing at the warrior with a sword who rushed at me, I saw others struck by arrows. Now that they were on foot my archers were more accurate. The Lithuanians could not focus on the arrows for there were horsemen trying to kill them. The Lithuanian's sword struck my poleyn. The blow hurt my knee but my sword swept upwards and hit the pagan in the head. His skull was split in twain from the chin to the top.

I wheeled Blaze and pulled him around so that I rode across their line. His hooves skidded slightly on the ice and his back end came around. One barbarian thought to take advantage and rushed at me. He seemed to be surer footed than we were. His swinging pike came down at me but I met it with my sword. As Blaze's hooves found purchase, my horse was able to move forward. The Lithuanian was too close to us and one of Blaze's hooves smashed into his shin, breaking his leg instantly. He fell and rolled down the slope. I had learned my lesson and

I did not try any further fast moves. I walked Blaze steadily. My men had split the pagan warband and they had been forced to turn across the slope to face us. Our archers now had free rein. When the Earl brought his handful of knights to join us, the skirmish was ended. The pagans fled. Their flight cost them another fifteen men as our archers sent arrows into unprotected backs.

We had lost men. Five sergeants at arms had died in the attack. All of mine were still whole and for that I thanked God. While Alan and his archers ensured that the trail through the wood was clear the sleds were brought slowly down the slope. Our dead were slung over their horses. We would have to find a time and a place to bury them. The pagans were stripped of weapons and treasure. When we returned home there would still be a war here in Lithuania and Sir Bengt and his brother knights would have a better chance if the weapons of the enemy were denied them.

I rode with the Earl and Sir Bengt as we followed the sleds down the slope. The Earl swept his hand across the white ice around us, "I do not envy you your task, Sir Bengt. These people do not wish to be converted and this is a harsh country in which to fight."

The Swede nodded, "It is a hard and unforgiving country but once Vilnius falls then the rest will follow. The Hochmeister prosecutes the siege forcefully, my lord, to end the war."

I shook my head, "I am sorry, Sir Bengt, but the siege was a half-hearted affair. Three towers to take those walls? You were losing more men outside the walls than would be dying of hunger within. Your knights were at Acre when that fortress fell. The Turks had many towers there. It was a lesson which should have been learned."

He was silent for he knew I was right.

We stopped six miles from the attack on the far side of the forest. We found a deserted village. The fires still had warm ashes and so we knew that the attackers had come from the village. They had taken their food but not their kindling and we had good fires with seasoned wood. We were almost warm. We set guards and we found some earth which was soft enough to dig. We buried our dead.

Sitting around our fire, after the priests had spoken over the dead, we were in sombre mood. The Earl was reflective, "I will have less coin to lay out when we return to England but I would that those men we lost were alive and I had to spend it."

This was a new Henry Bolingbroke. He had changed. It was as though being plunged into the icy world of Lithuania had tempered his steel. "I shall choose my wars more carefully next time."

Sir Bengt said, "You do not regret your crusade do you, my lord?"

"Sir William here is right, Vilnius will not fall and that means our crusade has failed."

"Not so, lord." Sir Bengt pointed to Harold Four Fingers. He was seated with Magda and her son whose name we had learned was Pyotr. The three were laughing as Harold amused them with tricks. "As I recall from the Bible there is a tale of a pair of sons. One is profligate but his father is pleased when he returns. There are two souls which have been saved. Who knows how many of the others have been redeemed. This is not a war which can be measured in gold but in souls saved. Two is not a great number but I will take that as a start. When I go to meet my God, I can hold my head up and know that I did all that I could."

I admired his belief but I wondered at the cost. The cold and the battles had cost us more than forty men dead. Others were crippled. John of Aldgate had lost his left hand. His life had been saved by the freezing air but the sergeant at arms who had followed Sir Walter had a bleak future.

It took three more days until we reached the fortress that was Königsberg. This was a bastion in the north of the Grand Duchy of Lithuania. It was not as strong as Marienburg but it was a formidable copy. Concentric walls and a square keep were well built. The mighty walls and sturdy gates must have seemed like a prison to the captives. The laughter of the journey was now replaced by fearful expressions. It was as though they were entering a prison. The nuns and priests who were there to educate the captives were not prepared for them and that gave us an extra day where we had to guard them. An empty warehouse used to store wheat was given over to them. It would not delay us by much and Sir Bengt felt that our presence would make the transition easier for them. We stayed in the barracks of the knights. Being winter a large number had headed east to raid the lands that were still pagan. Ralph was pleased that we would not be leaving soon. He fretted about the animals. The extra few days would enable us to feed them up and for them to recover from the rigours of the journey.

Two days after we had arrived Harold Four Fingers, looking nervous and anxious, approached the Earl, Sir Bengt and I. I had rarely seen Harold anxious about anything. Despite his ancient injury he was as confident in battle as any man. He spoke to me but his eyes glanced nervously at the Earl, "My lord, I have a boon to ask."

"Ask away, Harold. You are the most loyal of men. If it can be granted then I will do so."

"Magda and Pyotr would live with me. I wish them to come to England." He looked at Sir Bengt, "Thanks to you Sir Bengt, I have learned enough of her words and she wishes to live with me. At least I think she does. She spoke words I did not understand."

I looked at the Earl who seemed disinterested and then said, to Sir Bengt, "Perhaps, Sir Bengt, before we make a decision you could speak with the woman and ascertain the truth?"

"Of course."

They left. "Earl Henry, if she does wish to come home with us will that cause a problem?"

"A problem?" He shook his head, "I cannot see why. She would travel on your ship and would be your responsibility when we reached England. For the life of me I cannot see why Harold would encumber himself with a pagan and her urchin!"

He did not understand my men. He thought their whole life was war and fighting. He did not know that they were men, as he was, with the same desires and needs. "They say, lord, that if you save a life that it becomes your responsibility. I know that my men believe that."

"I do not. If I save a man's life then that man should be grateful to me. You are grateful to me for your elevation are you not? You are happy to have a larger manor? I owe you nothing for that; in fact, you owe me!"

It was not the same thing and I realised the futility of argument, "I am grateful, my lord, and you may be right."

Harold and the Swede returned and the look on Harold's face confirmed that she did wish to come to England with him. Sir Bengt, too, was smiling, "I now understand the woman's decision. She is of the old religion and when Harold saved her son's life, she believed it was the work of the Norns."

"The Norns?"

"In the old days people believed that there were three sisters who wove spells. They determined our past, our present and our future. The people called it *wyrd*. You would call it fate. The woman believes that she cannot leave Harold for their threads, hers and her son's are connected to his and if they are separated by the sea then the threads would be broken."

The Earl asked, impatiently, "So, a broken thread, what of it?"

Sir Bengt said, "The thread, my lord, is their lives. She believes their lives would end."

The Earl laughed dismissively. I knew that Harold and my men all believed in fate as something which determined a man's life. It explained otherwise inexplicable deaths on a battlefield.

Harold shook his head and turned to me, "Well, lord?"

"Of course, you may bring them with us but they are still pagans. That may cause problems in England."

"Lord, we came to Lithuania to save souls. Perhaps God has given me these two to save. I will make her my wife so that Pyotr has a father and I will strive to help them to come to God. I know that I am not a godly man but perhaps this is my chance to become one. I am content."

When we left, to head to Danczik, there were tears from Magda, for she was leaving her friends. I also saw that some of the women looked enviously at Magda and her son. The two had a future. For the rest they would be little better than slaves. The best that they could hope for was to be taken on as servants in someone's home.

The one hundred and fifty miles to Danczik were relatively safe. We were in the heartland of the lands of the Teutonic Knights. More, we were travelling along the coast and the sea had yet to freeze. The air was milder. It was wet but not as cold. The men who did not own one had bought seal skins capes when we had been in Königsberg. We were all drier. There were even patches where we could graze the horses along the way. Ralph was happy.

We were a day away from Danczik when John of Aldgate rode up to me. He was with Natty Longjack. Natty had been wounded and when we had been in the camp at Vilnius they had been tended by the same priest. A friendship had grown. Natty spoke, "Lord, John of Aldgate has lost his master and lost his hand." He gestured to the head of the column where the Earl and his household knights rode. "John has spoken with Sir Walter's squire and the Earl. He was told that he is of no use to them and when they land in England, he will receive his pay and that is all." He shook his head, "That is not right, lord."

"There is no compunction for either the Earl, nor Sir Walter's family to provide for a crippled soldier." I knew my words were harsh but so was the world and the sooner John of Aldgate realised that the sooner he could get on with his life.

John of Aldgate nodded, "I seek no charity, my lord. I lost my left hand. That does not mean I cannot do my job." I cocked an eye at him. He smiled, "Strap a shield to my stump and I can protect myself."

"And hold the reins of a horse at the same time?"

His face fell, "No lord."

Natty looked pleadingly at me. I knew what they wanted. I thought of the men I had known as a child. The ones who had not survived whole had gone back to England to become beggars. There was little sympathy for wounded warriors. "John of Aldgate, what is it that you wish?"

"I wish to be a warrior still but you are right, my lord, I cannot ride and fight."

I nodded, "But if you do not have to ride you could defend a wall, or my home, could you not?"

They both brightened, "Aye, lord, I could."

"Then, John of Aldgate, if you wish to join my company then there is a place for you. You will be the sergeant at arms of my new hall at Weedon."

"Thank you, lord!"

I knew that the Earl would think me sentimental, foolish even, but I cared not. I felt good about myself. I had done two Christian acts. For me the crusade had been worthwhile.

Part Two
Irish War

Chapter 10

The Komtur of Danczik was pleased to see us. He made us more than welcome. As we dined in his castle he said, "God, it seems, smiles on you, Earl Henry. There are English ships in the harbour. You may not need to commandeer ships. They came to pick up Baltic timber but there is none to be had. A French fleet arrived a month since. The English ships have been waiting for a week in the hope that more timber would arrive. I told them that none hew timber in winter."

The Earl's face lit up. He sent Edward, now fully recovered, and Geoffrey to arrange the passage. "That means we will be home a month early. We might have missed Christmas by a month but we will be home."

The Komtur said, "If you had waited another month then the harbour might well have been frozen over. You could have been trapped here until spring."

"Then God has truly smiled upon us."

'The Maid of Heart' was one of the ships in the harbour. Her size meant that the Earl did not want her and so we were reunited with Captain Peter. I left it to Roger of Chester and Ralph to see to the loading of the horses. The Earl had allowed John of Aldgate to keep the sumpter he had ridden across Lithuania. It took all day to load the ships and I took the opportunity of visiting the market with Sir Bengt. We had grown close in the months we had been here. The Earl had increasingly closeted himself with his knights. The loss of Sir Walter had had an effect on them. I went to buy items we could not get at home and I sought presents for Eleanor. She prized practicality and so I bought well made pieces of furniture. Sir Bengt ensured that I was not robbed.

"I should have liked to visit England, Sir William. My family's connection with England is strong."

"Visit any time you like, Sir Bengt, I will make you welcome."

"I fear that I have given my life to the order now. My life will end here, in Lithuania."

I shook my head, "I see that there is still some pagan in you."

"No, William, it is just that I have seen divisions between the Order and the Polish King. He has only recently converted to Christianity. I fear that we will end up fighting over the corpse that is Lithuania."

"Then leave the Order. Go home to Sweden. Marry."

"I am the youngest son. The land has gone to my brother. I could not hire my sword. I have committed to God and I will die in his service," I was sad. Sir Bengt meant what he said. He would die without wife and issue. He would fight for the Order. My life was better. I had a wife and children. On the journey home I would think long and hard about that conversation. It filled me with sadness. Sir Bengt was but a little younger than I but he had given up all freedom of choice. It made me more determined than ever to be the master of my own destiny.

We bade farewell and left on the morning tide. The Earl was heading for London but we would travel in convoy until we reached Hart-le-pool. He took me aside before we sailed, "You have served me well again. I will send the coin I owe to your home in Stony Stratford. With it will be the deeds to Weedon. If you stay close to me, William Strongstaff, then who knows how high your star may rise."

I was not certain if he was trying to suborn me. He knew of my oath to the King and that I would never betray him. I decided that ignorance was best. "I will always be loyal, my lord. I owe you much."

He seemed satisfied and he boarded his ship.

This time there would be no short cuts. We would not risk the pirates. We sailed in convoy and our ship, as the smallest, was relegated to the rear. I did not mind. I had much to occupy my mind. Our three new friends were made welcome. My men took advantage of the warmth of the horses below decks and did not venture on the deck where icy winds blew. The close confinement meant that Magda and Pyotr had lessons in English while John of Aldgate came to know his new shield brothers. I was alone with John, playing chess with the new set I had bought in the market. They were made of bone and were Viking figures. They were well carved. One set was stained red.

"Well, John, that was an experience."

"Aye lord, I have been on crusade. I need not go on another."

"You did not approve?"

"Those women we took captive should have been allowed to live the lives they wished."

"But they will be converted."

He shrugged, "A man's beliefs are his own. If they choose not to go to heaven then that is their choice. How many men who died Christians will not go to heaven for they did not confess before they died?" He lowered his voice, "Does that sound as though I am blaspheming?"

I shook my head, "No and I agree that there are some parts of our belief that I do not understand. I have to believe that our God is kinder than the priests make out. If you do good then I believe it matters not if you have not confessed; God will take you."

He brightened, "Truly?"

"As you said, John, a man's beliefs are his own. We all look deep within ourselves. I believe that I have not yet committed an act of which I am ashamed, not of my own volition anyway. I did not enjoy massacring the men in Ukmergė but I was obeying my lawful lord. If that was a sin then there is no hope for any of us. We all obey our liege lords!"

We sat in silence. I said, "Checkmate!"

We set the board up again. John fingered the white king, "And King Richard, lord, what of him?"

"What do you mean?"

"He is our ruler. What if he commands us to commit an act which makes us sin?"

"The King and the Queen are happy in Eltham Palace. He has shown no desire to order us to do anything of which I might be ashamed."

"But you were his bodyguard."

"And protecting a King is a sacred office. I never had to commit any sin while I watched him."

"And now you serve him and you serve the Earl." He moved his pawn. "One has the throne and the other desires it."

I did not answer for a while. I picked up my knight and moved it. The Earl's words as we had parted were still dancing around inside my head, "We cross that bridge when and if it comes. I, for one, hope it does not for that knot is too hard for me to untangle."

It was as we neared the Scottish coast that the weather improved. It did not become any warmer but the wetness went from the air and my men at arms and archers ventured forth from the hold. I saw that Harold had his arm around Magda and that Pyotr held his good hand. It was meant to be. It was as we passed the mouth of the Tyne that the Earl left us. They headed away from the course we had chosen to take a more southerly course. We headed south and west towards the mouth of the Tees and the harbour of Hart-le-pool.

I stood with the captain as we passed the harbour of Seaham. "You have been well paid, Captain?"

"Aye, Sir William. You need not fret. I have the coin from the Earl. We found no timber but this cargo will suit me."

"Yet your men will have to clean the hold again!"

He tapped his nose, "It is winter, lord. The straw, hay and dung are worth coin to the farmers. It is like gold. It is an extra piece of profit."

I liked the captain. He had learned to make the best of what came his way. The attack by the pirates had shown me how parlous was the life of a sailor.

As we landed the horses I spoke with Ralph. "And the horses? When can they travel?"

He smiled for he had become far more confident. Physically he had grown but I saw the makings of a man within. "I have thought of that, lord. If we walk for one day that will allow all of us to get used to the land. We need not rest them."

I nodded, "And there is a ferry at Stockton. If we walk there it is but twelve or so miles. It will cost us to cross but that matters not. We will save thirty miles."

And so we walked. There was a road. It was maintained by the Bishop of Durham. I knew not who was lord of the manor of Stockton but if we could not be accommodated then a night camping would not hurt. In the event Sir Richard of Stockton proved to be a most hospitable host. He was a grandfather with grey hair. His wife, Anne, was too. His son was lord of Norton and Sir Richard enjoyed an easy life. The castle looked big enough to house a large garrison but there were just eight men to guard the walls. He was happy to accommodate crusaders.

As we ate that night he said, "Times are easier now than in the time of my forebears. In the time of the Warlord this castle was oft times attacked. Now, thanks to the effort of the Percys and the Nevilles, the Scots are limited to cattle raids along the Tyne valley."

"Then you have a good life here?"

"Aye we do. We have a good market, the best for miles around. But what of you? Did I not hear that Sir William Strongstaff was once the bodyguard to the King?"

"I was but that seems like another life now."

"And you have come from crusade? Two truly noble enterprises."

"Yes, my lord, I served with the Earl of Northampton in the Baltic."

"He is the King's cousin, I believe?"

"Aye, lord."

"Then you have achieved much to serve the two highest men in the land. I fear my life has been dull by comparison. Raising a family and watching over my manor have been my lot."

The next day as we headed south, I wondered how many other men there were like the lord of Stockton. They were knights who could wield a sword but rarely had to. Then there were knights like me who seemed to be forever drawing their sword in anger. Perhaps I was due for some peace. I doubted it for I was still a warrior at heart but I had had enough of slaughtering those who were not warriors. We left Stockton and headed for Middleham. As we rode, I said, "Well, Ralph, son of Ralph, you will soon be back home. Are you pleased to be so close to your home and family?"

"In truth, my lord, I am conflicted. I would like to see my mother, father, brothers and sisters but I feel that I have seventeen more brothers and I do not want to leave them."

"Then you have a decision to make over the next few miles. Do you come with me and say farewell forever to your home, or do you bid farewell to us? There is no middle way."

"I know, lord. I have until we pass Richmond Castle to make up my mind."

Red Ralph greeted me while his mother and sisters greeted young Ralph. "How did he do, lord?" There was concern as a father from Red Ralph as well as the concern of a warrior.

"He is his father's son and he is a warrior. He knows horses. He has slain men with his bow and with his sword. He did not flinch and my men are happy for him to be a shield brother."

There was a look of joy on Red Ralph's face. He nodded, barely able to speak, "Then that is all a man can ask. I am in your debt, Will."

"You owe me nothing for I would be lying in the dust of Spain if it were not for you, Old Tom and Peter the Priest."

My men were happy to be in the barn for it was warm and they had English beer. They had missed it. Magda had become their cook and she helped Mary prepare the food. John ate with my men and so I, alone, ate with the family. I saw Ralph looking nervously from me to his father and then, finally, to his mother. When we had eaten and the platters taken out, he went out to fetch in some logs. He banked up the fire. I said nothing but supped the fine ale. Eventually Red Ralph said, "Come son, spit out the words which hide in your throat, lest they choke you!"

I smiled for Red Ralph had not changed. He was as perceptive as ever.

His son nodded, "Aye father. I have killed and I am now a man." I saw his mother's hand go to her mouth and his brother and sisters giggled as though he had sworn. "I like the life of a soldier and, with your permission, I would follow Sir William."

Mary said, quietly, "No."

Red Ralph put his hand on hers and shook his head, "Wife, the carrot is out of the ground. You cannot return it. Our son has seen a little of the world and wants more. He has tasted battle and he is not afraid. If we made him stay, he would come to hate this life and then to hate us."

"But we will never see him again!"

"That is quite likely but he will live and, if he serves Will Strongstaff, then I have no doubt that we will hear of him again. Who knows if we will never see him? Can you divine the future? We gave him life. Give is the word. We cannot take it away by making him stay here."

She began to weep, "But he is my bairn! He is my first born. He is my little Ralphie!"

Young Ralph was close to tears. He put his arm around his mother, "And I will always be that boy but I am a man grown. I will not be foresworn and make a promise which I cannot keep but if it is possible then I will visit with you. How is that?"

I suddenly felt guilty. It was not of my doing but I was breaking up this happy family. "Mistress Mary, I will need horses from time to time. What say I send your son to buy them? He is a good judge of horseflesh. That way you can see him. It will not be regular but better than naught."

She grabbed my hand and kissed it, "My lord, you are the kindest of men! I thank you! Forgive a foolish mother!"

I thought back to my mother who had been taken from me. I understood her feelings better than she could possibly know. Ralph went with his mother to pack his chest. I spoke with Red Ralph. "If you wish he can become my second squire. He knows horses and it would not take much to train him."

He nodded, "I am just grateful that all is well in my house. If he could become a squire then that is elevation beyond my wildest dreams but if he were just to be a sergeant at arms then I am content."

"Whatever happens I will let you know. It was not empty words I spouted. I will need horses and I would rather buy them from someone I trust."

"You could never tell a lie, Will Strongstaff, not even to save a life. You are a knight with honour and I am glad that you are my friend."

We had no snow on our way south but we had a wind which had followed us from the Baltic. As Harold Four Fingers said, "It is a lazy wind, lord. It cannot be bothered to go around us and so it goes through us!"

Magda had been surrounded by English words and had learned enough of our language now to be able to speak to us. Pyotr was fluent. I suspect it was because he was so young. He would grow up English.

He had already picked up some choice phrases from my men. How strange would that be, a barbarian boy growing up and speaking English?

My wife was so pleased to see us arrive back early that she did not even notice we had grown by four for the first few hours. John and Ralph did not eat with us. They knew that I wished to speak with my wife. I told her all and left nothing out. Eleanor knew my heart. She knew that which troubled me. She patted my hand when I had finished, "You are a good man, Will. You did not need to go on a crusade to show that you are a Christian." She nodded to the chest of coins I had brought back. "And to be paid for doing God's work is no bad thing either. That will come in handy. I have a Reeve for this manor. John's father, Jack, is a good man and we can trust him. All we need now are the deeds to Weedon and we can move."

"In winter!"

She laughed, "This from the man who has just spent months in the land of ice and snow? If we go now then when the spring comes, we can plough and plant. The last bad harvest we had was a warning! Let us heed it!"

In the event the deeds and my payment did not come for two months. My wife fretted but I did not worry. Henry Bolingbroke and his father were the richest men in England. The money he owed me was nothing to them!

As soon as the deed and my stipend were delivered by Geoffrey, my wife was eager to ride to Weedon. I pointed out that we had no real idea about the accommodation. She agreed to let me go with Ralph and John first. I deliberately went with just two men. I had seen nothing in the village which made me worry about our safety. A fat old French priest would not worry me. The deeds to the manor had been signed by the Abbot of the monastery in France. I had no doubt that some deal had been done and Henry had exchanged one of his manors in France. The church might have been able to extract taxes from a manor in England but the opposite was not true. When we had been at the siege of Vilnius Edward had told me that the Earl had tried to go on crusade to the Holy Land and asked the permission of the King of France. The French King had refused. Now I saw why he had been so generous with the manor. He had done a deal to exchange one manor in France for one in England. I had a number of documents including an account of the monies received by the monastery in Bec. As we neared Weedon, having stayed at the Earls castle at Northampton the night before, I wondered if the message had reached the fat priest yet.

The journey was only eight miles and we reached it well before noon. Spring was almost upon us and men were in the fields preparing them for the new planting. It was a prosperous looking manor. The manor house was not fortified but it was four times the size of my own. When we dismounted and watered our horses the priest and his curate emerged. I think he must have recognised me. His manner told me that he had not yet had news of our arrival. That was good. The deeds and the letter from the Earl informed me that everything in the manor was mine. The priest and his curate would have the clothes on their backs. All else belonged to the manor. I had been told that it was in my power to allow him to be the parish priest if he so chose.

He strode over, "Have we met before, my lord?"

"I passed through here last year on my way to crusade."

He beamed, "It is good that you do God's work. Feel free to use our water."

I nodded and took off my riding gloves. "The last time I came here I sought only water. Now I come upon the orders of the Earl of Northampton who is also the Earl of Derby." The flicker of a frown passed over his face. "Could we go inside for the chill of this wind reminds me of the Baltic."

He had little choice in the matter for I was a knight of the realm. He made the best of it. "I pray you enter. Thomas, go and prepare wine."

"Yes, father." I saw that the curate was young and where the priest was corpulent his assistant was lean.

Inside the hall was well apportioned. There was no Great Hall but there was an adequate looking feasting hall. I was taken to what looked like his study. It was a large room but there were just two seats. Ralph and John were forced to stand. It was a deliberate act on the part of the priest. He was trying to show his authority.

I smiled, "I am Sir William Strongstaff and you are?"

"Father Raymond d'Iscarte, guardian and God's reeve of the manor of Weedon." He smiled back.

The pleasantries would end soon enough. I took out the deed and the letter which was addressed to the incumbent of the manor. It bore the seal of the Earl of Northampton. "And that onerous burden has now been lifted from your shoulders. The monastery of Bec in France no longer owns this manor. The Earl of Northampton does and I am the newly appointed lord of the manor."

The curate, Thomas, walked in with the wine. He looked at the face of the priest. "What is wrong, Father Raymond?"

Ignoring the young priest, he shouted, "This is robbery! You are trying to steal my home!"

I handed the letter from the Earl to the young priest, "If you would read this out loud, for I fear Father Raymond may choke if he tries to read it."

Father Thomas read the letter. The Earl had couched his words carefully. There could be no misinterpretation. The manor was mine and the Abbot was happy about the arrangement. When it was read, Father Raymond slumped in his padded seat. His voice was quiet, "This is my home! Where will I go?"

"You are welcome to stay."

His face brightened, "Here?"

"No, for I have a wife and family. I will need a parish priest and I have the authority to offer it to you."

"A parish priest! I think not." He sounded appalled that he might have to work!

"Then you will have to return to the monastery in Normandy." I saw his eyes dart around the room. I turned to Father Thomas. "Will you be accompanying Father Raymond?"

"I er that is…"

Father Raymond shook his head, "No Thomas. I do not wish to be burdened by another mouth to feed."

The young man's face fell. I said, "Then would you do me the honour of becoming parish priest?"

"Of course, my lord!"

I wanted rid of father Raymond as soon as I could. "Is there a sumpter?"

"Yes, my lord."

"Ralph, go with Father Thomas and prepare the sumpter. I am certain that Father Raymond would wish to be on his way as soon as possible."

I saw Ralph grin as he left.

"I will need a wagon for all my things, Sir William."

I shook my head and proffered the deed. "As you can see, save for personal items such as clothing all else belongs to the manor. John and I will help you pack although as a parish priest I cannot imagine that you will have much."

"You mean I will not be allowed to do so privately?"

"I will need to make an inventory of all the items, Father Raymond. This has to be done properly. I came early to give you the opportunity to ride to Northampton. There is a chapter house there and you will have the opportunity to prepare for a new life back in Normandy."

When we accompanied him to his chamber, we watched his every move. Either John or myself kept our eyes on him the whole time. I knew he had chests secreted for his eyes kept glancing to the floor in his sleeping chamber. Ralph came in and said, "Lord we have a sumpter and an ass if Father Raymond needs it."

The priest gave an angry look which Ralph cheerfully ignored. I said, "Take Father Raymond's bag for him. If you would like to take a jug of wine for the journey, Father?"

He looked annoyed but still took the jug. He placed his bag on the ass and clambered on to the back of the sumpter. He waddled down the road to Northampton. I turned to John and Ralph. "Go and look beneath the bed of the priest. There will be chests hidden beneath the boards."

Father Thomas said, "How did you know?"

I laughed, "I have searched the houses of greedy men before now." As my men left me, we walked back into the hall. "I trust that you are more honest than Father Raymond."

"Honest lord?"

"You will learn, Father Thomas, that I value honesty more than anything. Speak the truth to me and all will be well." He said nothing. "You are bound by the confessional but your eyes saw that he was not sending all of the money he collected to the monastery." I took out the account. "I am no farmer but even I know that this manor should yield more than this."

His shoulders slumped, "You are right, lord. Dismiss me now for I did nothing to stop him."

"Nor could you. I do not blame you but the church in Bec. Today we have a new start and a new beginning. You will see to the spiritual matters of the parish and I will see to the rest. Now, while my men search, sit and tell me of the manor. I wish to know about all of those who are in my care."

John and Ralph joined us after a while with four large chests. I sent them out to stable our horses and prepare food. I had learned that there were four household servants. I would see them soon enough. The next day I would ride abroad and introduce myself and then I would send for my wife. I had much to do. I was no longer just a knight. I was now a banneret. When I rode to war it would be beneath my own banner. The next step would be to baron. My miraculous journey continued.

Chapter 11

The first years at Weedon were harder than I had expected them to be. The farmers were happy enough for there was little difference to them except for the fact that there had been no archery training. I insisted upon the application of the law. They complied. This had been a law for some time. The priest had gone but they barely noticed his departure. Father Thomas had held the services. Father Thomas looked after their spiritual needs but there were forty men of the manor who had little military training. I set my men at arms and archers to training them. I hoped we would not have to use them as the levy for they had not picked up a bow for some time. Whatever we did would be an improvement. My wife saw to the farming. That was not hard for her. She enjoyed it and she was comfortable with the task.

I, on the other hand, had to deal with the taxes and the courts. Stony Stratford had so few people that we had rarely needed an assize. Here we had one every quarter. In the first year one man had to be hanged for murdering his wife. It was distressing. In many ways the man, Andrew, reminded me of King Richard. He could be deliriously happy one moment and depressed the next. His death, when it came, must have been a relief to him. I gave his farm to Harold Four Fingers. None of my other married men objected. They all had houses which were attached to the village and were content for each had a small plot at the rear where they could grow vegetables. Seven of my men were married and soon some of their wives were with child. It changed each of the men. They were still warriors but they now had a solid tie to the land, my land. Stony Stratford still prospered. Jack was a good reeve and my wife's fortune grew. I say my wife's for I felt she had done all the work. I was still a warrior.

When I had time I worked with John, Ralph and Tom. I had promised Tom that I would train him in the art of war and a man did not lie, especially not to his son and heir. I had told Red Ralph I would help Ralph become a squire and I did so. It was hard combining the training and the running of the manor. If it was not for John, I could not have managed it. When I was busy with manorial duties, he continued their training. As our workers harvested our second crop, I spoke with John while Ralph and Tom sparred, "I am sorry that I am not yet able to offer you a knighthood. I would have to speak to the Earl and he is in the Baltic once more."

He laughed. He was a young man now. If he was not a squire, he could have had any of the maidens in the manor for he was handsome and all were in love with him. A squire could not marry nor could a bachelor knight without the permission of his lord. "Lord, I am elevated far beyond that which I dreamed. You have given my father a position which makes him important. Even if you were not to make me a knight then I would still be well rewarded. I am content.

I had been lucky with him. I was also fortunate with my men. The four men who had been married when we arrived had all sired children by their wives: Harold Four Fingers, Alan of the Wood, Jack War Bag and Lol son of Wilson were all fathers. Others had married women from Weedon. Coming into contact with the fathers of maids during weapon practice had an effect. David of Welshpool, Natty Longjack and Geoffrey of Gisburn were all married to local girls and their wives expecting. It tied them to me even closer than they had been. Father Thomas grew into his role. Father Raymond had used him as a dogsbody. I used him as a priest and my parish benefitted. He had a genuine interest in the people of Weedon. They grew to like the two of us. They had resented me when I came for I made their men work on Sunday after church and Father Raymond's parsimonious ways had alienated them from the church. We both won them over.

Despite the hard work and erratic winters, we prospered and we grew closer. My wife was happy for we were rich beyond her wildest dreams. The coin I had brought back from the Baltic and the money we had found in the hall meant that we could have four bad winters and still we would not have to endure hardship. All was well.

And then, not long after we had planted our fields for a third time, a messenger came from King Richard. He needed me. I had not heard from him for years but I did not hesitate. I was summoned to Sheen Manor, his private home on the Thames. The King had built a hunting hall and he and Anne of Bohemia spent many days there with just their servants. I took my men at arms, squires and Tom whom I was training as a page. This would be a chance for him to see the greatest in the land.

Sheen Manor was upstream from London. It was a country house rather than a castle. King Richard had loved Eltham but London had begun to spread out and impinge upon his castle. When he had been young the peasants under Wat Tyler had revolted. That event had given him a fear of the common people. He was a good king but he feared his people. It was part of the complex puzzle that was King Richard. He liked his privacy. He had been on the throne for seventeen years. He had been married for twelve years and thus far God had denied him children. I wondered if that was the reason for my summons. I had been close to both of them. I had been the man responsible for foiling the assassins' plots in the early years of his reign. I was looking forward to seeing them both, especially the Queen. She was a lovely woman both from within and without. I wondered if I was summoned so that they could tell me she was with child. That would set the seal on a peaceful England. I hoped that was the reason for I knew the joy which children brought. I decided I would mention Peter the Priest to her when I met her again. She was a kind woman and if she gave her patronage to the alms house then life would be easier for my friend.

As we neared the manor, I sensed that some darkness lay upon the hall. A black standard hung limply from the hall. Roger of Chester said, quietly, "Does this mean the King is dead?"

"We would have heard while we travelled south. This may be one of the King's moods. You know how he was."

"Aye lord." Roger and my men at arms had escorted the King in the months before Radcot Bridge. He knew him well.

Although it was just a manor there was a strong guard there. I had been King Richard's first captain. The second, Mavesyn, had almost done for the King and so he had chosen more wisely. Dick of Craven was grey now but he smiled, albeit wanly, when he saw me. "The King will be glad you came, my lord."

"Dick, what is it?"

He shook his head, "That is not for me to say, my lord. The King will speak with you. What I will say is that it is good that you have come. He needs you and you alone." He waved over a page, "Henry, here will take you to him. I will take your men to the barracks. It is good to see you again, Roger of Chester."

"And you Dick!"

My men at arms knew Dick and his guards well. They spoke the same language for they had experienced the same troughs and peaks as they guarded the monarch. I took my squires and son with me. As we walked, I said, "The King and Queen may wish to speak privately with me. You must honour that privacy."

John said, "Aye lord. All will be well."

The page took us to a feasting hall. It was not large and looked more intimate than any I had seen before but it was lit by two solitary candles. The King was seated on a throne and, despite the warm weather outside, was seated on a large chair before a fire. More, he was shrouded in black. The room was shrouded in darkness save for the King on his throne.

The page said, quietly, "Your majesty, Sir William of Weedon."

The King looked up for the words had sounded loud in the tomb like room. He leapt to his feet and waved a hand to dismiss the page. He hurried towards me and threw his arms around me, "You came! I knew you would. You have come too late but that is God's will for he has cursed me!"

To my dismay he began to sob on my shoulder.

Behind me I heard John say, to Tom and Ralph, "Let us withdraw and watch the door." I heard the door close as they left.

I patted the King's back. I did not know what else to do. I allowed him to weep. When he had done, he sniffed and then pushed himself away from me. He said simply, "Anne is dead, Will! The Queen has died. I sent for you when first she became ill." I saw in the light from the fire that he had a gaunt and haunted look on his face. He looked like a hunted animal. He looked around as though someone might be following me then, taking my arm, he led me over to a table which had a black sheet upon it. He pulled it back and I saw, beneath, a mummified body. I knew it to be the Queen. "She died of the plague." It took all of my strength not to run screaming from the chamber. The plague killed all it touched. He stroked the mummified head, "Why did God not take me too? How did I survive? God must hate me to separate me from my Anne. He can be a cruel God. I cannot take my own life for then I would not join her. She was shriven and died with a smile upon her lips." He looked up at me and smiled, "It was she asked for you to come. She knew she would die and she said you would bring me comfort. Can you bring me comfort, Will?"

This was not an easy subject for me. I thought back to the crusade. I thought of those who had lost as the King had lost. "She is, as you say, lord, with God and she is at peace. She has no pain and, as she was shriven then she is in heaven."

"But I am not with her!" He suddenly looked around, "Robert died two years since, you know?" I knew whom he meant, Robert de Vere, Earl of Oxford. "Did God take him too or was he murdered? Either way it shows that I am a cursed King."

I put my arm around him and began to guide him towards the door. I needed him away from the body of his wife. My intimate gesture, in itself, could be seen as a treasonous act but the man in the room with me was as sick as any plague victim. "You are not cursed, King Richard. For the last seven years your kingdom has seen peace and prosperity. That is down to you and your good Queen for you rid yourselves of those who would use and abuse you."

We were near to the door and he stopped, "You never liked Robert did you, William?"

"It was he who had me dismissed, my lord. The Queen liked me."

He looked back to the shadows on the far side of the room, "She had a good heart. We tried to have children you know. That is why I think I was cursed for she could not conceive. You have children?"

"Aye lord, sons and a daughter."

"Then you are truly blessed."

I opened the door and the light from outside made me shade my eyes. The King tried to return to the hall. I held him firmly, "No, King Richard, your wife is dead and she must be laid to rest." He turned to look up at me and I saw terror in his eyes. I also saw how thin and gaunt he was. "You know that she would wish it done well."

His eyes began to fill with tears and he nodded, "Aye you are right. You are always right."

"You will eat and change into more regal attire and we will plan the funeral." I saw the page and my squires standing close by, "Henry, we will have food. Is there another room where we can dine?"

"Aye, lord, in the western range."

"Then when you have organised the food fetch us there. The King and I will go and meet some old friends." I was in a foreign land here. This was not what I knew. The King liked and trusted my men. Perhaps their comradeship might bring him from his stupor. If England's enemies knew of his state then the country could descend into anarchy and chaos. I could not allow that. I now worked the land and knew that the poor people could not have their peace and prosperity snatched away by this tragic act. When we emerged from the hall into the courtyard, I saw the sentries stare at us as though they had seen a ghost. Dick of Craven and Roger of Chester approached.

Dick bowed, "It is good to see you, my liege. The sun smiles upon you."

The King nodded, dully and I said, "See, Highness, it is Roger of Chester."

The pained look on Roger's face told me that he, too, saw the change in the King. "It has been some years since we rode with you around England, King Richard."

He seemed to see Roger, "The Queen was fond of you and your men, Captain. You were as loyal and trustworthy as your master. Would that the rest of England was so loyal."

I nodded, "And they are, Highness. Come, let us have food and then plan how you will lay your wife beneath the ground." I had much work to do.

Over the next two days I worked as hard with the King as I had worked on anything. His courtiers, advisers and priests had retired for they were afraid of his temper. The presence of my men seemed to give the King some stability. He decided he would have a double tomb built in Westminster Abbey. His darkness meant that he still saw his own death as something that was almost imminent. Perhaps he thought he carried the plague within him. After four days we put his wife's body in her carriage and we rode, in dark of night, to Westminster. The King's priests had ridden to prepare the Archbishop and the church rallied around the King. While she lay in state we went to the Palace of Westminster. As Dick of Craven told me, just moving the King from Sheen Manor was an achievement. Now we had to make him a king once more. The measure of his mood was that, on leaving the manor, he had it razed to the ground. It was as though he was burning all trace of the disease and the pain of losing the love of his life.

John of Gaunt arrived at the palace. He had finally given up on his goal of becoming King of Castile. The attempt had cost him money. He might be the richest man in England but that was not enough to buy him a kingdom. He arrived at Westminster with his own advisers. He spied me in the ante chamber. The King was going over the finer details of the funeral with the Dean of the Abbey.

King Richard had granted him a further title of Duke of Aquitaine to go with the Dukedom of Lancaster. I bowed as he approached, "Your Grace."

"I am pleased that you are here, Sir William. The Queen was a good influence on the King and you appear to be another. My son speaks well of you. Tell me all."

I had known the Duke in Castile and I had known his brother, the Black Prince, better for he had been my lord. I trusted him. This was no Robert de Vere nor Michael de la Pole. John of Gaunt had lost any ambition to be the King of England long ago. That did not mean he would not wish to see his son as King but I could trust him. I had to, for who else was there?

He had his men guard the door and I told him all that I knew and all that I feared. He nodded, "You are an honest man. Your plain roots do you proud. There is no deception within you and I believe you have it aright. We must steer the King in the right direction for England depends upon it. First, we bury the Queen. I liked Anne and she was a good influence. Then we see about giving him a purpose. He has been indolent for too long. The Percys and the Nevilles gain glory fighting the Scots and the King does nothing. He needs something to drag him from this pit into which he has thrown himself. Leave this with me." He stood. "We will need you and your men to accompany the King. He will be preoccupied with the funeral for a month or so. Return to your home and settle your affairs. Hire another twenty men; equal numbers of sergeants and archers. You have a good eye. Return here within a month and we will go to war."

I was confused, "Go to war, my lord? With whom?"

He smiled, "There are many enemies out there. Let us find one the king can defeat eh?"

"My lord, should I not be here for the funeral?"

"A Queen has died. This will be a ceremony filled with the nobility of the land. These are my people. If my son was here, he might help me but I am comfortable with them. You can do more good by hiring men and horses to fight for the King." He waved over one of his squires and took a purse from him. He handed it to me. "If this is not enough then ask for more when you return. A month, mind, no more. We will act quickly and drive Anne from his mind. I will find him another bride. A King without an heir is vulnerable. Now go. I will say your farewells."

I was dismissed. As we headed north to my home I thought about the coldness of the Duke of Lancaster. He had praised the Queen and dismissed her in the same breath. The King would barely have the chance to mourn and there would be another bride. However, the nearer to my home I came the more I realised that this was the right thing to do. If I had not gone to Sheen Manor then he might have fallen into such a pit of despair that he would never have risen.

It was getting on to dark as we passed Northampton. "Roger, I would have you ride to Northampton tomorrow and see if you can find ten sergeants for me. I have coin to pay them. You had better have the seamstress we use make thirty more surcoats."

"Aye lord."

"Ralph I would have you take David and Wilfred and ride to your father's farm for I need twenty horses." I smiled, "I will be keeping my promise to your mother." Ralph had visited twice since he had moved to Weedon, a third visit would bring joy to Mistress Mary.

Tom asked, "And what do we do, father?"

"We fit you for war. I know not where we fight but you will need a hauberk, helmet and shield. You have not needed them hitherto but when we go to war you shall."

"Can I have armour?"

"You will not need armour and besides, your body is not yet strong enough to carry it. Ralph will buy you a better palfrey." I turned to Ralph. You will not have long, Ralph. We leave in less than four weeks' time."

My wife was upset at the death of the Queen. She had never met the lady but I had spoken of the couple so often that, to my wife, it was though a friend had died. "And you go off again, my husband?"

I nodded, "Aye and I take our son with me."

"Just so." I heard resignation in her voice. She was not as Mary, Red Ralph's wife, had been for she knew that Tom would not be a farmer. Harry was seven and I think my wife was preparing him to be the farmer. I suppose I had put my efforts into making my eldest the warrior.

That night I spoke with John of Aldgate and Alan of the Wood. "John, I know not how long we shall be away. You know better than any the vagaries of war."

"Aye lord."

"I devolve to you the training of the men of the parish. Do not relent. The Earl of Northampton is abroad but if he should return to join us in this war then he might call out the levy and they need to be prepared. The last thing we need is for them to be slaughtered because they are unprepared."

"Do not worry, my lord, they will be. I may not have your skills, Alan of the Wood, but I know how you have trained them and I can crack the whip if needs be."

"And you, Alan, go to Lincoln. We need ten archers. You know the sort of men we require. You have a week to bring them back here for we have to make them our own. I know not where we go to war but I want us all to return and that means fighting as one. We will be protecting the King once more."

"And there is no nobler task. Fear not my lord. Old Tom is a good friend and he will find the men that we need."

The next morning, I rode around my tenants for I wished them to know the task I had been given. It was a sign of the bond which had developed when they all gave me their complete support. There were no doubtful looks and sideways glances. They looked me in the eye and I saw into their souls. My penultimate call was to Martin the Smith. When I had first come to the village, I was pleased that there was a blacksmith. Edgar was my smith at Stony Stratford and he was happy there. I would not uproot him. Martin worked mainly as a farrier but I discovered that he had such a love of metal that he could turn his hand to the making of armour.

"Well, Martin, I have a task for you which you may not be able to complete. If you cannot then I will understand."

He grinned, "A challenge, my lord, is something I enjoy. Speak on."

"I need a hauberk for my son Tom and a sallet."

He looked at Tom. He had grown a little and his chest had filled out but he was not yet a man grown. "He has some growing to do. The hauberk and the sallet will last him but a couple of years, lord." He was thinking of the expense.

"I know."

He looked at his workshop. He had metal. We had brought back old swords from the crusade. All had been of poor quality but, over the last years, he had used some for ploughshares and other farming implements. He still had metal left. "The helmet is not a problem, lord. It is the mail. I have the metal but it takes time to make a hauberk and I am guessing that you will need a coif. I cannot see how I would have the time to make both. A hauberk would take a month or more. I could manage a coif."

"We go to war, Martin. I would not have my son put at risk."

Just then John slapped his head, "My lord, I am a fool!" He rushed off.

"Well, let us measure Master Tom for the sallet and the coif. Those I can begin."

I took out a purse and placed twelve silver coins on his bench. "This will pay for the coif and sallet?"

"Aye, lord, that is plenty for you gave me the metal and I owe you the labour."

"You are a skilled man and we pay for such skill."

John ran back in. He was carrying a heavy sack. "When you came back from Castile you brought this, my lord. It was intended for me, I believe, but we found a better one after we defeated the men who took the manor of Stratford. It has been with the other old weapons in the store room." He pulled out a hauberk. It was too big for Tom, that much was obvious but it could be adapted.

Martin smiled, "Here, Master Tom, let me try it on you." With John helping they draped it over his shoulders. I saw him wince at the weight. It had long sleeves which covered his hands and the bottom reached the floor. It was also too wide. Martin nodded approvingly, "We can make the sleeves into mittens, lord. I can take the mail below the knee and use that to make a coif. The hardest part will be to make it slimmer. I do not want to damage the integrity of the whole."

"For now, make it shorter and convert the ends to mittens. We need an aketon making for him. When he has the aketon we shall see how the whole fits together." I turned to John, "Thank you, John. You are a good squire."

John and I had all the war gear we needed but Tom had little. We had him some good buskins made. I knew not where we would be fighting but strong footwear was essential. As John had reminded me, we had collected many serviceable weapons over the years. I had a good short sword and scabbard which I gave him and he chose a ballock dagger as his second weapon. He would not need a spear for, now that I was a banneret, I had a standard. Tom would carry that. When they were done John went with him to make the shield he would need.

Roger of Chester took five days to find the men we needed. They all had their own swords and helmets. Most had a shield but they would need to have my staff painted upon them. All had a hauberk. Some were made of mail and longer than others. They were obviously ones which had been passed down to them. We would not look as uniform as the men of the Earl of Northampton but they looked like warriors all. They ranged from one who looked younger than John, James Jameson, to Oliver the Bastard, a grizzled old veteran. Roger introduced them: Gilbert of Ely, Uriah Longface, Dick Dickson, Mark the Minstrel, Stephen of Morpeth, Will of Stockton, Ulf the Swede and Richard son of Richard.

"Mark the Minstrel?"

The man was a tall blond warrior. He bore scars but his name suggested other. "Aye lord, I got the name in Castile when I fought for the Duke of Lancaster. I sang as I slew the Spaniards. I find singing gives me a rhythm. If it causes offence..."

I waved a hand, "Sing away!" He smiled and nodded. "You are hired by me for a war. I know not yet where we fight nor whom we fight but we fight for King Richard and the Duke of Lancaster." They looked relieved. "When it is over you may wish to serve another. If not then I will try to find the payment for you." I nodded towards my hall. "The purse strings are my wife's domain." They smiled. For the next fortnight we prepare for war. "Your shields will match your surcoats. The cloaks will be here by the end of the week. There are spare weapons in the armoury. Take what you wish. Your horses will be here shortly and, for the rest, you will train with Roger of Chester and learn to fight our way."

The archers took longer to find. Northampton was a major castle and sergeants at arms gravitated there. Archers often did not seek a new paymaster. Frequently, they would eke out a life in the woods hunting, illegally, for game. Most enjoyed that solitary life. However, Alan found the men we needed. This time they did not have any semblance of uniform about them. Alan assured me that all of them had had experience in campaigns. He even knew three of them from Castile. Two had served with the Earl of Northampton in the Baltic. The other five were unknown. Alan had tested their skill and attested to it.

I gave them the same speech as I had to the men at arms. "You will be equipped as men of Weedon. I know that archers are often independent men. When this campaign is over if you wish your freedom then it will be granted. I will try to find employment for all others."

They nodded. Alan had already told me that one was quite vocal, it was he, Much Longbow, who spoke, "That is well spoke my lord and we are all grateful." He pointed to his buskins which were heavily scuffed, "As you can see, lord, we have had hard times."

I nodded, "If that is your way of asking for payment up front then ask. You will learn that I prefer straight words for that is what you shall receive from me."

"Again, my lord, fairly spoke and I am suitably chastised. Payment would not come amiss. We will not run."

Alan of the Wood growled, "For if you did your corpse would never be found!"

The others laughed at Much's obvious discomfort. They would do.

Our assembly was complete. My men rode in with horses. Red Ralph was also with them. He grinned, "There were many horses and, besides, I had a yearning to see this fine manor. It is impressive, Sir William!"

I laughed, "None of that Sir William nonsense or I shall set the dogs upon you. Come meet my wife and children. This is well met!"

It was a merry feast we held. Red Ralph had always been witty and now, with the benefit of an easy life and a comfortable wife he was even funnier. My wife roared at his tales of campaigns. My children had no grandfather and Red Ralph was old enough to play the part. He loved children and, as his were grown, he played the grandfather with funny voices and games. It was an enjoyable time for all, then after he left, we began the work that would make my company a fighting force to be feared!

Chapter 12

When we reached Westminster, it was as though a new hive of bees had begun to produce honey. As I went, with John and Tom, to the King's side I could not believe the speed of the servants as they whirled from room to room. Leaving my squires outside the hall I entered a maelstrom of the great and the good in the land. The King was transformed. Gone was the sallow, haunted figure grieving for his wife. In his place was a whirlwind.

The Duke of Lancaster saw me and came over to me. The King was busy in conversation with a man I later discovered was Gerald FitzMaurice FitzGerald, Earl of Kildare. The Duke said, "You have the men?"

"Aye, lord."

"Good. We go to Ireland."

"Ireland? Was not Robert de Vere the Duke of Ireland?"

"He was and he made a mess of that too. He allowed the Irish to defeat our knights and it emboldened them. They have begun to reclaim parts of their lands. Cathal mac Ruaidri Ó Conchobair, King of Connaught, is seen as the most serious threat. He has joined with another of their petty kings, Maelsechlainn Ó Cellaigh, King of Uí Maine. The Irish seem to have kings where we have barons! The Earl of Kildare has brought us this news and the King is transformed." He pointed, "Is this the same man who was drowning in a sea of despair?"

"It is a miracle, my lord, but…"

"But is it just temporary? Aye, Sir William, I fear that too. Now that you are here things will improve again. He asked for you often. I told him why you left him and he is mollified." Lowering his voice, he said, "You were the King's bodyguard and I know you to be an honest man and so I will tell you this. When we buried Queen Anne the Earl of Arundel insulted the King by leaving the funeral early. The King struck him. I fear the enmity from the time of the Lords Appellant may surface once more. I have counselled my son and he is chastened but my brother Gloucester and Warwick are still dangerous men. They are not here and that tells you much. Watch for treachery!" He put his hand on my shoulder and guided me, "Come, let us go and listen."

The Earl of Kildare was speaking and I heard the passion in his voice, "They raid, King Richard, and they burn and pillage."

"Do they have castles?"

"There are some in the west but none can compare with those we have in The Pale, Ulster, Wexford, Kildare and Ormond."

"Which begs the question, my lord, why have the knights in those castles not sallied forth and destroyed these raiders? The Irish will become emboldened and that will make them harder to quash!" The Earl looked abashed. "Do you have men armed with the war bow?"

"We use crossbows, lord!"

"Then it is no wonder that you have lost so much land!" He looked up and suddenly saw me, "Will! At last someone other than my uncle who speaks sense. If you were to take Ireland what would you do?"

"I would use horsemen to pin down the Irish and then have our archers slaughter them. They wear no mail!"

The King laughed, "See? A humble man at arms who is now a knight knows more than one who can trace his lineage back to the time of the first Henry!" He waved over John of Gaunt, "Uncle, we know the problem, now we need the solution. I wish an army gathered at Chester and a fleet to take us to The Pale. I leave for Chester within the week. The army follows at utmost speed."

The Duke of Lancaster recognised the size of the task he had been given but he smiled and said, "Yes, King Richard!" for he knew that this was part of the recovery of the King.

The King led me away to a chamber attached to the hall. He nodded to Dick of Craven who closed the door behind us and stood guard. "I was sorry that you were not at the funeral. Anne would have liked that. She was very fond of you. You were the only knight she ever truly trusted."

"I wished to be there but your uncle sent me on an errand."

"I know. He appears to mean well although I suspect his motives. You know that he still harbours ambitions for his son." I said nothing for it would be futile. The King saw daggers in shadows. His eyes flickered nervously from side to side. "I now have the Kingdom in my own hands. They think they are safe but I will have my vengeance on them. First, I will show them all that I am a warrior like my father and my grandfather. They challenge me because I have never fought a war." He looked at me with pleading in his eyes, "When I faced down the mob that was braver than a battle was it not? I had no armour and I faced down an army who wished my death! They did not see that as courage. I will show them!"

I wondered who 'them' were. "Show who, Your Majesty?"

"Why my uncle, Gloucester, along with Warwick and Arundel! They killed my friend Sir Simon and drove my dearest ally, Robert de Vere, from my land. They humiliated me and put fetters upon me. I am King of England and I will have no fetters! You will help me, William. You have kept your oath and that is rare." He gave me a sly look, "Keep your eyes and ears open. Tell me all that they say about me. I trust only you and my guards."

I did not like this position. I was no spy. I just nodded. I was loyal to the King but the loyalty stopped at murder.

"I will have you at my side when we ride to Chester. You and your men will accompany my guards on the ship when we sail to The Pale. If they send assassins, they will find Will Strongstaff!"

I should have been flattered by the King's words but I was more concerned about the manner in which he had spoken. The Duke of Gloucester was of royal blood. How could he wreak vengeance on him? I liked it not. He was being duplicitous. He was feigning friendship with John of Gaunt while plotting against him. Henry Bolingbroke had confided in me and I believed that he harboured no treacherous thoughts. With Anne dead and no new Queen at the King's side then all Henry Bolingbroke had to do was wait and he would be King of England. After I left him, I went to the Abbey and I prayed at the tomb of the Queen. I asked for God's help. I could not ride the wild horse that was King Richard without help. I was treading a fine line. If I fell then it would be my head I would lose and, worse, my family would lose all that they had worked for. I could not allow that to happen. John and Tom also prayed. I knew not what was their prayer. A man's prayers were private.

I left the Abbey and sought out my men. "We will be heading for Chester. The King would have us and Dick of Craven's men to guard him. We have a great responsibility. The archers will guard our baggage. If there is trouble on the road then you will be best placed to react to it."

Alan of the Wood nodded. "And where do we fight, Lord? Wales?"

"No, Alan, we fight in Ireland."

Much Longbow shook his head, "They are wild men there, lord!"

Alan shook his head, "We have fought Irishmen before, Much. Have you?"

"I have heard terrible tales of what they do to men when they capture them!"

"And do you know that they fight without armour? That they have piss poor swords? And they use hunting bows with stone tips?"

He looked abashed, "No, Captain!"

"Then I suggest that you listen more and speak less. Sorry, my lord."

I smiled, "Questions I can handle. We leave within the week. One thing I do know about Ireland is that we cannot rely on a ready supply of arrows. I know we have plenty but buy as many others as you need. I will find the coin."

"We just need shafts, lord. We each have our own feathers and we have many tips."

"Good. At least this will not be a cold war!"

Roger of Chester shook his head, "Just a wet one. I am glad I still have my seal skin cape!"

It was not just the King who left London. The Duke of Lancaster brought a hundred knights with him, Thomas le Despenser brought twenty knights. The Earl of Rutland brought twenty. The Earl of Sheffield would meet us on the road and we heard that the Earls of Kent and Huntingdon were also on their way. We would pick up men north of Stratford and more in the Welsh Marches. The Duke of Lancaster confided in me that six thousand men would be crossing the Irish Sea. I was just glad that the voyage was a short one and we were landing in The Pale which was safely in our hands.

As we rode John asked, "Lord, who is the Earl of Chester?"

"There is no Earl of Chester. The title goes to the Prince of Wales. That was the King. If he had a son then he would be Prince of Wales. The knights of Chester will be joining us. They are the most loyal men in the kingdom save our company."

Tom had the furled banner in his hand. It could have been with the horses but he was inordinately proud of it. His mother and some of the women had sewn it. Magda, who had helped told Harold Four Fingers that the fact our women had sewn it would make it stronger. My wife had made the sign of the cross but Magda was adamant. She spoke of how the women in her village would weave and that there were spells in the wool they wove. That was witchcraft. Magda had shocked Eleanor by shrugging. Her people believed that witches were a force for good. So far Harold had failed in his attempt to convert her.

The King waved for me to ride next to him. He had four squires with him and they had all been chosen by the King. They made room so that Blaze could ride next to his courser. "When you were in the Baltic, William, I understand that you fought savages."

It was an over simplification but he was right, "They were barbarians, lord, and many fought half-naked."

"Then why did my cousin fail to take Vilnius?"

"He was not in command, my liege. The King of Poland made mistakes."

"But were the barbarians easy to kill? They must have been if they had no armour." He was genuinely interested.

"The opposite, sire. They fought on beyond all hope with limbs missing and mortal wounds." I knew why he questioned me, "The Irish are different, for they believe in God. Their priests will bless them before they fight. They have poor armour and weapons but they love to fight. If we were not there, they would fight each other and slaughter their neighbours. It is how they are. You were told that there were many kings and there are. Ulf the Swede told us that he had fought in Ireland as a mercenary. He had fought for the O'Connor clan. The chief of that clan had aspirations to be a king. Ulf fought in mail but no matter how many of the enemy he slew there were always more to fight. If you kill their chief then they may retire to lick their wounds and to appoint a new chief but, if not, then they will keep fighting."

"Then how do we stop them?"

"Simple, destroy their homes and threaten their families."

"That has no honour in it."

I nodded, "You did not ask what is the honourable way to stop them. If you had I would have said nothing can stop them."

"You seem to know a lot about them."

"I spoke with the Earl of Kildare's knights. They told me. I like to know what sort of enemy will face me. Once you are beyond The Pale and the Earldoms then you are in a land which has not changed for five thousand years. They still have hill forts and clans who are fiercely loyal to each other. These two Kings have done something unusual. They have managed to forge an army from clans which hate each other. We will need to slaughter them when they attack and, if they try to regroup, then we sack their villages and take captive their people." Part of me remembered the four women who had chosen death rather than be used by the King of Poland. I hoped the Irish were not like that.

When we reached Chester my men and the King's guards were housed, with the senior lords, in the castle. The rest camped. Some ships had been gathered but not enough. The King spent an increasing amount of time with men like the Earls of Huntingdon, Rutland, Kent and Nottingham. All had remained loyal when the Lords Appellant had inflicted their vengeance on the King. All had suffered equally at their hands. Now the King was using those men to become his replacement for the Earl of Oxford. At heart he still thought of me as a bodyguard.

After three days the King, now more decisive than I had ever seen him, made an important decision. "The crossing is not a long one. We use the ships we have and we ferry the army across. This will give me an opportunity to examine the borderlands and to decide the best way to attack the Irish!"

And so I was amongst the first to land in Dublin. With one of the finest castles on the island we were safe. A series of small castles at places like Athboy, Kells, Kilcock and Trim ensured that no Irish army could get close to the King. We had almost a thousand men landed and we rode west to view the border. The land was green. I saw hills which the Irish called mountains but it looked to me to be perfect country for horses. We had come in summer and that gave us four months to subjugate the Irish and return to England.

Gerald FitzMaurice FitzGerald, Earl of Kildare, led us. He and twenty of his household knights formed the vanguard. We stayed at the Earl's castle of Kildare.

As we ate that night in the huge feasting hall the impulsive King asked, "Tell me, Kildare, how do the Irish fight? Do they array their men in battle lines as we do? Knights in the centre protected by archers and men at arms?"

"The Irish fight in a strange way, King Richard. They like to arrange a battle. They send emissaries and they agree a battlefield and decide numbers. They turn up and fight until one has lost so many men that they flee. As for order? They do have knights but few of them. It is the lords of the clans who emulate us. King Cathal mac Ruaidri Ó Conchobair and his sons as well as chosen oathsworn have mail hauberks and ride war horses. We might meet twenty or so. They have chiefs who are mailed. Those do not use cavalry as we do. Their horses are hill ponies. They use them to get to a battle. They fight dismounted."

"Then they will not be ready if we ride forth to meet them. If we rode tomorrow how many men could the Irish muster?"

"You mean, my lord, how many Irish warriors are close enough to fight us?"

"Aye, if we rode forth tomorrow how many men would face us?"

"Many hundreds, Your Highness."

"Then let us tempt them. Let us make them see who rides abroad in their land. If we can we will bloody their nose."

"Is that wise?"

I thought King Richard would turn on the Earl but, instead, he smiled. "If we bring them to battle in the next few days then we will win. If we retire to Kildare what will they then do?"

"They will bring every warrior they can to drive us hence. They will try to organize a formal battle."

"By which time the Duke of Lancaster will have landed the rest of our men and instead of the Irish facing a thousand men it will be eight thousand. I want a single victory to destroy their armies and then we can destroy their homes so that they cannot rebel again."

I was impressed. He had listened to all that had been said. It was a bold move. He was trying to make a name for himself as a commander. It was what his cousin, Henry Bolingbroke, had tried in Galatia and the Baltic. Henry Bolingbroke had failed. Would King Richard succeed?

There was a moment then which marked a change. "Sir William, I shall not need you and your men tomorrow. I will lead my knights and those of Kildare. My guards can guard my baggage and you and your men can be a reserve."

I did not argue for there was little point. I was disappointed but I did not think that the Irish would be foolish enough to attack the King of England. In the event I was proved wrong.

We rose and rode forth. The King ordered all of our banners to be unfurled. He was making a statement to the Irish. We crossed from Kildare into the land ruled by the Dempsey Clan. They supported Cathal mac Ruaidri Ó Conchobair, the King of Connaught. We saw no scouts and the King had none out but we must have been seen for, at noon, as we watered our horses, we saw men gathering on a hill some two miles from us. In the time it took for us to mount and move towards them the numbers had been swollen by reinforcements. The hill side was soon filled with a mass of men.

The King shouted to Dick of Craven to guard the baggage and he led two hundred knights, their squires and some sergeants forward. He had archers but they rode behind the men at arms. He had ignored his own words to the Earl of Kildare. It was though there were two demons inside the King and they were fighting. He led over five hundred mounted men. The two hundred archers could have been deployed and they would have guaranteed us victory. The King did not use them. John of Gaunt had not reached us yet. The King was trying to prove that he did not need the aid of the House of Lancaster to win. The line of horsemen was two hundred men wide. It meant it was a shallow line. The Irish on the hill were in a mass of men but I estimated the lines to be thirty or forty deep. I made a decision. I would disobey my orders. I would not be a reserve.

Turning to my men at arms and archers I said, "Follow me!"

I was riding Jack and I spurred him. I did not intend to charge. I just wanted to threaten the right flank of the Irishmen. I had just forty-three men with me but twenty of them were archers and we could do some damage.

The King and his knights were approaching the Irish properly. They had their spears raised and they were cantering rather than galloping. They were keeping their lines tight and riding boot to boot. The Irish had just formed on the hill as they had arrived. Their chiefs and kings were gathered on the top. Some men in the front rank had spears but others did not. The King and his knights had a chance. A slight chance but a chance nonetheless. I worried about how the Irish might fight. The King and his earls rode mailed horses but the Irish were brave enough to throw themselves beneath the horses and use their knives to gut them.

We rode hard. I had no intention of charging the Irish. I saw some of the knights on the left flank looking over to me as though I was stealing their glory! I was not, I was trying to save their lives. When we closed with the right flank of the Irish, I saw them turn their shields, spears and swords toward us. A third of their men anticipated an attack from us. We would attack but not in the way they anticipated. When we were two hundred paces from their line I shouted, "Halt! Dismount! Horse holders!"

We had practised this and five warriors grabbed the reins of the horses. I drew my sword and swung my shield around. John and Tom stood behind me. Ralph was one of the horse holders. My men spread out in a thin line.

"Alan, you know what to do!"

"Aye lord, Unleash the wrath of God on these barbarians!"

"Tom unfurl the banner let them know who we are."

As Alan shouted, "Release!" the King's line hit the Irish. There was a clash and clatter of metal on wood and the crunching of bodies broken by hooves. Horses neighed and men screamed. It was the sound of primitive battle. The combination of the joint attacks confused the Irish. Alan managed two more flights before those with shields raised them. The forty arrows killed or wounded more than twenty. His third and fourth flights had the same effect. By the eighth flight the wild Irish had had enough and they ran at us. I had no opportunity to see what the King was doing. We had our own battle here. In the two hundred paces they had to cross Alan and his archers killed or wounded fifty more men and then they hit us. The arrows had thinned them so that the Irish tribesmen did not hit us as one. Even so the wild men of the west threw themselves at our swords. Many of the first of them died without striking a blow.

I blocked the blows of their swords on my shield. Some were so poorly made that they bent. Spears were thrown at us from those advancing. They had fire hardened tips. They sounded dangerous as they rattled off helmets but they did no harm. I slashed my sword sideways. I struck flesh. I raised it to strike down and saw that it was bloody. All the time the arrows sent from behind us slowed down the advance so that the twenty or so men who reached us were easily despatched. The next twenty or so were also sent to their deaths. They stopped attacking and fell back out of arrow range. That gave relief to Alan and his archers.

I glanced to my right and saw that the knights, supported by the men at arms, had pushed the Irish up the hill but it had been at a cost. I saw unhorsed knights. We had done what I intended and I shouted, "Mount and reform."

We hurried back to the horse holders. Ralph held Jack's reins while I mounted. We formed two lines. They were not long lines but the Irish must have thought we were going to attack. I turned and shouted to the King's archers, "Archers, join us!"

The Captain of archers had been waiting to get into the battle. He had seen what Alan had done and he galloped over with his archers. There were two hundred horses. They were liveried and, as they covered the three hundred paces to us the Irish must have thought they were more men at arms come to charge them. A horn sounded and the Irish began to disengage. They were not mailed men and they scurried from the battle. The King and his knights had exhausted their horses. There was no pursuit. When the archers joined us, I sent them to help the King. They were despatching the Irish wounded. We walked our horses towards the Irish we had slain.

We dismounted and my men went amongst them collecting the weapons and helmets. Some of the Irish were chiefs and had old fashioned torcs around their necks. Others wore battle bracelets made of silver and gold alloy. All was collected. My men would share it out later. My archers collected arrows. Only shafts which were broken would be left. They would take the fletch and the heads. All of my archers could make arrows. A good archer made his own missiles. Ralph came back towards Tom and I, he had four swords and a couple of helmets. "That was not much of a battle, lord. They did not stand long,"

"That was not a battle. That was an encounter. They came to see who we were. When the Irish fight they arrange a battle. The King's attack unsettled them. He did not fight it the way he should have but we won and it will allow the next part of the campaign to be fought successfully."

A horn sounded and we headed back to Kildare. I saw that many knights were riding their second horses. Destriers had died. The knights who had lost them would not be happy. We had not fought knights. Had we done so there would have been ransom which would have paid for the horses. We might even have captured horses. The few horsemen had been riding hill ponies. We reached Dick of Craven first. He shook his head, "You fought the battle well, Sir William. The King should have used archers."

"Perhaps he will use them later."

We reached the castle and a rider was sent to the Duke of Lancaster to ask him to bring the rest of the army as soon as he could. The King was enough of a realist to know that it would take some time to ferry all of the army from Chester and then to march them across The Pale and then Kildare. I had displeased the King by my action and I was not invited to the feast in Kildare Castle. I did not mind, I enjoyed the company of my men.

Dick of Craven came to join us at the fire later on. He brought a jug of the wine from the feasting hall. He chuckled as he poured it. Roger of Chester said, "What amuses you, Dick of Craven?"

"When the lords were eating one of the Earl of Rutland's knights asked why the King did not do as you had done and use archers to support the attack! The silence that fell upon the hall sounded like thunder! I thought the King's head would burst it was so red and angry. Sir Henry was sent from the hall but he was just speaking what the others were thinking. There are many knights who lost horses."

Harold Four Fingers asked, "The King made a mistake and others paid. It is not right."

Dick of Craven shook his head, "Curb those thoughts and do not give them voice, Harold Four Fingers. That is treason. King Richard can do no wrong. He is King." He stood. "I just thought I would bring you the wine, Sir William, and the news that others think you did right."

When Dick had gone Roger divided the treasure, little though it was. The swords would be returned to Weedon and given to Martin the Smith. He would use them for more mail. I called over Alan of the Woods and Stephen the Tracker. "I do not think there will be a battle tomorrow. I know not what the King intends but I would know what is out there. I want you two to lead my archers in two hunting parties. One goes south and west and the other goes north and west. Find where the Irish are gathering."

They nodded and then went to choose their men. They would mix the old and the new. My archers also had to become as one.

"Ralph, did the horses suffer today?"

"No, lord. They are rested and this is good grazing."

"We will not have to use them for a few days. I have ordered the archers out tomorrow. When they return, we will need to rest their horses."

"Aye lord. Do I have to stay with the horses each time we fight?"

"You are keen to fight?"

"I am here to learn to be a warrior, I could hold horses on my father's farm."

I nodded, "You make a fair point. I will let you fight the next time we meet the Irish."

As I lay down on my fur and pulled my cloak up around me, I wondered just how long it would take the Irish to gather enough men to fight us.

Chapter 13

When my men returned it was with the news that there was no sign of the Irish for more than thirty miles. The horses were lathered and the archers weary when they walked their horses back into the camp. I went to the castle to report to the King. He made me wait for an hour. I watched the hourglass being turned. It was another punishment. The King had more faces than a man looking in a cracked mirror. When he did agree to see me, his face was stern.

"Your Majesty, I sent my archers to seek the Irish. They are not close to the castle."

"Then my victory, despite the fact that you disobeyed my orders, is complete." I said nothing and the King said, "You disagree, Sir William? Answer me."

I was in dangerous territory but I had trained the King. Even though it might cost me I would answer him truthfully, "King Richard, we slew two hundred men on the battlefield. My men and I counted the bodies of just four chieftains. Where are their knights? Where are their kings? We caught them by surprise. It is my belief that they are gathering their forces to fight us on ground of their choosing. It was a victory but not the one you sought."

He frowned. It was a sure sign that he was thinking. He then rose and said, "I thank you for sending your archers out. I will send for you tomorrow when I have had the opportunity to discuss strategy with my lieutenants."

I had gone from being a close confidante to a messenger. The unpredictable and erratic King of England had returned. This time I could not blame the late Earl of Oxford. The worm in the King's head made him hard to predict.

The Duke of Lancaster arrived the following day at noon. The camp grew tenfold. The good grazing which Ralph had spoken of would soon be gone. The King did not send for me as he had said. I stayed in the camp with my men. It was the following morning when one of the King's pages, Peter, found me. The King and his uncle were alone and the door closed behind me.

"The King has told me of your action the other day in the skirmish. On reflection he thinks it was well done." The King would not apologise but his uncle would do it for him. "We are going to take the army into Connaught. If the Irish will not bring their army to battle, we will take the war to them. We would have you and your company twenty miles ahead of the vanguard."

I gave the Duke a sharp look, "We are bait, my lord?"

The King said, "I told you uncle, Will might be low born but he has a mind as sharp as any. No, Will. I would not lose you and your men. Let us say that we are hunters and we wish you to start the prey. You and your men are more than capable of dealing with any warband you might meet and, if you meet their army, then you are quick enough to return and tell us. If you pass settlements then sack them. Burn their homes and their crops. Slaughter their animals. We will make them fight us."

Despite the King's words I knew that I was bait. I was no longer needed to protect the King for he had a new coterie of knights and lords he was gathering around him. They were the new Robert de Vere. I just hoped that none were as ambitious as the Earl of Oxford had been. "We head west, my lord?" I looked at the Duke.

"Yes, Sir William. We head for Galway. You do not go as the only knight. I have a young knight who would follow you. Sir Henry of Stratford is serving with me. He brought just his squire. You know the knight I believe?"

I smiled, "I trained him."

"Good, then he can follow your banner. He married the daughter of Marie de St. Hilaire of Hainaut. She is a lady of my acquaintance."

I hid my smile, Marie de St. Hilaire of Hainaut was his mistress. Sir Henry had done well for himself. "He is a good knight. He and his squire know their business."

The Duke gave me a wry smile, "I am pleased that you approve. We leave the day after tomorrow. We would have you and your men on the road before dawn. I will supply you with four riders to keep us informed of your progress." And with that I was dismissed.

I did not mind the isolation. I was not reliant on another. Oft times the Blue Company had had this role and within the Blue Company, Red Ralph and Peter the Priest were always the scouts.

We had spare sumpters but now I regretted not bringing servants to lead them. We would have to waste men at arms or archers to do so. It could not be helped. When I told my men that Sir Henry and Peter were to join us, they were delighted. They had seen little of Sir Henry since he had been knighted, but for the years he had been trained by me, he had been part of our company. Peter was an old soldier and was never happier than when he was with my men at arms.

"John, take down the tent and send it to the baggage. We will not need it. We leave our chests here with our spare surcoats. We will go dirty if we have to. We take cloaks and all the weaponry we can muster."

"Aye, lord, come Ralph and Tom we have work to do."

Tom asked, "Where do we sleep then?"

John laughed, "You will learn to make a hovel. It can be cosy enough. We had them in the Baltic and they were warm even in the ice."

I went to speak to Alan and Roger. I had just explained our task when I heard hooves behind me. I turned and saw Sir Henry, Peter and two servants leading Sir Henry's war horse.

He dismounted. His grin told me that he was pleased to see me. He had grown into a man. He was now about twenty-three years of age and looked like a confident warrior rather than the diffident youth who had come to me. "Good to see you, my lord. A banneret now!" He gave a mock bow.

I laughed, "I can still give your coxcomb a clip!" I embraced him, "Good to see you too and congratulations on your marriage."

He blushed a little, "Thank you, lord. I have a beautiful wife in Marie and she is with child which is a double cause for congratulations. It is why I left my men at arms to guard my home. The memory of Captain Mavesyn still haunts me."

"It is good to have you and you too, Peter."

"It is good to be back, my lord. This is Jacob and Abraham. They are servants but they can handle a sword if they have to."

"Good. Sir Henry, walk with me and I will tell you of our task and what we have learned of the men we fight."

When we had finished, we returned to the camp where my men were cooking our supper. I had been honest with Sir Henry. He did not have as much experience of war. "This will be the first time I have drawn my sword in anger since Radcot Bridge and the race to Stratford. I hope I have not forgotten how to use it."

"You will not but I should warn you these warriors we war against will not seek to take you prisoner. They will gut your horse and then try to butcher you. If you can take their head with one blow then do so."

He lowered his voice, "Then why does the King fight them?"

"They challenged his authority. This is a message for those in England and across the border in Scotland. This is King Richard flexing his muscles and exorcising the death of his wife from his mind."

"It was a shame that she died. She was a real lady."

"Aye, that she was and she was good for him too. Enough of that. We must put our mind to hunting Irishmen. When we ride, I will send Stephen the Tracker and my best six men ahead of us. With you and your men we now have almost fifty and that is a good number. Your Jacob and Abraham can lead the sumpters with our war gear. If we have to fight then it will be against scouts. If we find an army we are to report back to the King."

This was a land without real roads but with few hills and even fewer woods then it was an easy country to cross than had been the Baltic. We could see for miles, once we crested the pimples that they called hills. The problem was that the enemy could see us and they wore no mail for the sun to reflect off mail and helmets. It would be hard to see them but just as hard for them to ambush us.

We found the first hamlet just twenty miles from our setting off point. My archers had found it on their scouting expedition. I sent the Duke's rider back with the message that we had found the first settlement. It had just twenty huts. I had my orders. I had disobeyed one and got away with it. I would not disobey a second. When Stephen the Tracker reported it, I said, "We attack. Do not harm the women and the children. Drive them off. We slaughter the animals and burn the houses."

"And the men, lord?"

"If they fight us then we kill them."

Harold Four Fingers shook his head, "Then we will slay them for they will not sit idly by while we destroy their homes." Harold had changed since he married and had his own farm, I wondered how much longer he would wish to fight.

I sent my archers in two wings to the north and south of us to prevent us being surprised. I left Ralph and Tom with the horses along with Sir Henry's two servants. The rest of us formed a long line twenty-four men wide and I dug in my spurs. I would not ride beneath my banner. There was no need. None of us wore helmets and my shield guarded my left leg. We trotted rather than galloped. In my heart I wanted them to flee and then I would not have to kill them. We were seen when we were four hundred paces from them. I saw them run. I thought at first, they would all leave and escape us and then I saw that there were two pigs and an old cow which were lumbering down what passed for a road in these parts. Four men held spears and swords and awaited us. There would be blood. My men spread out in a wide line.

I had learned a couple of words from the Irish who lived close to the castle. I shouted, "Surrender!" as we approached. I did not catch the answer but from the gesture I suspected it was a negative reply. Two of the men on the flanks of the Irish suddenly turned and fled. Twenty odd galloping horses will do that to a man who is untried. I saw that the other two were older men. I watched as the taller of the two lifted his spear in two hands. He meant to spear me over my horse's head. I let my reins hang. Jack would keep running until I pulled on them. I was wearing gauntlets and, as he lunged at me, I grabbed the shaft and pulled it over my horse's neck. When he lurched forward, I used the flat of my blade to smash into his nose and face. I broke his nose and rendered him unconscious. I left him lying in a pool of blood. When I looked Roger of Chester had split open the head of the other. He had not risked his own life.

We reined in. The two pigs and the cow had been left. My men slew them and then began to butcher them. Others looted the huts. There was little of value in them save that each had a small pot of coins buried in the floor. We took them and burned the huts. We left most of the butchered animals for the rest of the army and took choice cuts with us for our supper. We left within an hour of our arrival. The smoke would act as a marker for the army. I did not doubt that they would probably camp there. The army moved more slowly than we did. We found two more villages before dark but they were deserted. Those who had fled us had warned them. I was glad. We burned them. One had a field of wheat growing. We burned that too.

We camped that night on a small lump of land which rose from the undulating land around us. It afforded clear line of sight. The Duke's replacement rider found us. His horse was lathered. He had ridden hard.

"His lordship is pleased my lord. He thanks you for his supper. He is fond of beef."

I was happier knowing that the Duke was with his nephew. He was a moderating influence. The King needed that. We roasted pork and beef on the fire. The livers and kidneys had also been taken. They cooked quickly and my men loved them. They did not bother with hovels for the skies were cloudless. It would be chilly but we had furs in which to lie and our oiled cloaks would keep off the wind.

Sir Henry said, as he ate the juicy pork. "This is not the sort of war I imagined."

"Nor me but I agree with the King and the Duke. This is the best way to bring this rebellion against the King's authority to an end."

"Is this his land?"

"The kings of Ireland all acknowledged, in the past, the right of England to live on their island. They accepted his authority. When Strongarm came here two hundred years ago with three hundred knights and conquered their land they knew they could not stand up to the might of knights. Had King Cathal mac Ruaidri Ó Conchobair not been greedy and seen his chance to steal land then we would not be here."

The next day brought us to their first stronghold. It was at a place we later learned was called Beannchar na Sionna. Two ridges met and there was a settlement and a hill fort with a palisade. It was too large for us to take and so we sent the rider back to the army. We made a camp three hundred paces from the walls.

The people lined the palisade and hurled abuse at us. As Roger said, wryly, "They shout and curse, lord but I see that none have the courage to ride forth and face us."

I nodded, "Alan, bring our archers. Let us see if we can stir them to battle."

I dismounted and handed my reins to Tom. I did not bother with my shield or helmet. John and I, along with Sir Henry and Peter, approached the walls. My archers lined up one hundred and fifty paces from the walls. Four arrows flew at us. They were ranging arrows. The best of them fell ten feet from Stephen the Tracker. He walked up to the arrow, which had a flint head, picked it up, snapped it in two and, spitting on it, threw it to the ground. He then walked back to the other archers. Each one chose a good arrow, a swallow tail. The men on the walls did not know that they were being targeted. They assumed that our archers had bows as poor as theirs. My men each had a bow which was six feet long and made of yew. A man had to train for at least ten years to be able to pull it. Alan gave no orders. He just looked down the line when he had nocked. He nodded and released. It would have been comical had it not been tragic. The men on the walls watched in fascination as the twenty arrows soared. By the time they realised that the arrows would not fall short it was too late for twelve of them. Twelve heads disappeared from the walls. The other targets survived because they had a shield and had had the wit to raise it. The other defenders all ducked below the top and instead of heads we saw shields.

I began to walk back. "They have seen our power. Let us go and eat. Roger, send four men to the far side of the hill fort. They may send for help!"

"Aye, lord."

It was the King himself and twenty of his knights who first arrived along with the Earl of Kildare. In all there were a hundred warriors. He dismounted and looked at the walls. "What have you done, Sir William?"

"We have sent men to watch the west gate. My archers slew a dozen or so of their men. I thought to wait until the rest of the army arrived. They will surrender."

He nodded, "Come, Earl Gerald, bring that tame Irishman and we will go and speak with them."

I said, "My liege, go no closer than the broken arrow you see. They have the range."

He smiled, "I will heed your advice but if the arrow of a barbarian could penetrate this plate then I would have the head of the weaponsmith who made it!"

I walked behind the King and waved Alan of the Wood to accompany me. His arrows would be faster than any Irishman who tried to kill my king. With the Earl and the King was an Irish lord. He wore a surcoat. I had learned that many of the local lords and princes would ally themselves with us in the hope of advancement. He shouted something. Those in the hillfort responded. The King spoke to the translator and so it went on until the King turned, "They have decided to die. So be it. My conscience is clear. They have the misguided belief that their King will save them. They are in for a rude awakening when their town is burned and their men beheaded!"

The rest of the army had joined us by dawn. Most would be in no condition to fight but the King hoped that the sight of our superior numbers would make them surrender. They did not. In the late afternoon the King ordered all of the archers to line up. He was going to send a message. He looked at me, "Sir William has given me good advice. He thinks our archers are the best in the world. Captain Alan, let us see what ten flights sent into the hill fort can do!"

Alan of the Wood looked at me and I nodded, reluctantly, for I knew what he intended. Richard was the King and we could not refuse an order. Two thousand arrows descended into the hill fort. Those who were in their homes were the lucky ones but the children who were playing, the women who were grinding wheat and those standing and discussing the attack were not. They died. When the arrow storm had ended, we could hear the cries from within. Some were cries of those who were hit but others were of mothers who had come from their houses and seen their children and aged parents slaughtered.

The gates opened and four men, bare headed and open handed emerged. They spoke their language. It was translated and, turning, the King simply said, "It is ended. They have surrendered. Sir William resume your scouting. We have wasted enough time as it is!"

We were spared the sight of the children who had been killed. Alan and his men were grim faced. They had not enjoyed obeying that order. They could kill men but the King had ordered them to kill the innocent. A new, ruthless King was emerging. His standing amongst my men plummeted.

As we headed west, he said, "If we meet a real enemy, my lord, we will struggle. We have but forty flights each left to us. We can make another fifty with the ones we recover when we return to the fort but that is all." The ten flights had used a fifth of their supplies and they had not had the opportunity to recover any.

"Then let us hope we need them not. Send Stephen the Tracker and his men ahead of us."

We rode steadily and it was just an hour or so later when they galloped back to us. We had seen no sign of people since leaving the hill fort. There were abandoned villages dotted in the distance. We had not the stomach to torch them. If the King wanted them destroyed then he could do it.

"My lord, we have found the Irish. There is an enormous army. They have mounted knights and many banners. They filled the land ahead of us. We could not begin to count them."

Just then a couple of hundred warriors on hill ponies rode over the small crest towards us. "Alan of the Wood ride back to the King and warn him. We will bloody their noses and follow you."

"Are you sure, lord?"

"You have no armour and will be faster. Do not fear. We shall not be long behind you."

"Form line. Ralph and Tom behind me. When I shout 'turn' then do not hesitate."

"Aye lord!"

I pulled up my shield and drew my sword. Behind the horsemen I saw banners as they rose over the crest. Alan was right. It was like a sea of faces. It was hard to discern where one man began and another ended. There was no order to it. It was as though the whole nation had risen. The only horsemen I could see were the ones on hill ponies who galloped towards us. We could outrun men on foot.

As we waited, I said to Sir Henry. "Now we know why they were holding out. They expected their King to come to their aid. Perhaps King Richard was right to use the arrows. Had we not reduced the hillfort then we would have been trapped between the army and the defenders." I did not convince myself but at least I could justify, partly, King Richard's act.

The Irish ponies closed rapidly with us. The riders' feet almost touched the ground. They were much smaller than our horses.

"We wait until they are forty paces from us. We hit them and then retire. No heroics. We hurt them and then fall back. Ride to the left!"

My men all chorused, "Yes, lord."

As soon as they were forty paces from us, I spurred Jack and he leapt forward. I know not what the warriors thought we would do. What we actually did confused them. My sword hacked through the head of the first Irish warrior for his skull was at a perfect height for my sword. Even as I pulled Jack around to my left, my bloody sword continued its sweep and hacked into the back of a second warrior. Our sudden attack had emptied more than sixty saddles. We could have destroyed them.

"Turn!"

As I turned, I managed to stab an Irish chieftain in the back. I saw that Ralph and Tom had obeyed me and were heading, a little slower than I might have hoped, towards the distant hillfort. I glanced over my shoulder. The survivors of the attack were milling around. They looked at the hacked and maimed bodies which littered the ground. Barely seventy remained in their saddles. Many had been slain but some had been wounded. Others had been thrown from their saddles by our bigger horses. When the Irish army passed the skirmish, it would be a warning for them.

We reached the hill fort in a shorter time than it had taken us to reach the enemy. My archers had arrived and warned the King about the Irish. Even as we approached, I saw the lines being prepared. When we rode in the lines parted and allowed us through. The Duke and the Earl, along with the Earl of Kildare awaited me. "Well, Sir William, what can you report?" I heard the hint of fear in the King's voice.

"The Irish are coming. I fear they have been using the time since our skirmish to gather warriors from all over the island. If we show a line of steel it may halt them."

The Duke said, "I will order the archers into the hill fort. They have the range to loose over our heads. We can dismount the men at arms and have them present a wall of spears and shields."

"And what of the knights, uncle! They are our most powerful weapon!"

I knew he was wrong. The two hundred archers we had were the most powerful and they had shown it already. The Duke smiled. "King Richard, we withdraw our knights to the other side of the hill fort."

The Earl of Kildare said, "They will negotiate first. It is the Irish way. There will be no attack this afternoon. Your wall of sergeants will make them stop and they will seek a truce."

The Earl was proved correct. The Irish stopped three hundred paces from us. The wild warriors beat their shields and chanted. Some dropped their breeks to expose themselves but the kings and their knights conferred. They camped. The Earl looked pleased with himself. "We have the night to prepare."

Chapter 14

When morning broke, and it was a grey one, Irish emissaries in the form of priests, approached. "We would speak with the King!"

"I am the King. What is it that you wish?"

"The King of Connaught wishes to have conference with you. You may bring a bodyguard and advisers. He swears that there will be no treachery."

King Richard nodded, "Uncle, Kildare, you will come with me. Dick of Craven, I would have ten men with me." He looked at me, "And you Will Strongstaff. I need your wits and your blade. I fear treachery."

The Earl of Kildare said, "There will be no treachery, my liege!"

"When men have sneaked into your bed chamber and tried to kill you and your wife then you can speak to me of no treachery. Will Strongstaff can be trusted to watch out for the life of the King."

I walked behind the King as did Dick of Craven. We would not talk. We were there to watch for knives which might flash from beneath cloaks. I saw that there were three kings waiting for us. A bishop and four chieftains were there also. The bodyguards all had bare tattooed chests. They had paint upon their faces as though to terrify us. On their heads they wore high domed helmets and, in their hands, they held long war axes. They did not frighten me.

We stood in silence and it was broken by King Cathal mac Ruaidri Ó Conchobair. He was as old as John of Gaunt. He wore many rings on his fingers. About his neck he had a golden torc and his helmet was golden too. I doubted that it was pure gold. More likely it was a silver, copper, gold alloy. The hilt of his sword was elaborately decorated and I doubted that it was a weapon to be feared. His breastplate shone. It was made to look like gold but I suspected that it was iron coated with copper and burnished. The King was a showman. He was trying to impress.

The King spoke our language well. That was not a surprise. His neighbours were English. "King Richard you have brought an army into my land and slain my people. I ask you why?"

The King stared deep into the King of Connaught's eyes. His voice was filled with steel. "Do not speak with a false tongue to me, you barbarian! For all your polished copper you are but little removed from the half-naked men who guard you! You attacked Kildare, Ormond and The Pale. You thought us weak and we are not. We are puissant and we are strong. Have you forgotten that all the kings of Ireland bow their knee to me!"

There was silence and I could see that the Irish had been badly advised. They thought Richard to be an ineffective king. Perhaps their dealings with Robert de Vere had misled them.

The Irish King flushed, "Perhaps we need to renegotiate that arrangement, King Richard. You bring a large army here but ours is ten times your number."

"And it could be a further ten times that number and I would not fear you. Bend the knee or fight. That is your choice."

King Richard had taken them by surprise. He had not come to speak of peace but of war. They looked at each other. King Cathal mac Ruaidri Ó Conchobair was their leader but he began to doubt himself.

King Richard pushed his point, "This is a good place for a battle. We have eaten well and we are ready to fight. What say you? Will you fight or will you bend the knee and quit the field?"

I think he might have bent the knee had not King Maelsechlainn Ó Cellaigh suddenly spat out, "We fight you! You are no man or else you would have already sired a child! You are a lover of men and as such we despise you!"

I wondered if the unpredictable King Richard would erupt from within and rise to the bait but he did not. He nodded, "Then we fight! You have priests with you, confess now, for if I have my way, none of you will survive the day!"

As we walked back, he said, quietly, "Will, Dick, what did you make of the bodyguards of the kings?"

"They look to be hard men but any of our sergeants could take them. They wear no mail."

It was as though he had not heard Dick. He turned to the Duke, "Uncle, your plan is a good one. We will have the archers in the hill fort. Earl Gerald, you and five of your knights will fight with the men at arms. They need a leader. Your standard will draw them to you. Dick of Craven, you will dress in my spare surcoat and wear a visored helm. You will stand with my standard at the rear of the sergeants at arms."

I looked at Dick who shrugged and said, "It will be an honour, Your Majesty."

We reached our lines and the Duke began to give his orders. The Irish were still forming up their lines and our men at arms and knights were already drawn up before the hill fort. "Ralph, fetch Jack. We mount on the eastern side of the hillfort. Send Tom to stand by Alan of the Woods. This is no place for him."

We passed through the men at arms. I saw Roger and my men, "Do you fight with us, lord?"

I shook my head, "The Earl of Kildare will command. The knights will be led by the King and we will attack when the Irish are committed." I lowered my voice, "Dick of Craven will be the bait to draw them on. He will be dressed as the King."

Roger's head slumped forward. He and Dick had served together. He knew what it meant. The Irish would try to get at the King. They would send their best warriors and they would find but a sergeant at arms. His surcoat might be the King's but the plate he wore would not be. He would be sacrificed.

The King needed to use every knight and squire for his attack. We would be vastly outnumbered. However we would have an advantage of men in our mounted charge. A charge by heavy horse was irresistible. The squires would form the rear rank of the four. Without Dick of Craven the King insisted that his uncle and myself flanked him. We took our horses to the hill fort's south western slope so that we could view the battle and best judge the moment to attack.

I saw Dick of Craven now attired as the King. He and the rest of the King's guards made their way through the serried ranks of sergeants to stand at the rear of the three lines beneath the royal standard. I saw that Roger and my men jostled their way to stand close to him. The Earl of Kildare stood with his five knights and amongst his own men at arms in the second rank. There were more men at arms gathered on the western side of the hill than I had seen in a battle since the war in Castile. Even so they were outnumbered many times by the mass of Irishmen who now began to advance. The Irish sent half their men in the first wave. There were over five thousand men but it was hard to judge for their lines were not even. They had banners but I did not know how many men they represented. I estimated the number.

The Duke had fought in more battles than I had and he made a keen observation. "They are using this first attack to probe for weaknesses. They hope to make inroads into our lines and then send the second attack thence. They will keep their mounted men for the end. I do not think they know we keep our knights here."

Once again, their knights and kings did not advance. They sat on their horses looking like English knights. The difference was the hundred or so bodyguards whose half-naked bodies gleamed in the sun which just peeped out from behind grey clouds. The elevation of the hill fort would allow our archers to loose their arrows over the heads of our men. Thanks to the King's slaughter of the innocents they would not have as many arrows to thin the numbers as they would have wished but I saw, from the speed with which the Irish approached that the archers would have a shorter time to kill them. I was not close enough to hear the individual commands given by Alan but I saw the two hundred arrows sail high into the sky and, while they were plunging down to tear into flesh a second two hundred rose and began to fall. I saw the effect immediately. The Irish shields were but simply made and they did not stop the arrows. Worse, the first flights caught the Irish with their shields held before them. Alan had spread his archers in a long line to maximise the area he could target. As the arrows continued to fall they struck more and more men. The weight of arrows was towards the centre of the line. It looked like a farmer had taken his scythe to a field of wheat and swept it across. The odd warrior in the line had been lucky enough to survive but, after a few flights, where there had been a thousand men there were now just thirty or forty staggering forwards. Not all the rest were dead but they were, effectively, out of the battle. The two wings of the Irish struck our sergeants at arms. Their best men, those who had been the bravest and the most experienced, now lay dead or wounded. When the warriors on the flanks struck, they were met by walls of steel which held them.

The Irish leaders had not prepared as well as they might but now, they reacted. I heard horns sound and the second attack began. This time the men in the front ranks had shields and they came more slowly. They were trying to protect themselves from the arrows. I was aware that Alan had stopped sending arrows. The King was too, "Why have the archers ceased their attack?"

"I am afraid, King Richard, that they may run out of arrows if they continue to expend them at the present rate. I am guessing they save the rest for this next attack."

The Duke nodded, "Besides they could not send them for fear of hitting our own men. The two battle lines are now joined." He pointed. The Irish and the sergeants led by the Earl of Kildare were now engaged in battle. Spears probed, swords flashed. Metal hit wood and mail. Although our men had armour and shields there were so many Irish that, inevitably, some of our sergeants fell. When an Irishman fell, five raced to take his place. When a sergeant fell there would be a single man to step forward. Already, in places, our three lines were now two. It took longer for the second attack to reach us and all the time the perimeter of sergeants' spears grew fewer. When Alan's archers sent their next flight, it had an effect. It halved the attackers but the slower approach and the shields bore the brunt of the attack.

The King said, "It is time."

We turned our horses and rode down the slope to join the knights. We took our place at the head of the column. John and Ralph were behind me. The standard would be next to that of the Duke. The King's standard was with Dick of Craven. The enemy would think that the King was one of the Duke's knights. They had similar surcoats. Both displayed the lions and the fleur de lys. John handed me my spear and the rest were handed spears and lances by their squires. With our arming caps, coifs and helmets the sound of battle was muffled but we could still hear it. We had no sight of it. The Duke lowered his spear to signal the advance and we began to trot. The ridges lay to the north of us and we rode parallel to them. We would be hidden from the Irish. Once we had cleared the western edge of the ridge we would turn and begin our charge. We would have just eight hundred paces between us and their kings. It was a bold strategy. The Duke was counting on the fact that, while the Irish army would be greater than ours, we would outnumber the kings and their guards and we would be attacking them from their flank.

When we emerged, we were just a hundred paces from the main Irish attack. The warriors were milling around the south western end of our defences. Our men were holding and the Irish were so engaged that they did not see us. We began to canter and our war horses ate up the ground. As soon as they began to thunder it had an effect. The warriors felt the ground shaking. Some of those at the rear of the Irish line feared we were going to attack them and they turned and began to flee. As they did so, they were struck in the back by the arrows of our archers. Horns sounded for their leaders had seen the threat. They knew that we were attacking their kings. If they were calling back their men then it was too late for we were already closer to the kings than their rear line and we were mounted. If they had charged us with their knights then there might have been a chance that they would have stalled our attack but they did not. Their bodyguards formed a wall before us. I saw that they had shields but they were not large ones and they were not uniform. Some were round, some rectangular and some oval. They would not be able to lock them. There were just two hundred men and we had a line one hundred men wide. We rode with our spears and lances held in the air. When we were just one hundred paces from the line the Duke shouted, "Charge! For God, King Richard and England!"

As I lowered my spear, I spurred Jack. I preferred the slightly shorter spear to a lance. The end was easier to control and here the extra length of the lance was unnecessary for we were not facing lances. We faced bodyguards with shields, swords and axes. I knew now why the King had asked me about the bodyguards. He realised we would face them first and I had trained him well enough for him to know that you sought an enemy's weakness. The kings and their knights had withdrawn forty paces behind their bodyguards. I knew not if that was so that they could run or charge us when we broke through their lines.

I pulled back my spear as I approached the line. I saw the man I would kill. He had a large oval shield and held a long-handled war axe. He was screaming at me. I gambled that the shield was like the ones the other Irish used and just made of a simple board without lamination and metal. As he raised it to protect himself, I rammed my spear at it. It splintered and broke the wood driving long slivers into his face and chest. The spear continued and entered his chest. The head scraped off bone and then, as it struck something vital, the head broke and he fell dead. I was already dropping my broken shaft and drawing my sword as I pulled back on Jack's reins to make him slow and rear. His hooves clattered down on the shield of the man in the second rank. I heard a shout as the shield and the man's arms were shattered by the impact. As the shield fell, I brought over my sword to hack into his neck and he fell. There was no one between me, King Richard, the bulk of our horsemen and the line of Irish knights and kings.

Not all of our knights had broken through. I saw that one of the Earl of Kent's knights had been dragged from his horse. I wheeled Jack and rode at the two Irish men who were raising their weapons to slay him. My sword slew one but the second hacked his axe across the chest. John, holding my spare spear, rammed it into the Irishman's head. The knight had died but he had been avenged.

The King shouted, "Charge their kings. Let us end this!"

Even as I turned to obey the orders, I saw that the mass of Irishmen had disengaged from the attack on our sergeants and were streaming towards us. That was the moment when King Cathal mac Ruaidri Ó Conchobair should have charged us but he had seen his bodyguards slaughtered and, instead of charging, he fled. Their horses were fresh and ours had charged. They were blown. The Duke took charge. He knew that with a start of fifty paces we would not catch them, "Turn and face the others! This battle is not yet won!"

Ralph was still with me. I saw that he had drawn his sword. He held the reins and the standard in his left hand. He was a good horseman but he had yet to be tested in a battle. I shouted, "Stay close by me!"

We turned and cantered towards the Irishmen who were hurtling towards us. They had to be weary. They had run to fight. They had fought and now they had run back to fight us. Carrying a sword and a shield wearied a warrior. I dug my spurs in and rode towards a knot of warriors who had small shields and swords. They had to be from the same clan. Sir Henry was with me and his squire, Peter. In a confused mêlée such as this you concentrated on one target at a time. You relied on your squires to watch your back. That is what Sir Henry and I did. As we closed, I waited until the last possible moment to spur Jack. His sudden burst of speed took the leading Irishman by surprise and his tired arm was still raising his sword and shield when my blade took the top of his head from his body. I back slashed down at the next warrior and my sword cut into his neck and shoulder. John still rode with his horse guarding my left side and he brought his sword across the arm of the next Irishman who saw my left side exposed and thought he had me. Henry and Peter slew two more. Suddenly the one whom John had struck leapt from behind me. His right arm was half severed but he held a dagger in his left. He used the body of a dead comrade to leap up onto Jack's hindquarters. I felt his arm come around my chest to pull me from my mount. I would have died had not Ralph slashed his sword across the man's spine. His back arced and he fell from Jack's back.

"Thank you, Ralph." I turned to view the battlefield. The Earl of Kildare was leading the sergeants and archers to attack the rear of the Irish line. With horsemen to the fore and a mass of horsemen behind them the Irish knew that they were defeated. Their kings had fled and they joined them. They ran and we began a hunt which took the rest of the day. We chased them at the pace of a weary man. They stumbled and fell. When they rose, a sword would end their pain. We stopped because we did not wish to kill our horses. We had killed many Irishmen but more had escaped. They would return to their villages and tell the tale of the day the King of England's wrath was visited upon them.

There was little joy in our victory for we were exhausted and we had been as butchers and not warriors. The sensible knights dismounted and walked their horses back through the body littered field. What little there was evaporated when we found Dick of Craven's body. He and six of the King's guards had been hacked to pieces. Dick's head had been taken from his body. Roger and my men at arms were laying out their bodies when we returned. As the King followed us, I saw genuine remorse. He knelt by the bodies of his dead men and he bowed his head in silent prayer. His ruse had worked but at what a cost. Dick was irreplaceable. As the Captain of the Guard he had been the last barrier between the King and an assassin. Now that barrier was gone.

The enemy dead were stripped and their bodies piled inside the hill fort. We pulled down the palisade and made a pyre from it. As the sun set, we burned their bodies. While we watched it burn the King said,

"And tomorrow we will fill in the ditches with the ashes. This hill fort will be no more." The people who had lived there had been sent hence. No doubt they were still heading towards distant parts of Connaught to be as far away from the dreadful English as it was possible to get. After we had buried our dead we ate. None had an appetite but we knew we needed to put food in our bellies. I sat with John and we flanked Ralph. Tom had watched the battle and he was silent.

"You saved your lord's life today, Ralph. What would you have as a reward?"

He gave a wan smile, "Nothing, my lord, for I did the least of all. Your arm must be weary for you must have slain more than twenty men this day."

"I did not keep count but I know that I was wielding an iron bar and not a sword by the end. John, you will need to put a good edge on it."

Tom said, "Let me do this, father, for I just watched men die this day."

I nodded.

Ralph asked, "Will we fight again?"

"The kings escaped and we will follow. I know not if there is a stronghold in Galway but the Irish King made a mistake when he insulted King Richard. There will be a price to pay and it will be a most terrible one."

They asked me no more but I knew that the King had changed. He had turned from mourning the memory of his wife to destroying his own good reputation. He was beginning the journey from king to tyrant. I saw it that day at the battle of Beannchar na Sionna.

Part Three
The Tyranny of King Richard

Chapter 15

We left the next morning with the hill fort destroyed and the smoke from the fires still hanging in the air. We had lost many men. It was not just Dick of Craven and his loyal men who had died. There had been others, knights included. Only our archers had been spared losses. We headed west. As we rode, we found the bodies of those we had slain and then the bodies of those that had succumbed to their wounds. It was almost dark before the road was clear. Some had fled a long way to die alone. The corpses acted as a marker to the lair of the kings. We found them the next day. Perhaps they thought we would have given up the pursuit or maybe they over estimated the numbers who would have rallied. As soon as we were seen the gates of the stronghold opened and the Bishop of Galway came out to ask for talks of peace. I was a warrior and I was not involved.

We were ordered to pillage the town and the countryside. Galway was a rich town. By the time we had finished it was impoverished. We emptied warehouses and the homes of the rich merchants. We took food from granaries and the abattoir. We took pickled fish from the fish quays. We left nothing. We were a vengeful army. We had all lost friends and King Richard's army took it out on the men and women of Galway. Even while the King of England was discussing the peace terms the Irish were being punished. The peace talks went on for two days. It gave us the chance to heal our wounded and to help our horses to recover. The terms were harsh. The Irish Kings who had fought us all had to swear not to attack the English earldoms. In addition, hostages were taken. They were women, daughters and sons. They would be housed in the castle at Dublin. Of course, there were other Irish Kings who had not fought. There was no such surety for them. The Uí Néill from the north of the island had kept dangerously quiet.

The Earl of Kildare expressed his doubts about the northern clan but the King, who was in an ebullient and confident mood, dismissed them. "We have shown the Irish who rules this land. I want columns of our men to return east and, on their way back to Dublin, destroy any castles which might offer opposition again."

I was sent with the Earl of Kildare and his knights. We were given the southerly route home. We were lucky. There were few places which were strong enough to defy the King. We destroyed four hillforts on the journey home. None of the hillforts were occupied. It took a month for us to complete the journey. The King and his uncle headed to the north. He intended to intimidate the Uí Néill clan. King Richard did not care that his victory had been paid for by the blood of many English knights and men at arms not to mention thousands of Irishmen, he was determined to exercise his authority.

I confided my fears to Sir Henry as we headed back to Kildare. "He has used Ireland to test his power. I fear that he will return to England and try the same."

"But there are no rebels in England."

"There are those who not only challenged him once but won. I think he will punish them. The Queen is dead and there is none, save John of Gaunt, to rein him in."

We left the Earl in his castle and made our way back to Dublin and The Pale. We had taken great quantities of treasure. Most was in the form of swords, helmets and some mail but we had taken torcs, coins and jewels from dead chiefs. The money John of Gaunt had given to me to hire the men was now spent and I had to pay for my men. Costs were incurred as we had to pay for food while we awaited the King's pleasure.

The Earl of Kent arrived next, a day or two later, and he informed us that the King had disbanded the army and we could make our own way home. Of course, he had neglected to send the funds for us to do so. Some of the weaponry was sold to fund our voyage home. We were still well in profit. We arrived back in Chester and headed back to Weedon. As we rode, I asked the new men if they had decided if they wished to stay with me. Some told me that they were happy to do so but a handful of them wished to seek their fortune elsewhere. It was not an acrimonious decision on their part. They were warriors for hire. The four were all sergeants. The archers were happy to stay on with me. Alan of the Wood had explained that they would not be paid the same rate but that did not worry them. I now had to find out if the three manors, Weedon, Stony Stratford and Whittlebury could fund the extra men. By the time we reached Weedon, six months had passed since we had first left. Harry and Alice had both grown and there were new people working the land. It had been a good harvest and all was well.

We paid off the four men and I sold the metal to Martin the Smith. It would fund my men for another six months.

Life settled into an easy pattern for the next six months. My new men found life in Weedon suited them. Some of the new men married. My wife parcelled up the farm which had belonged to Old Harry and his wife. They had died without family and it was a big farm. Old Harry had allowed it to lie fallow for a couple of years before we arrived. My wife now saw an opportunity. Six of my married men were offered the tenancy of six small farms. None was big enough to support a family but, with the stipend, I paid them they were all better off. It was an astute move on my wife's part.

When, some months later, we visited Northampton to buy more surcoats, we heard news which surprised me. The King had become betrothed to Isabella of Valois. She was seven years old and the youngest daughter of the King of France. It was part of a truce with France. As we rode home, I pondered the decision. It was a political marriage but what the King needed was an heir and he had none! A seven-year-old bride might be a political help but it would not bring him a son. He was in a difficult position. The marriage was planned for the next year. We also heard that the King had had the body of Robert de Vere brought back to England and he had built him a tomb. It was said he wept at the sight of his dead friend's mummified body. That concerned me as much as anything.

While in Northampton I was told that Henry Bolingbroke had finally managed to go to Jerusalem. He went not as a crusader but as a pilgrim. The cynic in me saw the political side of the gesture. He was preparing himself for kingship.

It was the following year, not long after the marriage of the King to Isabella of Valois that I was summoned to Northampton to meet with the Earl of Northampton. I had not been invited to the wedding of the King. My wife had expected an invite but I had not. I knew that the King viewed me as a warrior. I was not a noble. I was there to be used in time of war and then dismissed. The Earl of Northampton had been invited and I was summoned to his castle when he returned from London.

He had with him his son, Henry of Monmouth. The young lord had spent more time away from his father than with him. When I arrived at the castle I was greeted as an old friend. That had not been the way we had parted on our return from the Baltic. Then I had almost been dismissed. I had with me John, Ralph and Tom. Whenever I was summoned to the side of Henry, I knew that some request would be made of me. However, he was my liege lord and I could not refuse him.

He smiled and that was always a bad sign. This is your eldest? Thomas isn't it?"

"Tom, my lord."

"Tom, just so. And this is my son, Henry. The last you saw of him, Sir William, he was but a babe and now he has grown."

"That he has, my lord."

"Henry, this is the man who trained the King to be a warrior and trained me. He guarded the King too. This is not a knight who fights at tourneys. This is a warrior."

To be fair to the young lord he looked at me with respect. That was not always the case with lordlings. I bowed, "It is good to meet with you, my lord."

The Earl of Northampton looked over at John. "And has John been dubbed yet, Sir William?"

I shook my head, "No, lord."

"Is he not ready yet?"

"Oh yes lord, he is ready but…"

The old Henry Bolingbroke smiled, "But you did not wish to offend me by doing so. Then that is easily remedied. I have a ceremony at the end of the month. Fetch him here and he shall be knighted. You are a banneret now. You should have a knight to follow your banner. What say you, John? Are you ready for spurs?"

"I am, my lord." I saw, on his face, the worry. How would he afford a courser, the plate? Whence would he get his squire? I gave him a nod. We would have to work that out later. My wife would have to change the accommodation. He would no longer be able to share a room with Ralph. He would need his own quarters. He would require a coat of arms and his own surcoat. All of this was rushing through his mind. I knew it because when I had been knighted the same thoughts had terrified me.

"Good. And now that you need a squire I would have you train my son, Henry of Monmouth. He can be a sort of squire to you. You need not worry about making him a knight. I have better qualified men to do that but you are the best to teach him how to survive on a battlefield. Your home is close enough for his mother and I to visit although his mother spends more time in Monmouth. I give him to you for a year."

The act seemed well thought out and planned and I wondered if this was the reason I had been given Weedon. Henry Bolingbroke was a complicated and deep man. I would not put it past him to have planned this all those years ago. I smiled, "I am happy but you should know, my lord, that my home is simple. We do not have fine dining."

Henry of Monmouth grinned, "Do not worry about that, lord. I do not need fine food. And I shall be Henry, my lord, for I need to learn from you. You are the master and I shall be your apprentice. It will be good to see how those who serve England live."

I liked the young lord. He was not like his father. He appeared to have no guile about him, "Then all is well."

The Earl handed me a bag of coins. "He has his own horses and James, his servant, can see to his needs. He will need armour for training and a training sword. When he is full-grown, we shall buy him plate."

I nodded, "And when shall I come for him?"

"You take him now. I hope to see an improvement in his skills by the time John is knighted."

Eleanor would not be happy. She liked to prepare. It could not be helped.

"Henry, take the lord's entourage to help you pack. You can get to know them. I would have words with Sir William."

When we were alone, he poured us some wine, "You were with the King in Ireland?"

"I was, my lord."

"My father said he acquitted himself well."

"He led our men in battle, lord, and the Irish were defeated."

"There is a hint of criticism in your voice, Will."

I smiled, "No, lord, as you know I am a warrior. The fighting I understand but I am less confident with the strategies which are used by the great and the good."

He seemed mollified. "And now he takes a seven-year-old as a bride." He lowered his voice and gestured towards the door through which his son had just passed. "You know that you may be training a future King of England. I may never attain the throne but if my cousin has no children then Henry of Monmouth will be the next King of England. You have a great responsibility upon your shoulders, Will Strongstaff."

I shook my head, "Then give it to another, lord."

"The Black Prince was the best judge of warriors and he chose you to train both my cousin and me. You are perfect because you have neither affiliations nor obligations to any. Your blood is not touched by your betters and that makes you the ideal choice. You are not related to the families of England who wield the power. Keep your eyes and ears open, Will. There are plots and there are conspiracies. Know that I have no intention of harming my cousin. I do not wish my cousin, Mortimer, and his cronies to attain the crown and I will do all in my power to keep the King safe. When I heard that you were with the King and my father in Ireland, I knew that they would both be safe. I know that my son, a future King of England, will be as safe with you as in the Tower of London!"

James, Henry's servant, was an older man. He was almost my age and I recognised him as having formerly been one of the Earl's men at arms. As such we got on well. Riding the short journey back to Weedon I was largely silent. I had much to ponder. Despite my own choices I was now back in the centre of the struggle to keep and hold the crown and the throne. Henry Bolingbroke was right. The King had ruled for a long time and had no heir. His bride would not be able to conceive for six or seven more years. Anything might happen in that time. Young Henry of Monmouth might well be the King.

John nudged his horse next to me. Ralph and Tom were chattering like magpies with Henry. "Lord, the Earl does me great honour but I know how much it costs to be a knight. I have saved coin from the wars but it will not be enough. How can I find a squire? What about a war horse?"

I nodded. This was a healthy distraction from my fears about my own future. "The squire is easy, if you will have him. Ralph is willing and he is good with horses. I am certain that his father would have a courser for you. You do not need it yet. You have time to garner the coin. If you wish to go to war to earn coin then I will not stop you. I am your lord but I have known you too long to be an awkward one. Plate? Speak with Martin and see what he can do. Your mother and father will be proud of your achievement. Your father is now an important man. As reeve of Stony Stratford, he has more coin. Ask your mother to make your surcoats. When I was first knighted that is what I did. This knighthood is something to be embraced and not feared."

"What of you, lord? Who will be your squire? You were training Ralph."

"And I will train Tom. He is willing and he will like the elevation. There is little likelihood of war in the near future. He has time to learn."

When we reached my hall I knew I should have sent Ralph ahead to warn my wife. When she was introduced to the young lord her face, when she caught my eye, was as black as thunder, although she smiled at the young lord. Henry was perfectly polite and I think his smile and charm disarmed her. While Henry and his servant were shown their new quarters, I told my wife all. She was pleased that John was to be knighted for she liked both him and his parents. I did not tell her about the possibility of Henry becoming King. That would have been too much for her.

Our training began the next day. I gave John a week off so that he could tell his parents and I allowed Ralph to return to Middleham. His father would be pleased and he could begin to look for a courser for John. I used my men at arms to help me train Henry. His enthusiasm and attitude endeared him to my men. He was no soft lord. He relished the hard work and the rough banter. He reminded me of me when I had been with the Blue Company. Throughout his life he had this ability to get on with ordinary folk. I had it because I was ordinary but he was the son of one of the most powerful and richest men in England. He was heir to both the English and French thrones. Yet he never used that to his advantage. When Harold Four Fingers put him on his back while showing him how to wrestle, he laughed and asked for my sergeant at arms to show him how to do it. He was battered and he was bruised at the end of each day yet he never complained. He admired my archers more than any. He tried to pull a bow but he could not. If he was going to be an archer, he would have begun training many years earlier. It did not stop him from trying and he spent hours each day at the butts. Alan of the Woods and my archers also took to him. I realised this would not be as hard as it had been with King Richard. Of course, then I had had Robert de Vere to upset the applecart. I had Henry all to myself and I moulded him to be a warrior. It was a measure of the youth that when the men began calling him Hal, he did not object and actually relished the name for it marked him as different from his father. While he was at Weedon he was Hal. When he returned to his father, he became Henry of Monmouth once more.

At the end of the month we headed back to Northampton. My wife insisted on hiring a carriage to take her and John's parents to Northampton for the dubbing. "We can stay in the town. We might not be allowed to see the ceremony but it is right that his mother and father see him with his spurs!" There was no arguing with my wife when she was in that sort of mood. Martin had made the spurs for John. They were my gift to him as well as a fine scabbard for his sword. His livery was to be a simple red and blue one. It was mine without the staff. As he told me, he had not done anything to merit anything more. He was what he was because of me.

There were others to be knighted and, after the ceremony, while John left with Tom and Ralph to meet my wife and John's parents, the Earl took us to the inner bailey. He waved over a servant who had two wooden practice swords. This was unfair for young Henry had had no warning that he was to be tested. To be fair to the youth he grinned and took the sword. His father took the other. Henry Bolingbroke had been trained by me but that had been some years ago. The Earl tried a flurry of quick blows. Henry of Monmouth deflected them all and, using his feet, moved out of the way of the last one. He was barely breathing while his father was almost out of breath. His father raised his sword to bring it down on his son's head. Had it connected then the young lord would have had his skull split open. Roger of Chester had spent hours with the youth and it paid off. Henry of Monmouth blocked the blow and then spun around to land a blow on his father's buttocks. The Earl looked shocked and I feared he would be angry. Instead he shook his head and began to laugh. He threw the sword to the ground and put his arm around his son's shoulders.

"That will do, Will Strongstaff. That will do. Another eleven months will see him ready to ride to war!" His servant came over and the Earl took a purse from him and threw it to me. "A reward for the good work." He shook his head, "Bested by my own son who has yet to shave." He wagged a playful finger at me, "Will Strongstaff! You have not lost your touch!"

My wife, John and his parents stayed in Northampton in an inn and celebrated. I rode home with Tom, Ralph and Hal. It was a big day for both Tom and Ralph. They were now squires. Ralph had seen that John had begun from a similar position to himself. The possibility of knighthood was there. Tom was different. Weedon was a hereditary manor. When I died the title would pass to him. The Earl had told me that was as a result of being a banneret. His father, the Duke, had insisted upon confirming the title for my work in Ireland. Of course, it meant I had to provide more men when we went to war. I was glad that so many of my men had chosen to stay with me.

Over the next months Hal grew both in size, for he ate hearty meals prepared by my wife, and also from within as a warrior. He became better with a bow. He would never become as good as even Ralph but the bow gave him a broader back and stronger arms. He joked that I was adding to the expense of his plate and mail. I had joked back that his father could afford it. Ralph was good with a sword but soon Hal could defeat him. Tom also took part and he improved as well.

My life as lord of the manor meant I had duties there too. It was late November when we heard that there were bandits in the woods to the north of Northampton. Travellers had been robbed when they were on their way north, to Lincoln. Women had been abused. The King's highways had to be kept open. The Earl was not in the castle, he was visiting his wife in Monmouth, and so we were asked to help the Earl's men to hunt them down. It was the nearest we had come to war. We wore no mail and we carried no shields but we took our swords and my archers. With Harold the gamekeeper's dogs we set off at dawn. If women had not been involved then my archers might have been reluctant to hunt them for they had lived beyond the law for a time. Women had been abused and their merchant husbands beaten. That had broken the code of the bandit and for that they would be punished.

We left the road close to the path which the victims had told us the bandits had taken. They had told us that there were twelve of them. It was a risk to take Henry of Monmouth but his father wanted him prepared. This would do it. We had hunted game but that was never the same.

Stephen the Tracker liked the young lord and he took him with him to show him the tracks they had found. "See, Hal, the indentation there at the heel. It has a mark in it. I saw it by the road. That means it is the same man who came this way. The prints we follow could have been a couple of bands. This tells us that it is one. They are following in each other's tracks and that shows they are careful."

"Won't the dogs find them, Stephen?" Hal knew the right questions to ask.

My tracker laughed, "Dogs are stupid animals. If they have the scent then they might be able to follow. We know their prints but not their smell. No, Master Henry, the dogs are to put the fear of God into them and make them run. Then we will have them!"

We moved another half a mile into the woods and then Stephen held up his hand. He looked to me, "My lord, they are close. I smell fire." He pointed to the north. "That direction."

Hal's lesson was over. This was serious business. We were hunting bandits, "Alan, you take half the archers and sweep east, Stephen take the other half and sweep west. We will give you a count of five hundred and then set the dogs loose."

They set off. We dismounted and tied our horses to the trees. I detailed ten of the Earl's men to watch them. I cared not that they felt slighted. My men were better and I knew it. We only had twelve men to hunt and we had more than enough with us for that task. I counted off the numbers and then nodded to Harold. He let the four huge dogs go and they hurtled off through the woods. Drawing my sword, I ran after them. My men at arms, Ralph, John, Hal and Tom followed me. I heard shouts and cries from ahead. Suddenly four men rushed towards us. They had bows and swords.

"I command you to lay down your weapons I…"

I got no further. They nocked and drew in one motion. I stepped behind a tree as three arrows thudded into it. I spun around the far side and reached the nearest bandit as he nocked a second arrow. John had run towards a second bandit and struck him on the head with the flat of his sword. I hacked down at the first man's right hand. I half severed it and the bow fell to the ground. Tom, Ralph and Henry ran to the other two so quickly and had their weapons at the men's throats that they dropped their bows and fell to their knees.

One of them looked up when he saw the youths who had taken them. He shouted, "These are nothing more than pups!"

Tom and Ralph just stared at him but Hal backhanded him so hard that he fell backwards. "And pups have teeth! You are not a man! You are less than the soil beneath my feet for you prey on the weak. If I were the lord, I would hang you now."

I said, quietly, "But you are not and the law of your uncle rules this land. Men died for the charters. They will be tried." I turned to the man, "And then they will be hanged!"

When we reached the camp, we saw that one of the dogs had been slain and that the rest of the bandits lay riddled with arrows. Alan shook his head, "I am sorry, lord, we tried to take them without this but they fought and when they killed the dog…"

"Make no apologies. Had you slain them all it would have saved the hangman a job." I pointed to the captured men. "Dig graves and we will bury your friends here. Roger, have the men search for what they stole. We may be able to return it. Ralph, Tom, Henry, go fetch the horses."

We left the bandits in the gaol at Northampton. They would await the Earl's pleasure. My men asked if they could have a drink in one of Northampton's inns. As they deserved it, I acceded. When John said he would stay with them Hal looked at me pleadingly. Roger said, "If you leave Hal with us, lord, we will watch over him You have our word."

Harold Four Fingers nodded, "Aye lord, he has done well."

"Very well." I could not see his face but I knew his thoughts, "You, Tom, will return home with me. I will not risk your mother's wrath!"

My men did not stay late in Northampton but the ride back was many miles and they arrived back after dark. I saw that young Henry was the worse for drink. He was not falling over drunk nor vomiting but he had the giggles. Sir John looked at me apologetically, "I am sorry, lord. He hid his state from us. He seemed to be able to match Ralph beaker for beaker. When he slipped from his stool, we knew he could not and came home."

My wife smiled and ruffled Henry's hair, "Every young man goes through this. I daresay my Tom will one day. It is good that he had those about him who would watch over him. He has learned a lesson and will be better for it. Come, Hal, I am not your mother but I will put you to bed. Ralph, give me a hand. Tom, stop grinning and fetch water and a pail. I would not have a mess on my floor."

My wife had a good heart.

Chapter 16

The months flew by. Hal learned his lesson and when the unmarried warriors went to the ale wife in Weedon he was more temperate. He and Ralph were good looking young men and the unmarried girls of the village took a shine to them. Their company was sought. After my wife spoke to me, I took the nephew of the King to one side and counselled him, "Henry, you know that one day you might be King?"

"I do, my lord, but the King is hale and hearty, that day, should it ever come, is many years hence."

"Even so you do not want the mistakes of youth to come back and haunt you. I hear that you have dallied with the maids of the village."

He smiled, "My lord, have you read of my family? The first King Henry had so many bastards by so many women that he made one the Earl of Gloucester. It is said the Earl of Kildare is descended from one of my grandsire's offspring. However, you offer good counsel. I will be careful."

"Then let me put it another way. This is my manor and I am responsible for those in the village. No matter how noble your seed I would not have it in any of my maids. Do you understand?"

He smiled, "Of course, my lord. Their loss will be the gain of others. You are a good lord of the manor. My time here has been productive."

"I know for you are now a good warrior. If you were not noble born then you could hire out your sword."

"That is not what I mean, my lord. Your men are the best at making raw metal into steel. I have seen that which I could not see while at Monmouth or Northampton. I have seen the men who would fight for England. I know how they think. Even my father does not know that. He speaks of their courage but he does not know what makes them fight. You do and now so do I. When we sit and talk, I hear their hearts. You are a better leader of men than my father." He smiled at my face, "Do not deny it, lord. My father is a great leader and can command nobles but you have the touch with those who do the real fighting. I am learning that."

My time with the young man, who was becoming as dear to me as my own sons, was nearing the end when the Earl of Northampton arrived unannounced. My wife, who was rarely panicked, ran around the kitchen like a headless chicken when his men approached, "Peace, wife, he comes to see his son is all. Wine, bread and cheese, that will suffice."

The Earl had a serious face. "Will, dismiss all but my son. I have news to give to you."

My wife had laid the table and she shooed all from the room in which we dined each night. "Father, what is it? You look so serious."

"The country dangles on a knife edge. The King has finally extracted his revenge. His uncle, Warwick and Arundel have all been arrested. Arundel's brother, the Archbishop of Canterbury, has been exiled for life. The Duke of Gloucester is imprisoned in Calais, Warwick in the Tower and Arundel in Carisbrooke Castle. There are trials taking place of those and others who upset the King. My cousin means to have vengeance. There are plots and conspiracies. William, you and Henry need to be careful. Trust no one. I am pleased that you are here and away from the murky waters of English politics. Perhaps my son's misdemeanours in Northampton's inns are a price worth paying." Hal gave his father a sharp look and he smiled, "You think I would not find out?"

It was not only the King who had spies. I wondered if James had reported to the Earl?

"Do you wish your son returned to you, lord?"

He shook his head, "God's Blood, no! He is safer here than anywhere. My father watches the King and I seek his enemies. This is a storm through which we pass. I pray that we will all survive." He stood, "I go to watch the King's enemies for they are England's enemies. I would have you watch your backs. Treachery is all around us."

After he had gone my wife, my knight and my squires returned. Their faces were filled with questions. I sighed, I could not tell them all but I had to warn them. "The throne of England is threatened from within. We have enemies abroad but, at this moment there is a conspiracy to overthrow King Richard. Young Henry may be in danger. We keep a good watch for strangers and those we do not know." We told our men to be vigilant and then resumed our work on making Henry of Monmouth into a complete warrior. I had just a couple of months left to do so.

We paid frequent visits to Northampton. Although the Earl was not at home for much of the time, we knew his trusted lieutenants and knew that the news we would be given would be accurate. It was there that I learned the fate of the men who had been arrested by the King. Arundel had been executed while Warwick had confessed to all and was now incarcerated upon the Isle of Man. The news of the King's uncle was more sinister. He had been prisoner in the castle at Calais. His gaoler had been the Earl of Nottingham, Thomas Mowbray. I did not like Thomas Mowbray. He had been a leading opponent of the King and had been a co-conspirator with the Lords Appellant. He had managed to ingratiate himself into the good offices of the King. He was now Earl Marshal! The Duke of Gloucester was murdered while in his charge. The King had had his vengeance. He had told me he would and now I wondered where he would stop.

Returning to Weedon I reflected on the way the King had changed since the death of his wife. Not only had the three leading enemies of the King been either killed or imprisoned, all of those who had served them had also had their lands forfeited. The King had revoked some of the laws passed by Parliament. The war in Ireland had yielded him enough coin so that he did not need to go with a begging bowl in hand. The lands he had taken from his enemies, Gloucester, Arundel and Warwick had also made him rich. He had shaken off the fetters of Parliament and he could rule as he wished. There was no Anne to guide him and advise him. He now surrounded himself with those who agreed with all that he said.

Nearing our home, I said, "Well, Hal, you are almost at the end of your time with me. In a month I will return you to your father. You will re-enter a noble world."

He laughed, "Sir William your family and your men have more natural nobility than any of the fawning courtiers who surround the King."

"Be careful for that could be construed as treason."

Shaking his head, he said, "Nay, lord, for I impugn those who fawn and not the King. He is my uncle and I am loyal to King Richard."

"Good."

"I would ask a favour. When I am knighted and a lord, when I come into my properties then, should I need a captain of men, I would deem it an honour if you would serve me."

"That day is some way off but aye, God willing that I am still hale when that time comes, I will follow your banner and gladly for I see, in you, one who could lead men and that is a rarity."

As the time came for Henry to prepare to return to Northampton the mood of my men changed. They had enjoyed training the youth and his company. Roger and Alan came to me just a week before he left. Henry was with Ralph and Tom exercising their horses. "Lord, the men grow a little restless. They are warriors. Our work with Hal is done and they wonder what awaits them. They like not this inactivity."

I nodded, "I, too, yearn for action. I am a soldier and it is in my blood. When we visit with the Earl, I will ask him of any lord who needs us to fight for him."

"Not all feel this way, lord, "Harold Four Fingers and the other married men are content with their lives and the rest, David, Natty, Geoffrey of Gisburn wish to guard your home with John of Aldgate."

Alan of the Wood nodded, "I also, lord, have a bairn and a second on the way. My days of wandering are gone. Stephen the Tracker can always lead the men."

"Thank you for your honesty and it is good that my home will be guarded. We will speak more on this when we are in Northampton and I know the Earl's mind."

In the end we did not go to Northampton. Henry of Monmouth and the Lord of Weedon were summoned to Westminster to meet with the King and the Earl of Northampton. If this was a visit to the King then we had to go and be ready for court. I chose ten of my men at arms to accompany me and we chose our best horses. My wife ensured that all of us had, not only a set of clothes in which we would travel, but also two other good changes. She wanted her son and her family to look their best. She included Hal in this.

The day we parted she was tearful and young Henry looked emotional, "My lady, you have been as a mother to me. Nay, I will say more. You have given me such love and affection that I feel as Tom does. You are a good woman and I was lucky to have had you to watch over me. I will never forget it."

She kissed his cheek, "Nay, Master Hal, you have been a delight. My children are all better for having been in your company. I wish you well for I see your star rising."

We headed down the road to London in sombre mood. Speculation about the King and his reasons for our invitation were pointless. None knew the mind of the King these days. He was no longer the young man I had trained. I had done that which I had promised his father and if I did no more then I would have kept my word. I remembered his words all those years ago at Eltham. He had invited the Duke of Gloucester and those who wished him harm to his palace. He had intended to imprison them. The Richard who had been guided by Anne would not have carried out such an act but this new Richard, who wielded a tyrannical sword might.

As we rode Hal appeared quiet. "You have a problem, Hal? Until I return you to your father, I am still your mentor and you know that I am discreet." I wondered if this was about the village girls. Right until he had left, he had enjoyed their company. He had sworn that their honour was intact but he was young and I wondered if there was an attachment.

"The Duke of Gloucester was of royal blood. Do you think my uncle had anything to do with his death?"

In one way I was relieved at the subject he had raised but in another it disturbed me for the thought had crossed my mind. "The Earl of Nottingham is ambitious. He was part of the conspiracy to unseat the King. It would not surprise me to learn that he did it of his own volition."

"But you do not believe it?"

"Let us reserve judgement. We will know when we reach the court."

"How so, Sir William?"

"If Sir Thomas did this without the King's knowledge then when we reach Westminster he will be under arrest."

"And if not?"

"Then we can only think the worst." I looked at him for his shoulders were slumped. I had learned to read what his body shape meant. "What is it that you fear?"

"My father and I are of royal blood. Are we in danger too?"

"Your father is now an ally of the King. Your grandfather advises the King. I believe that you are safe but if you wish me to find bodyguards for you…"

He shook his head, "I will speak with my father first." He nodded ahead to where my men at arms rode, "And besides I think I know how to judge men now. I did not just learn sword play with you."

We had been invited and so we were admitted to the palace. I only recognised a couple of the King's guards. Most of the ones I had known at Eltham had died with Dick of Craven in Ireland. They directed the men to the barracks and one of them took us to the palace itself where a page took us to our chambers. I passed many of the new favourites of the king: the earls of Rutland, Kent and Huntingdon, John Beaufort, John Montacute and Thomas le Despenser. They were dressed in their finery and looked to be in good humour. They nodded to me but spoke cheerfully to Henry of Monmouth. I knew that they looked down on me. I was low born. Henry was the nephew of the King and his company worth courting.

Henry showed his strength of character, "My lords, until I have seen my father, I am still the ward of this great knight. I beg your indulgence. I will speak with you when I may." It was a polite answer but it displeased the young men.

The page took us up some stairs, "My lords the King has placed your chambers adjacent to those of your father, the Earl of Northampton and Derby."

We had two rooms. That was almost a luxury. As we were shown the chamber the Earl's door opened. He walked to my chamber and when the page had gone waved us into my room. He spoke quietly, "The King is up to something but I cannot quite work out what. There is a rumour that he is favouring Edward, the Duke of York's son."

I asked, "Favours, lord?"

"It seems that the King has given up on siring an heir. Perhaps he cannot produce an heir. It may be he does not like women." I knew that for a lie. He and the Queen had been as close as any couple I had seen. I ignored it. "Whatever the reason he is looking around for someone to become the next King of England."

I shook my head, "This sounds like court gossip, my lord."

He shook his head, "Nottingham is here and he is closeted with the King. The Duke of York seeks to advance his son and many nobles think that the Lord Lieutenant of Ireland, Roger Mortimer, has a better claim than some others." He was talking about himself. "I want to warn you to keep your wits about you. Do not drink too heavily." He turned to me, "My father is here although he is not well. He says that the King still holds you in high regard. If you can discover anything then I beg you let me know. I do not like being in the dark."

I shook my head, "I have never been a spy, my lord. I will speak with the King but my oath to his father means that I can do naught to harm him. Do not ask me to, my lord. I am your liegeman but he is my King."

"Nor would I expect you to betray him but surely you want a King of England you can trust?"

"Aye, but I am no kingmaker. I am a warrior and I serve God, King Richard and England."

He nodded, "You are a good man, Will Strongstaff: too good for…" he waved a hand. "What will be will be. I am no traitor! I will speak with you later, my son."

When his father had gone Henry said, "That was well spoken, my lord. I know that my father hopes that I will attain the throne. If it is meant to be it will happen. I am still young as is the King and my father. Both are but thirty years of age. My grandfather lived to be sixty-four. I could have lost all of my teeth and hair before I climb the throne!"

I smiled for Henry had a wit about him which my men appreciated. I was not sure that his father even knew what a joke was. He was a most serious man!

We were summoned to the Great Hall the next morning. I had been surprised that the King had not held a feast. Instead he had eaten alone and we had eaten in the Great Hall. We had been seated amongst friends. There were suspicious looks flashed between groups of nobles. I had been seated with the Duke of Lancaster, his son and grandson. Ralph Neville the Earl of Westmoreland, was also with us. The Earl of Northumberland had not been invited and I took that to be ominous. My seating marked me as a member of the Lancastrian faction. I had little choice in the matter for Henry Bolingbroke was my liege lord.

When we arrived in the Great Hall the King was seated on his throne. His child bride was on a throne next to him. For one so young she seemed very self-assured. Perhaps that had been her upbringing at the court of her father, the King of France. The King waited until all were assembled. There were no chairs, we all stood. A clerk approached with a servant who carried many parchments.

The King stood, "Know that we have brought you here today for you are all the most loyal of my nobles. You are here to meet my bride and so that I may reward those who have shown their loyalty."

A murmur and buzz of anticipation raced around the Great Hall.

"Tonight, we hold a feast but, for now, we will give titles to those who deserve reward for our enemies have now been dealt with."

I looked at young Henry. The words were ominous. Had he had a part in Gloucester's murder?

"Firstly, we reward our great friend and supporter, Thomas Mowbray, Earl of Nottingham and, from this day forth, the Duke of Norfolk!" If the King expected a great roar of cheers and support then he was proved wrong. There was a deathly silence. Mowbray had betrayed too many people in the past for him to have much support. Nonetheless he stepped forward and took the parchment. It confirmed what I had suspected. The King was complicit in the murder of his uncle.

The next to be rewarded were all the lords who had signed the affirmation of the treachery of Warwick, Gloucester and Arundel. The Earl of Huntingdon was made Duke of Exeter, the Earl of Kent became the Duke of Surrey. Thomas le Despenser became Earl of Gloucester. John Beaufort became Earl of Somerset. Others were also rewarded with lesser titles. I could sense the growing disquiet of Henry Bolingbroke and his father. The Earl of Westmoreland was also concerned. I wondered why I had been invited to this gathering. The only reason I could divine was that it was to be close at hand in case there was trouble. The King knew I would protect him if someone tried to kill him. I looked at Henry Bolingbroke. His face was impassive but I could hear his breathing, he was angry. My hand was on my sword in case he should suddenly lose control and attempt to harm the King.

"And there are others who deserve reward. My cousin Henry Bolingbroke, the Earl of Northampton and Derby, has shown himself to be loyal. To him I give the Dukedom of Hereford and all that goes with it."

That was, probably, one of the richest titles he could have given any for the land around Hereford was amongst the most productive in the land. Only Gloucester was richer and that just had an earl. Henry walked up to receive it and his son, Hal, said, quietly, "That was a surprise. He has made my father even richer. Why?"

I asked myself the same question.

The new Duke of Hereford returned with a bemused look on his face. He turned to his father and said, "Now men will wonder what I did to be rewarded so highly." He was thinking of Mowbray's murder of Gloucester.

"You were loyal to the King."

I could see that Henry Bolingbroke did not believe his father. I thought we had done when the King said, loudly, "And we have one more person to reward. Once, I had hoped to reward this most loyal of subjects with a knighthood and a manor. That pleasure, it seems, was denied me by my cousin. Now I can reward William Strongstaff, knight of Weedon and Stony Stratford. Walter FitzArthur was also a traitor and he has paid for his crimes. He lost his head and now I grant his manor, Dauentre, to Baron William known as Strongstaff. Come Will."

I went up to greet him. The others had had a hand clasp and been given the parchment. King Richard embraced me. He said, in my ear, "You have been the most loyal of my subjects. You have suffered when I have been melancholic and I have forgotten to thank you. This manor is to make up for that." He moved back and added, smiling, "This also makes you my liegeman. As Baron I have first call upon your services!
"

Even when he was being generous the King was plotting. He had rewarded Henry Bolingbroke and, in the same breath, taken me away from him. I still had the two manors of Weedon and Stony Stratford as well as Whittlebury. I would reap the rewards but my service now reverted to the King. He had played the game better than the new Duke.

As I returned to my place the King said, "And now we will keep apart until it is time for us to dine. I daresay all of you will have much to talk about."

After the King had left there was an outburst of conversation from all in the hall. It was left to Hal to congratulate me, "I am pleased for you, my lord. This is a great step for you. I know that you will still be loyal to my father and the King! You are an acrobat, my lord, for you walk a tight line between two cousins."

I was forgotten. My reward was insignificant. Now Mowbray, the new Duke of Norfolk and, Bolingbroke, the new Duke of Hereford were rivals. I watched the arrows fly from their eyes towards each other. Their thin-lipped nods of acknowledgement meant nothing. In their hearts they were now enemies. The King had been clever. Had he just rewarded one then he would have created a rival for the throne. This way he kept all of his Dukes at each other's throats.

I listened. The Earl of March, Mortimer, was being spoken of as a possible heir to King Richard. He was in Ireland and therefore could not defend himself. It was worse than the gossips around the village well. I found myself sickening of it.

That evening, as we ate in the Great Hall, I asked the new Duke of Hereford if there were any opportunities for my men at arms to go to war. He laughed, "You have more than enough money Will. Why go to war?"

Hal answered for me, "Father do you not know this man who trained you? He is a warrior. His men are warriors. He needs to use his skills."

The Duke of Hereford shrugged, "Apart from Gascony, and that is now at peace, I know of nowhere which requires armed men."

Ralph Neville said, "Not true, my lord. Before I left my home the Sherriff of Westmoreland, John, Earl of Clifford told me that the Earl of Fife has broken the peace. My cousin, young Hotspur, is busy dealing with the Douglas Clan. I was going to raise men myself to go to the aid of those who live north of Carlisle." He smiled, "I would be honoured to have you and your men in our service. The Scots always bring much coin when they are ransomed."

"Then I will take you up on your offer. Where do you muster?"

"Carlisle."

"I shall leave on the morrow."

The Duke of Lancaster, whose lands were adjacent to Westmoreland said, "Make sure that you speak with the King before you go. It would be diplomatic to say the least. When he spoke of you, he did seem to make a point about you serving him."

"Thank you, my lord, that seems like sage advice."

That ceremony was the last time I spoke with John of Gaunt. He had been part of my life since I had been a boy in Spain. He could have made an attempt to take the throne from Richard but he never did. Like me he had sworn an oath to the Black Prince and he had kept it.

The next morning, while my men prepared our horses, I went with Tom to speak with the King. He was in his private quarters. I was admitted quickly. That surprised me. "Ah Will, come to thank me again?"

I smiled, "Of course, Highness. I did not expect to be rewarded. I was just doing my duty."

"As you have always done. You have thanked me and when I need you again, I will send for you. Do not be tardy!"

"Of course not, but I am here to ask if I have your permission to join the Earl of Westmoreland. The Earl of Fife has broken the peace and has raided the borders. The Earl has asked for me and my men."

His face was a mask. I had no idea what his response would be. When he gave me a broad grin, I was relieved, "Of course! The Scots need a lesson from time to time. Hotspur failed at Otterburn. You can show him what the King's man can do! Go with my blessing but do not stay overlong."

I gave my farewells and left with a lighter heart than I had had in a long time. For the first time in many a year I would not have to worry about politics. All I had to do was fight and I knew how to do that!

Chapter 17

My wife was delighted with my new title and manor but mystified as to the reason I was going to war, "We have coin! We have four manors! Why fight?"

Her words sounded remarkably like the Duke of Hereford's, "Because, my love, my warriors grow rusty. Apart from fighting bandits they have not used their skills since Ireland." I lowered my voice. I fear there is unrest in England. There are lords who seek to unseat the King from his throne. There may come a time when we need the skills of my men simply to survive."

"Very well." She understood that logic.

Sir John said, "I will prepare our horses, lord."

"No John, I need you to go to Dauentre. There is no lord there yet. You have a good mind. I will give you authority to act in my stead until I return. My love, you could go with him. It may be that you wish to live there rather than here at Weedon. The town has a market!"

That convinced her and I was able to concentrate on preparing my men and horses. Jack and Blaze had been retired and I had bought Caesar and Hart from Red Ralph. Caesar was a cross between a destrier and courser. He was magnificent. I had a full mail caparison made for him for he could carry it. Hart was a good palfrey and she had some courser blood in her too. Red Ralph had learned how to breed. We left my married men at Weedon. Ralph was the one who was most annoyed to have missed out on the opportunity to go to war. He would be with Sir John.

We rode north for I intended to stay at Middleham. I needed no horses but old friends like Red Ralph helped me to stay sane. The lords I served, young Hal apart, were unpredictable and their motives were always suspect. Red Ralph, Peter the Priest and Old Tom were different. They said what they thought and had no ulterior motives.

Red Ralph lived closer to the border than anyone else I knew and I spoke to him of the Scots. He shook his head. "They are wild men, Will. If you have fought the Irish then you know their soldiers for they are of the same blood. They have knights as we do. I heard that the Douglas who died at Otterburn was a particularly good knight." He grinned, "We might have found him hard to kill. They don't use archers and they like fighting with a small round shield called a buckler. They use it to punch you and the sneaky Scot will try to gut you with the dagger he hides behind it. Some of the Scots are quite well off. They have land in England. From what I heard from my neighbours most Scots dream of owning a piece of England. They want a piece of England but not the rule of an English king."

"Thank you for that."

"From what you say, Will, you don't need to fight. You have four fine manors. Wait until you have to fight!"

"You sound like my wife." I laughed. "Tell me Red Ralph, if you had to go to war today and to fight what would be the outcome?"

"Who do I fight?"

"You say the Scots are just wild, then make it them."

He hesitated, "It has been many years since I drew sword. If I am honest, I would probably last a few strokes."

"And that is why I must fight. The Irish campaign was years ago. Our skills grow rusty when we cease to war. I am not yet ready to hang up my sword. Young Henry has asked for me to go to war with him when he is old enough to lead. I would like that for he is a good lad. Besides my men wish it as does Tom."

"I am guessing my son is unhappy to be left at home."

"He is but when he does go to war, he will be able to handle himself." I lowered my voice, "And I fear that war is coming. The King is not yet dead and yet already carrion gather ready to pick the corpse to pieces."

"And you are now part of that world."

"I am."

When I left the next day, I felt sad. I was the last of the Blue Company who still plied his trade.

Carlisle Castle was a real castle. By that I mean it was a border fortress. It had been attacked many times. The Scots had taken it in times past but not since the time of King William of Scotland. The Nevilles and the Cliffords knew its worth and kept it well maintained. They patrolled the border. The Earl was already in the castle and he greeted me like a long-lost friend.

As he took me to the keep, I asked, "I spoke with others as I came north. The Earl of Fife has lands in the east. Why is he here in the west?"

He laughed, "Blame Henry Percy. He was so annoyed when the Scots claimed that they won the battle of Otterburn that he has been harassing them and taking back their cattle for the last seven years. The

Earl of Fife seeks to make us pay for what the Earls of Northumberland take!"

When we entered the hall, I saw many border knights already gathered. I was introduced to them all. They were a curious mix of older knights, my age and younger knights who were yet to be blooded.

"We leave in two days' time. The Earl of Fife is with his forces north of the Roman wall. Dumfries is their nearest castle. The fact that we have not yet reacted to their incursions has made them bold. We believe that he intends to strike south towards Hexham. If he does so he risks the wrath of the Percys. We will head east and hope to catch him close to the wall." He saw my face fall. "Do not worry, Sir William, we have good scouts."

"And how many men will we take?"

"When the muster is here there will be thirty knights, fifty men at arms and forty archers. Yours will be the only mounted archers we have."

I now saw why he had been so keen to offer me the opportunity to join him. Pinning the Scots down would be like trying to grasp quicksilver in your hands. My mounted archers could help the knights and men at arms to do just that.

Tom had now seen fourteen summers. He had a good leather jerkin studded with metal and he had a padded gambeson beneath. His bascinet was well made. The mail coif was as sturdily constructed as I had ever seen. Martin had put a great deal of effort into it. My son now had a longer sword and his shield was full sized. I hoped that it would be unlikely that he would have to fight but, if it was necessary, then he was ready. My men at arms would keep an eye out for him. I had not bothered with my own banner. I would ride beneath the Nevilles'. I was not here for glory.

We left and we were not to the fore. Tom and I rode just behind the Earl of Westmoreland and my men at arms and archers just behind us. The men of Westmoreland were the advance guard. We were not all mounted. The hardy hill men of the north ran behind the horses. These were men who lived and farmed on the fells. They were as tough a group of warriors as I had ever seen. They gave me hope that we could deal with the Scots. We took the road which had been built by the Romans and ran south of the wall. The Roman wall was still an imposing sight. We rode to the south of it and I could see that most of the stone still remained in place. It was not as high as I might have expected but Ralph had told me that it was wide enough for two horses to ride along it. More importantly there were only a limited number of places where mounted men, or men with stolen cattle, could cross. Two of the Earl's men were mounted on ponies and they rode along it. They would act as lookouts. They could see further ahead than we and would warn us of an enemy.

The Earl saw me looking towards them. "There is one part of the wall they cannot ride. The Romans cut a path for their foot soldiers in the cliff. At that point our men will ride towards us and then rejoin the wall further east. Other than that, they will have a good view."

"Do we face an army or a warband, my lord?"

"Warband. We will be evenly matched in numbers. They raid for plunder and they raid for vengeance. The Percy family have raided and pillaged their lands and they seek redress. It may be that the sight of us makes them flee. If that happens, I want your archers to try to cut them off and slow them down."

"I would not wish my men isolated."

He looked at me in surprise, "They serve you do they not?" I nodded. "Then they will be doing their duty."

"Nonetheless I will lead them. I will leave my men at arms with you for your plan is a good one but I am honour bound to stand with my men if I send them into enemy land and put them in harm's way."

"As you wish." He stroked his beard. "I can see now that you are low born. A noble would not worry."

I think my request had disappointed the Earl. Certainly, after that, he spoke less to me. The cynical side of me wondered if he saw me as a close friend of a future King and wished my friendship. My words had shown him that I was no politician. I was a soldier.

The two scouts disappeared from the skyline. There were trees and I guessed they had reached the cliff the Earl had spoken of. It seemed a long time before we saw them again and when we did, I saw them signalling, "My lord, your men."

He shaded his eyes and said, "They have found the Scots. They must be close to the Roman fort. The locals call it Housesteads." He reined in. "I need your archers to cross through the wall. My scouts will show them the best place to slow down the enemy. Are you certain that you still wish to ride with them? I cannot promise that we will reach you in time."

"They are my men, my lord. My son and I will share their risks." I turned in the saddle, "Stephen the Tracker, bring our archers. Roger of Chester have the sergeants follow the Earl."

I heard Roger's voice, "Aye, lord, you be careful now. If I don't bring the two of you back here ladyship will have my bollocks fried up for breakfast!"

The Earl shook his head, "You allow your men such informality?"

I laughed, as I spurred Hart, "My lord that is how we all talk to each other. At the end of the day our titles are just that, a title. It is what is within that makes or mars us."

We left the road and headed across the scrubland which lay between us. I fixed my eye on the two scouts. They had halted when they saw us leave the column. I had fifteen archers with me. The ground was open. There were no trails but we were not galloping. Stephen edged his horse next to mine. "And what is the plan, my lord?"

"We cross through the wall. Apparently, there are breaches along it. They were the gates in times gone by. When the Scots see the Earl and his men they will flee. Our task is to pin them down so that the Earl and the rest of our men can attack them."

"Do we know numbers, my lord?"

"The scouts will tell us."

Once we neared it I saw that there was a trail of sort which led up to the wall. We rode along it in single file. It climbed between scrubby trees and bushes. We emerged close to the wall itself. A path ran next to it. We headed east. The two scouts had dismounted and were drinking from their skins. They bowed, "The warband has just passed through the old fort, lord. They are heading for the road. My guess is that they are heading for Hexham and the abbey there."

"His lordship said you would know of a place to halt them."

"Aye, lord, The fort. This is the biggest gap along the wall for a few miles. There are little ones but they would only allow a man at a time to pass through. His lordship probably thought to hold them north of the wall but they have obliged us by heading to the road. We counted at least ten knights and squires. Their horses can only cross by this gate or the next one which is four miles along the wall."

"How many men in total?"

"More than two hundred, lord. The Scots are wild warriors and move without any order. Numbers are hard to estimate. There are no more than forty men on horses, lord."

"Then lead on."

We rode through woods. The path rose and fell. Then it began to climb and I saw a tower ahead on the left. The scout said, "That is the start of the fort, lord."

"Then let us dismount and walk our horses."

My decision proved to be a good one. The woods stopped and I saw the half-ruined walls of the fort. The scouts were right. This would be the best place to stop them. I saw the Scots. They had reached the road and were heading east. There was little order about them. They moved as a mob. Only the horsemen displayed any order. I also saw the Earl and his men. They were walking along the road not galloping. Once they began to gallop then the Scots would be alerted.

The hill fort was typically Roman and rectangular. I saw a gate and a gap in the south wall. The wall proper had just one gap in it. There were no longer any gates, they had long disappeared, but four men could ride through it. We entered through the west gate. I saw that rain had made a natural trough in the rocks. "Hobble the horses close to the water. You scout, what is your name?"

"Oswald, my lord."

"Well, Oswald, we will try to hold them here and use the natural defences of this fort. I want you and your companion to try to block the north gate. Use anything you can. Roll stones, cut some of the gorse. Do whatever you think will slow them. If they pass us, I want them delayed."

"Aye, lord."

I draped my cloak over Hart's back and took my helmet and shield. I walked to the south gate and peered through. The Earl and his men were now galloping and the Scots had seen him. The Scots must have decided that they were in danger of being caught and they turned to run back to the gate and escape north. The English archers on foot were heading directly across the scrubland towards the fort. The Scots were closer to the fort than the Earl. I shouted to my men, "There is a fighting platform. Fill it between the south gate and the fallen piece of wall."

"Aye lord, and what of you and Master Tom?"

"Why, we will stand in the gate and see if we can slow them down!"

"My lord you are as mad as a pail full of frogs. Come lads. Silent David, you take the west edge and I will be close to Sir William. Much and Garth, you go on the other side of the gate. Keep your swords handy."

I pulled up my coif and donned my helmet. I turned to Tom. He held a spear. "Your place is just behind me to my left. You will stop any from attacking that side of me. Strike hard. The first men will be mounted and mailed. Hit at the men's legs or the horse's heads."

"Aye father." I saw his face. He was afraid but determined, "I will not let you down."

"Good, for that means you will run when I fall. If you have to tell your mother that I died up here in the north then she will be a more formidable foe than any wild Scot."

He laughed, "Aye, you are right there."

I saw that the Scots had reached the track which wound its way up to the south gate. The Romans had chosen the site of their fort well. The ditch ran all the way around and the only way to cross it was by the gate. The only warriors they would see would be my son and I. The Earl of Fife and his men were cutting across the scrubland to get to us. The hill men archers were actually keeping pace with the horsemen. The Earl of Westmoreland had spread the knights and men at arms in a long line. They were like hunters beating game. The Scots, too, were spread out. They could not know about the ambush which awaited them. The horsemen were on the road but the mass of men, those on foot, were just heading any way they could to cross the wall. The broken section of wall would be where they would try to cross for the horses would struggle with the ditch and they would have to brave the gate and the foolish knight and squire who stood to bar their passage.

I drew my sword and kissed it. A shaft of light glinted off my sword and I was seen. I saw the leader. I took it to be the Earl of Fife for he had a standard bearer behind him and, even at six hundred paces distance, I could see that he had plated armour. None of his knights, and I counted eight of them, had spears. The leader pointed his sword at me and four knights began to gallop their horses up the slope. It was a steep one and they laboured. They overtook the Earl. They were going to clear us from the gap.

I shouted, "Stephen, wait until they are forty paces from us. I do not want them to know our numbers yet. They have no mail on their horses. One arrow for the horse and one for the knight. Can you do it?"

"Aye, lord. Consider it done."

I saw that the knights were poorer knights than the Earl. They had no plate. My archers had knight killers and war arrows. They would use bodkins for the knights and swallowtail arrows for the horses. The four knights had open faced helmets. Behind them I saw the other knights, led by the Earl of Fife. They were forty paces from the four who anticipated sweeping us from the gate. I saw that the Earl of Westmoreland had already caught some of the Scots on foot at the rear. I guessed that they were the ones who still had booty or were slower. They were hacked down.

There was no command from Stephen but I heard the whoosh of my men's arrows. The Scottish knights must have thought that we were either very brave or very foolish. They had raised their swords to strike us when all four were plucked from their saddles and the four horses were hit. One horse fell for the arrow had penetrated its skull. The others reared or pulled to the side. The riders fell.

I shouted, "Now Stephen, take out the others!"

Fifteen arrows, heavy war bodkins all, were sent towards the knights and mounted men at arms who were less than eighty paces from us. They could not miss. However, there were just fifteen of them and although the Earl of Fife's standard bearer and squire fell, the Earl's plate saved him and he closed with me. My archers did the right thing. They concentrated on the mounted men who were racing towards the wall. They left the Earl for me. I heard a wail from the Scots further down the slope as the Earl of Westmoreland's foot archers began to send arrows at them and the Earl led my men at arms to begin to harvest the Scots.

The Earl of Fife charged at me. He rode a courser. He came for my right side. That pleased me for it meant Tom would still be safe. The Earl did so in order to allow him to strike me with his sword. There was barely a gap and his horse would have to brush the wall. Perhaps he thought I would flinch but I was confident that the effort of making the rise would have slowed the horse almost to a walk. He tried to urge the horse through the gateway. The arch still remained and he had to lower his head. Even better was the fact that he had to swing his sword sideways. As his horse snapped at me, I lifted my shield above my head. The Earl's sword almost skittered across the angled shield. I had little to strike at and so I rammed my sword between his leg and his horse. My sword had a good edge and it sliced through the leather strap holding his stirrup. That might not have been a disaster but my sword also sliced along the horse's belly. The horse lurched forward and, as it broke through the gate and headed left, he was thrown from his horse.

I shouted to Tom, "Watch the gate!"

I knew that I was taking a risk leaving Tom alone but the Earl of Fife was still unhurt. My archers had thinned out the knights and men at arms. They were still coming up the track but more slowly as they were using their shields for protection. Two more horses had been struck and unhorsed their riders. I ran to the Earl of Fife and put my sword to his throat. "Yield!" He hesitated, "Yield or I will slay you where you lie!"

"I yield! I yield!"

I turned and ran. An unhorsed knight ran at Tom. My son showed courage. He stood his ground. He blocked the sword blow with his shield and then thrust at the knight's leg. The knight wore poleyns and was weakly struck. The blow did no harm. The knight raised his sword again. I did not hesitate. I did not care for ransom. This was my son whose life was in danger. Even as he raised his sword to end Tom's life I hacked down on his right arm with my sword. He wore mail but my sword hacked through it and broke his arm. The edge came away bloody. As he dropped to the ground, I raised my sword to end his life, "I yield!" The knight valued his life.

A man at arms and the knight's squire ran at us both. The man at arms had fishtailed metal plates and a kettle helmet. He was a grizzled veteran. I left the squire to Tom. Leaving the protection of the gate I ran at the veteran. The man at arms had a war hammer. He swung the beak like end at my head. Had I used my shield then he would have torn a hole in it and, worse, ripped it from my grasp. I hacked up and across with my sword. Not only did I deflect the hammer I hacked a chunk from the haft. I was above him and so I pushed at his face ramming my shield upwards as I did so. The edge caught his kettle helmet and the leather strap broke. The helmet flew from his head. As he looked up in surprise an arrow flew from the walls. It hit him square in the forehead and the tip emerged from the back of his head. I looked back and saw Much Longbow grinning. I nodded to him.

I turned to return to the gate and saw Tom duck beneath the swashing sword of the squire and then back hand his sword across the padded jacket of the squire. It ripped through the material and across his stomach. The squire looked in horror as his guts spilled forth. I joined my shocked son, "It is not yet over. Be strong."

We turned to face the Scots who still ran at us. The knights and mounted men at arms who had survived had taken off towards the east. Oswald had told me there were more gates there. That left the men on foot. As they struggled up the hill, they were attacked from two sides, my archers to the fore and the Earl of Westmoreland's archers, knights and men at arms from the other. They split up. Some ran east and some ran west.

The Earl shouted an order and my men at arms rode west while he led the others to the east. There were no enemies left for us to fight. The Scottish squire was still alive. He looked up at Tom, "How did you manage to kill me? You are a boy!"

Tom was too shocked to speak. The sight of someone, just a couple of years older dying before him had robbed him of words. I knelt next to him, "Make your peace with God, son. I am no priest but I can hear your confession if you wish."

"I am sorry I…" He died.

I was not certain if merely saying the word sorry would grant him admission to heaven but I had done my best.

I went to the knight whose arm was bleeding. "Was he your squire?"

He nodded, "My brother. He was twenty. When we returned home, he was to be knighted."

I shook my head as I tore part of the knight's surcoat to fashion a bandage for his wrist, "He was not ready. He was beaten by a squire of fourteen summers." I fashioned a tight bandage to stop the bleeding. "Tom, go to the horses and fetch honey and vinegar. I might save the arm yet."

By the time I had dressed and bandaged the wound our men were returning. I saw that the Earl of Westmoreland had gathered horses and brought with him two knights. He dismounted at the gate, "Bravely done, Strongstaff. You and your son are doughty warriors. I am sorry if I offended you with my comments about your birth."

I smiled, "No offence taken, my lord. I have two knights for ransom. As one is the Earl, I am guessing it will be a good one."

"Aye it will be."

"Then I beg leave to return home. I trust that you will send me what I am owed."

"Of course. Will you not stay to see them humiliated when they fetch the fortune?"

"That does not interest me. I have two horses. As soon as we can I would head for home. You have more than enough men to guard the prisoners have you not?"

"Of course. You are a strange man, Strongstaff. I have not met your like before." He headed to his men to give them orders.

My archers had descended the walls while I had tended the wounded knight. They had taken all that they could from the bodies of the men and knights they had slain. They took a further two Scottish horses which they used as sumpters. Finally, they retrieved every arrow that they could. They would salvage some flights and tips as well as some arrows which could be reused. Tom had searched the dead squire. He brought me his sword, dagger, purse, a crucifix and a ring. I shook my head. "They are yours but I would return the ring and crucifix to his brother."

"Aye father.

"And then fetch the purse, sword, rings, dagger and plate from the Earl of Fife."

The Earl had heard me, "But I yielded!"

"That gives you your life. Think yourself lucky I do not take the hauberk too."

My men and I were ready to leave before the men of Westmoreland. I bade Sir Ralph Neville farewell. "I think we will see each other again, my lord."

"Aye, I can see that. The ransoms will be sent to Weedon. Fare ye well."

Chapter 18

We spent the night at the abbey. The Abbot was more than happy to accommodate us. They had seen the approach of the Scots and had feared for their lives. As my men shared their booty, they expressed satisfaction. We had managed to do that which we had wanted. We had practised the art of war. We had lost neither man nor horse and come away with booty. That was the main reason I had left the Earl so quickly. We had done all that was required to keep my men and myself happy.

When we reached Middleham I left the Earl's horse with Red Ralph. I had wounded it and it needed healing. Ralph was happy to do so. Roger and Stephen dined with us and Red Ralph enjoyed every arrow and stroke of sword as they told of the battle. "Serves the Scots right. They will think twice before coming south again. You have done us all a favour, Will."

"I hope so. I will send Ralph back to you in six months to collect the war horse."

"Thank you, Will." He looked at his wife and patted the back of her hand. "Just think my love, my son may become a knight one day!"

I nodded and added more good news, "And that means a manor. You could have a farm on his land!"

Red Ralph shook his head, "When my son becomes a noble, he will not need people looking at the mercenary who was his father."

"Ralph that was me too."

"Will, you were made differently to the rest of us. The Black Prince saw that. He saw, in you, some nobility. Answer me true, if it was not for you would my son be a squire?" My silence was eloquent, "There you have it but when my son does have a manor then I shall die a happy man. The blood of Red Ralph will be noble. My grandchildren will want for nothing and that pleases me." We stayed for a few days in Middleham before we headed south.

After we reached Weedon we divided the goods we had taken equitably. The horses were part of the booty as was the mail and plate. Tom now had a good sword and I took the Earl of Fife's as a spare. It was a good one but mine was its equal and felt better balanced in my hand. My wife, for once, said little for she was just relieved that her son and husband had survived.

The first evening Tom was besieged by Harry, and Alice. They wanted to know how he had gained such a good sword. I sat before my fire and spoke with Eleanor while my son patiently answered their questions. "Is the hall at Dauentre better than this?"

She nodded and smiled, "It is, my husband, but I think I would prefer to stay here. I told John to be lord in the hall until you returned."

"I will ride there with some of my men at arms and archers. It is not right for poor John and Ralph to be alone. What of the burghers?"

"Oh, they think they are better than they are. They have a market and seem to think it gives them the right to look down on other folk." I now knew the real reason why she chose to stay in Weedon. She, like me, hated snobbery worse than almost anything. "All the market does is make them rich. You might want to bring the accounts of the manor here, husband. I am not sure that the reeve is an honest man." The manor might have a better hall but my wife was a practical woman, here we had friends. There we would have tenants.

I laughed, "Apart from John's father, when did you ever hear of an honest reeve? I will ride there tomorrow and take Father Thomas with me. Let him cast his eye over the accounts. He knows better than any a dishonest one. He worked with Father Raymond."

I left her and headed for the hall my warriors used. Not all of them lived there now. The seven who were married had their own homes. I spoke to the rest, "Tomorrow I visit my new manor at Dauentre. Sir John will live there and he will need men at arms to serve him. Sir John is still my knight and any who choose to live in Dauentre will still be my men. For one man at arms and one archer it will mean an extra six pennies a month as they will command the men for Sir John. Do not decide now. Talk amongst yourselves. The ones who would come be ready to leave at first light. Have your war gear ready."

Finally, I spoke with Father Thomas, "I am not sure I am qualified to look at accounts, lord."

"You can read and you know your numbers. You saw what Father Raymond did and can recognise fraud. More importantly, Father, you are a priest. If I looked at the books, I might be accused of being false. Your honesty cannot be questioned."

He nodded, "They do not know you, Sir William, if they think you would be false. A truer knight I have yet to meet."

Six archers and four men at arms came with me to Dauentre. I was pleased for that was a good number for Sir John to command and yet I had more left to me. While the men settled in, I went to speak with Sir John. "How is it going?"

He looked unhappy, "The townsfolk think I am young ..."

He hesitated and I said, "Come John, we have endured war, cold and near death. Whatever you have to tell me cannot be worse than that."

He nodded, "They look down on me because my father was a tenant farmer and," he took a deep breath, "they call you a mercenary."

"How do you know?" The fact that I had been one was irrelevant. They were insulting me and I could not allow that to go without action on my part.

"Peter was in the alehouse and they did not know who he was. They spoke freely."

"Then they are in for a shock. You now have men at arms and archers. Our authority will be established. I care not if they look down on me but they will obey and respect us. First, I will look at the accounts and then speak to the reeve. There is a town council and I will summon them. Is the hall in a fit condition?"

"Aye lord, when she came your wife and her women cleaned it. The burghers thought that marked her as being less than a lady."

I was beginning to become angry. Had King Richard given me a poisoned chalice? There was little point in having an argument with myself. "Sir John, take four of the biggest men at arms and fetch the Reeve and the accounts here. Make sure he is never alone. My wife did not trust him and she is a good judge of character."

"Aye lord."

When he had gone, I said, "Tom, we will stay here a few days. Go find a bed chamber for us and then familiarise yourself with the house. When the Reeve has come then fetch the archers and the other men at arms." Although I was angry, in many ways I relished the challenge. I would bend them to my will.

The Reeve was a man called Hubert of Dauentre. When he arrived, I did not like him. He had a permanent sneer upon his face. I saw Oliver the Bastard watching him. My man at arms looked like he just wanted to punch the man. He must have annoyed Oliver on the way over to the hall. I caught his eye and shook my head, this would be done legally. "Reeve, put the documents on the table. Father Thomas, be so good as to peruse them while I speak with the Reeve of my manor."

I used a formal tone and he gave a slight bow, "May I be the first to welcome you to Dauentre, my lord."

"Thank you, Reeve. How long have you been Reeve here?"

"Since always. My father was the reeve before me and his father before him."

"Then you are a good reeve; you have experience?"

"None has more and I can tell you now, my lord, that other manors have sought my service but I have remained loyal to Dauentre." His smug face told me that I should be respectful to him.

"Ah yes, Sir Walter FitzArthur was the lord."

The man was now in confident mood, "He was a noble man and came from a good family. I served him well."

I cocked my head to one side. Father Thomas looked up and he nodded. He had found the evidence. The tone of my voice changed. I put harshness into it and threat. "Sir Walter FitzArthur was a traitor and lost his head. It is why I am now lord here. Are you associating yourself with him?"

The Reeve was a cunning man who could think quickly and his attitude changed immediately, "And right glad we are to have you here, my lord."

"I put it to you that you stayed here not because you had better offers but because you were robbing the manor!"

"That is a lie! Who says so?"

Father Thomas said, quietly, "I do. I have looked over your accounts and see that a twentieth of each amount is missing."

He laid the document on the table. He had ringed the offending amounts. They were the amounts in pounds, shilling and pence of the fees collected. They were less than those from the smaller manor of Weedon!

Fee-Farm of town of Dauentre - £12 2 4,
Escheated lands of said town - £4 7 0,
Rents of the Manor of Dodford and Muscott - £13 2 6,
Farm of Norton - £13 19 0,
Profits of Mara and Welton - £18 0 9,
Profits of Staverton Manor and Park - £13 19 0,
Mills of Dauentre and River Nene- £11 0 0,
Annual profits of Fordham Manor - £10 0 0,
Profits of Wolfhampcote Hundred - £6 1 8,
Farm of Wolfhampcote Borough - £10 1 3,
Profits of the forest of Wolfhampcote £30 12 11 3/4,
Profits of escheater of Dauentre - £14 19 0,

"Had you been less greedy or cleverer you might have hidden the theft." Father Thomas looked at me and gave me a wan smile, "Believe me I know how to look at the accounts of a manor and I know how lords are robbed."

The man was bereft of words. I said, quietly, "Oliver, bind his hands. I will deal with him later. Secure him somewhere safe."

"My lord, I protest. I will complain to the High Sherriff of Northampton."

"You mean the Earl of Northampton recently promoted to Duke of Hereford? That Sherriff? The father of Henry of Monmouth whom I spent a year training? Good for that will increase whatever punishment I deem to be fair. The Duke hates theft."

He was taken from my hall. My men were rough with him.

"Sir John go and fetch the Town Council. I want them all here within the hour!"

"Aye lord."

"Father Thomas, take these four men at arms and search the Reeve's home. I have no doubt that he will have secreted his ill-gotten gains in his home. Fetch any papers that you may find there." When they had gone, I was alone until Oliver returned. I looked up from the false accounts. "Bring the rest of the men in here and clear the room. Put the table and chairs to one side. Leave just the master's chair for me. I want you to have my men stand behind me. Much Longbow came in. "Much, help Oliver and make sure your men have their swords ready."

"Trouble, lord?"

"There may be. Let us say I wished to be prepared in case there is."

When the council came in, I was seated on my chair with a goblet of wine in my hand. There were eight of them. All looked prosperous men. From what I had seen this was a very rich town and they had benefitted from it. I wondered if the theft went deeper than the Reeve. There would be little to be gained from investigating. I allowed a few moments of uncomfortable silence to hang in the air. I emptied my goblet and placed it on the table.

One portly man spoke, "The Reeve is not here, yet lord. We could not find him. He is a member of the council."

I nodded, "I know exactly where the Reeve is."

I stood and rested my right hand on my sword hilt.

"Good men of Dauentre, I have been appointed by King Richard of England to be lord of this manor. You do not know me. There is no reason why you should. I feel, however, that there are some things about me which you should now. The Black Prince himself appointed me the bodyguard of our King and I served as the Captain of the King's guard. I have thwarted attempts by assassins to kill our lawful King. I have fought and defeated his enemies." I let that sink in. They were uncertain of the direction I was taking. "I say all of this because your lord, Sir Walter FitzArthur, was a traitor. I have yet to discover how deep the treachery goes. If any of you conspired with the traitor then, believe me, I will discover the truth."

Some of them were actually shaking.

"Does anyone wish to confess?"

One of the older men dropped to his knees, "No, lord, we are all loyal men and true. I swear it."

I remembered Weedon. They had forgotten of their obligations to their King and country. "What is your name?"

"I am Harold Goldsmith. I make gold and silver objects, lord."

That explained his fine clothes. "When was the last time you practised with the bow?"

"What lord?"

"Am I speaking a foreign language? I ask you all, when was the last time you practised with a bow?"

The goldsmith rose to his feet, "Lord we are men of commerce. We do not practise."

"Then you are not loyal Englishmen. King Edward's edict of June thirteen sixty-three states that all of you should practise at the butts after church each feast and Sunday. Do you have a sword? A bow? Arrows?"

They shook their heads. I would not need my men at arms and archers. These were sheep, greedy sheep but sheep none the less. "This is a rich town but that does not excuse any of you. This Sunday Much Longbow here will be at the green and he will make a list of all the men who turn up with a bow and sword ready to practise. All those whose names are not on the list will be fined ten shillings for each Sunday that they are absent. If any man misses four Sundays then they will be brought before me at the assizes. Then I will not be so lenient. I also want a town watch. One of my men will be the captain of the guard but the men who watch will be from this town. Have I made myself clear?"

They nodded.

"You are the council and you will set an example. You will tell all of the men in this manor of my edict." I stared at each one, "And one thing more, this is my manor and I will not be cheated of any monies. The Reeve has discovered that and he is now my prisoner. I will appoint a new one. The new one will be a man I can trust. He will not be from Dauentre. I am unsure if I can trust men whose lord was a traitor and who disobey the law of Edward the Third." They all looked even more shocked, "I do not expect to be liked but, by God, I will be respected and any man failing to show respect to me, my family or my men will have to suffer my wrath!"

They left a great deal less confident than when they came in. Much shook his head, "I hope I never get the wrong side of you, Sir William."

"So do I, Much, so do I!"

My men found chests of coins and papers in the Reeve's hall. When I confronted him, he confessed. He had been able to hear what I had said to the Council. He pleaded for clemency. "That is not up to me. It is the Earl of Hereford who will hear this case. Until then you will be held here. If, of course, you can provide any information about others who were guilty of crimes against the Earl then that may well ease your sentence." He began to chatter, "Tell Father Thomas so that he may write it down and you can sign it."

By the time evening came I was exhausted. Sir John shook his head, "I could not have done what you did, lord. I am not ready for this."

"You are. Be strong with them. I will take the Reeve to Northampton and find another Reeve. I would have suggested your father but he is happy at Stony Stratford."

"There is one who is obvious, lord."

"Who is that?"

"Harold Four Fingers. He is happy to stay at home and you can trust him. He has a family now. His wife has made a fine farm at Weedon. With the land attached to the Reeve's home then she could do more. To be honest, lord, Harold is a strong character. He would manage the council far better than I. Father Thomas could help him with the numbers and accounts."

Sir John was right.

We left the next day, Tom, Father Thomas and the Reeve. I took most of the coin we had retrieved from the Reeve with me. I left some to pay the wages of the men I had left with Sir John. We stayed the night at Weedon. I spoke to my wife first and then Harold Four Fingers. As I had hoped he was delighted. He dropped to his knees to thank me. I shook my head, "Your thanks will be in doing a good job. There is no rush to get to Dauentre. Settle your affairs here. I intend to take the Reeve and his confession to Northampton."

I took Roger of Chester and four men at arms with me to Northampton. I was well known now and admitted to the keep. The Duke was not at home and so I handed my prisoner, the charges and the evidence to the castellan. Sir Richard, the castellan, seemed distracted. I thought that I was the cause.

As we headed back to my men and horses I asked, "Is this matter too trivial for the Northampton assize? I confess that I am new to the role."

He shook his head, "No my lord. If I might have a word."

I said, "Roger, go and fetch the horses. I would speak alone with Sir Richard."

"There has been trouble at court, Sir William. I can speak openly to you for you are a friend of my master. He and the Earl of Nottingham, now the Duke of Norfolk, had a disagreement. The Duke Henry said that Nottingham tried to suborn him to rebel against the King. He went to King Richard. When the Duke of Norfolk was summoned to the King, he explained away his words as misinterpretation. Duke Henry disagreed. The matter was sent to Parliament to be decided."

This was serious. "And when does Parliament make its decision?"

"It is today. That is the cause of my distraction. The Duke and his son are in London."

This was not my affair but I could not sit idly by. My fortune was tied with Henry Bolingbroke and his son. "I beg you send a message to my wife and tell her that I have had to go to London."

He looked relieved, "You go to the Duke's side?"

"I do."

My men were not surprised at my decision to go to London. As we rode, I asked, "But why were you not surprised?"

Roger laughed, "The castellan was tight lipped about the affair but his guards were not. The incident is common knowledge in the castle. It is said that the Duke misinterpreted the Earl's words."

His voice told me that he did not believe it. "You think there was no misinterpretation?"

"My lord, we have both fought alongside the Duke. We have seen a change in him over the last few years. He is loyal. The Earl of Nottingham? The man is more slippery than an eel. He opposed the King and then supported him. He was the one who killed the Duke of Gloucester, everyone knows that."

"On the orders of the King."

"Probably, lord, but the deciding factor is the quality or lack of it of the men he leads. I know them. A lord's men reflect the nature of the knight who leads them. They are treacherous to a man."

He had given me much to think about.

By the time we reached London, Parliament had decided. It was common knowledge and we heard it shouted from house to house. Parliament had decided on trial by combat. The two knights would fight and God would decide. Roger nodded, "Then it is a foregone conclusion. England's Parliament does that because they believe the Duke of Hereford. He is the better warrior."

The news was less than an hour old and we rode to the Palace of Westminster for the news would be taken there. The two men were waiting with the King. I had never seen so many men gathered at the palace. All wanted to witness this event. Had I not been so well known we would have been kept from the Great Hall. I had to leave my men outside but Tom and I managed to gain entrance. Once there I saw that it was filled with the great and the good. The Duke of Lancaster was there, standing next to his son and grandson. The Duke of Norfolk, Mowbray, stood with his supporters. The Dukes of Exeter, Surrey and York along with the Earl of Gloucester were also present. I moved to the side of Henry Bolingbroke. The throne was empty. The King was not there.

Hal looked up at me and smiled, "Sir William! You heard the news and came! My father will end the life of this snake."

His grandfather, John of Gaunt, did not look well. He coughed as he said, "Henry, God will decide."

Henry Bolingbroke was silent and he stared across the Great Hall at Mowbray. There was mutual hatred between the two Dukes. Trial by combat did not always result in death. This one would. The two had been rivals for so long that it was inevitable they would clash at some point. The buzz of conversation was like surf on a beach. The words seemed to hiss. No-one raised their voices. It was like a room of conspirators. When the King entered the hiss ceased instantly and all eyes were on him as we bowed.

He looked around the room. "Is the representative from Parliament come?"

An older knight stepped forward, "Aye lord, Sir James Beaumont. I have Parliament's decision." The King nodded. Sir James said, "Trial by combat!"

There was no surprise for we all knew the decision. The King said, "Norfolk, Hereford approach the throne." The two Dukes walked and stood before him. "This matter cannot be settled any other way?"

The Duke of Norfolk said, "My honour has been impugned. I demand satisfaction."

"And I am no liar. I will fight for my name,"

The Queen had come in with the King. She looked like the little girl she was. I had seen the King with Anne of Bohemia. They had been a very tactile couple. They had held hands. I now saw that the King had little interest in his new Queen. He patted her hand but it was in the fashion of a grandfather who has not seen a grandchild for some time. "You should not have to witness this, my dear. Go to your ladies and I will see you later." The Queen stood and we all bowed to the young girl. When she had gone, we all thought that the King was about to give the time and place for the duel. Instead he said, with a smile on his face, "We cannot allow two of our Dukes to spill blood. We forbid the duel. More, this disagreement has upset my lords and my land." That was not true as the land did not know of the disagreement. The King was playing a game. "Thomas de Mowbray, Duke of Norfolk, you are exiled for life. You return to England upon pain of death." His decree was greeted by a stunned silence. The King turned, "Cousin," he shook his head, "Henry Bolingbroke, Duke of Hereford, you are exiled from England for ten years. As surety of your good behaviour whilst abroad I keep your son, Henry of Monmouth, as my ward." He was taking Hal hostage! The King had truly changed. This was not the man who was King of England when Anne of Bohemia lived.

Hal's father dropped to one knee, "I beg you reconsider, Highness!"

"I have made my decision. Both of you are no longer Dukes of the Kingdom. Those titles are forfeit. When, cousin, your time of exile is over, we will reconsider your position. The two of you have a week to put your affairs in order. Henry, say goodbye to your father."

Hal embraced his father. Words were exchanged but they were so quietly spoken that none knew what passed between them.

"Henry, come with me, as for the rest, disperse. We have suffered your presence enough!"

Henry Bolingbroke looked to his father but the Duke of Lancaster was not a well man. He alone out of the assembled lords was the one who might have spoken out for his son but he had not. Henry Bolingbroke turned to me, "Will! You are the only one who can do this. I beg you go to the King and intercede on my behalf. Plead with him, beg him, do all that you can."

I nodded, "I will try, my lord, but I think that you overestimate my influence. Any I had died with the Queen. He is a changed man and we both know that."

"I know but I beg you try. I will be forever in your debt."

"Come Tom." I knew the palace well. I headed to the small hall the King liked to use. I recognised the guard on the door. Stephen of Andover was a good man. Somewhat dull of thought he was a reliable sergeant at arms. "Stephen, I need to speak with the King. Tell him that I wait without."

Had I not once commanded him, when he had been a young man, I think he would have sent me hence. Instead he nodded saying, "I owe you this, lord, but it may cost me my stipend." He opened the door and went inside. He was back remarkably quickly. He smiled a relieved smile, "The King will see you, lord."

When I entered, I saw that there were just two pages and a scribe along with Hal and the King. King Richard smiled. It was a genuine smile. He was pleased to see me. "You must be some sort of wizard,

Will. I was just dictating a letter to you. I was going to summon you to my side." He frowned, "You were in the Hall?"

"Aye Highness, I was here to deliver some news to the," I was about to say 'the Duke' and then stopped myself, "the Earl of Northampton."

He looked relieved, "Then you know that Henry is my ward. I would have you as his…" the word he sought was gaoler but he said, instead, "his protector. There will be those who seek to do him harm. You were once my bodyguard and I know that you have been training Henry. It will be no hardship will it?"

There were many reasons why I should have refused but far more reasons for me to agree. "Of course, Highness. Will I protect him at my manor?"

The King laughed, "I want both of you close to me! You will both be by my side at all times. This will be good for your son, Will. He can see how a great king rules this land."

I nodded, "Tom, go to Roger and tell him what has happened. Ask him to return with my war gear and clothes. It seems we will have a new home for a while." He looked up at me and, while my back was to the King, I mouthed, '*speak to Duke Henry, tell him the news.*'

Tom nodded and rushed off.

The King continued, "Will, you know your duties better than any. You and your son will share a chamber with Henry. He does not leave the confines of the castle without my permission. You may continue to train him. England will need young lords who can fight as well as you." He waved me forward, "We have heard that Louis, Duke of Orleans, plots against the father of our Queen, King Charles of France. We will need to do something about him when we have settled all the scores which remain in England. He threatens our peace. Godfrey, take our guests to their chambers. We will see you when we dine."

As we left the chamber, I put my arm around Hal's shoulders. "So long as I am here you are safe."

"But my father!"

"Is a resourceful man. This is not over. I can feel the spirit of your great grandfather, the Black Prince. He wishes me to watch over his land still."

Chapter 19

When Tom returned to us, he told us that he had told Hal's father the news. "He seemed quite happy about it, my lord. He said that so long as Will Strongstaff was by his son's side then Henry of Monmouth was safe."

"Good and now we make the best of a situation I could not have seen when I left Weedon this morning. We have little else to do and so the three of us will spend each waking moment becoming better warriors."

We had a week at the palace and then the King took his court to Shrewsbury where he summoned Parliament. There he shocked all by making the terms of the merciless parliament null and void. There would be no restraint which could be legally enforced upon the king. It delegated all parliamentary power to a committee of twelve lords and six commoners. The lords were all men recently appointed by the King. The King became, in that one parliament, the absolute ruler with no need to summon England's Parliament again. He had become a despot, a tyrant. Yet, as we rode back to London, he seemed the same man he always had been. He chatted happily to Hal and Tom. He seemed genuinely interested in their hopes and aspirations yet he was now a King with an iron fist.

We had Christmas at Windsor. I missed my family but I made the best of it for the benefit of my two charges. We had no snow and so, in the short days of December we practised still. It was February when we heard the news that John of Gaunt had died. Although he had been ill his presence had been a force for good. Had he not been ill then he might have prevented the Parliament of Shrewsbury.

We returned to London for the funeral. The Duke was buried in St. Paul's Cathedral next to his first wife, Blanche of Castile. It was a month after the funeral that we had the news that another who was seen as heir to the English throne, Roger Mortimer, was killed in Ireland. The manner of his death was suspicious for he had ridden forth in disguise, apparently, and been ambushed. Whatever the reason the King flew into a rage. He summoned the nobility of England. When assembled he told them that we would punish the Irish so that they would never rebel again. We set off for Chester. Our departure confused me for I had lived with him for many years and the King Richard who organised our Levin was not the one I had known. Strangely, the King not only took all of his nobles except for the Duke of York, he also took the crown jewels. Many thought the King was fleeing England. I knew that not to be the case. It was just that the King no longer trusted anyone. He ranted on about the Celts and their deceitful nature. He would punish the Irish once and for all.

That journey across England showed me the fawning and false nature of the senior English nobility. They agreed with all that the King said. There was no John of Gaunt to offer counsel. Whatever idea the King had was agreed upon. Once again, we sailed from Chester. We had fewer men this time but more knights and nobles. All the most powerful men in England were with us except for the Duke of Lancaster and the earls of Northumberland and Westmoreland. The Percy and Neville family kept their distance. That worried me. Hal and I sailed with the King. Hal was excited about the prospect of the war. He had yet to participate in one. Tom, slightly older and with more experience of war, deflated him, "My lord, it is not as glorious as you might think. These Irish we fight are almost barbaric. They will gut a horse just to unseat the rider. You will have to fight for your life."

I smiled at Hal's face. My son had shocked him, "Do not worry, the King will not risk you and the horses we use will be the King's." Hart was in the stables at Chester.

As we neared Dublin the King came over to speak to us. "When last I came, Will Strongstaff, it was the kings of the west who were troublesome. Now it seems that the clan from the north, the Uí Néill clan, are the ones responsible for the death of our cousin and the insurrection. We do not have as far to travel. Who knows, this may be over within the month."

He was wrong and, while we tarried in Ireland, events in France were sounding a warning for King Richard of England. His kingdom was threatened and he did not know it.

When we reached Dublin Castle Hal and I were left to fend for ourselves. The King had meetings with his lords. He needed to find out the extent of the rising against English authority. One day, as we walked down to the river, I spied some men at arms who were riding down the road. They had been on patrol. I recognised one of the sergeants. They were led by James Jameson. He had been one of the men at arms who had decided they wished to seek their fortune elsewhere. He reined in. Waving to his men he said, "Go stable the horses. I will report to the Captain of the Guard when I have spoken with their lordships."

He dismounted and I clasped his arm. When he had first come to me Hal would have been surprised at the informality but now, he took it as normal. "I am pleased that you found an employer."

He nodded, "Aye lord. I took ship back to Ireland and they needed experienced men here. I put to good use all that I learned with you. Now I command ten men. I would still rather work for you. Are the other men here?"

I shook my head, "I am here as the guard for the son of the King's cousin, Henry of Monmouth." That sounded better than gaoler.

He bowed to Hal, "Pleased to meet you, my lord. Are you here to avenge the death of the Lord Lieutenant?"

"We are. What do you know?"

"That it was strange. I was with him and we were riding towards Kells for we heard that a warband of the Uí Néill clan were raiding that land. One of the young knights of the Earl of Ulster, Sir James Fitzpatrick, suggested that they don Irish garb and scout out the Irish. Lord Roger was a game 'un, lord, and they went. They did not return and we searched for them both. We found his lordship's horse and later his body."

"And this Fitzpatrick?"

"There was no sign of him. The Earl took command and we chased the warband hence. When we found no trace of him the Earl assumed that he and his lordship's squire had been killed."

"Lord Roger did not take his squire?"

"No, my lord, Sir James said that it would be easier with just three of them."

"You think that Lord Roger was murdered."

He shook his head, "My lord, I am a sword for hire. I cannot pass judgement nor make comments. You are a clever lord. I give the information freely for I would not wish harm to fall upon you or the young lord who rides at your side. Watch your backs would be my advice."

He left us and Hal spoke to me, "I knew Lord Roger. He was a rival for the throne but I liked him. I think your man at arms is correct. He would be trusting enough to ride forth and scout. He would not believe that a fellow knight could be treacherous."

We turned and began to walk back to the castle. Suddenly this land seemed more dangerous than it had before we had spoken to James Jameson. "We will know the truth if we find the body of the Irish knight and his squire. Until then there is doubt. I will mention this to the King when we are alone."

I did not manage to find an opportunity to speak privately with King Richard until the next day. Henry, Tom and I rose early, as we normally did and the King was also breaking his fast. "Highness, if I might have a word?"

"Of course. Your chambers are to your liking?"

"We are more than comfortable. We need to have conference with you for we have learned disturbing news about your cousin, Mortimer."

He waved away the servants, "I do not know these men and do not trust them. I have also heard news. Tell me yours." When I had told him he sat back, "That confirms what I heard." He turned to me and looked afraid. "Will, there may be assassins abroad. I would have you stay close to me."

"And Henry of Monmouth?" He was next to me.

"Henry of Monmouth, I trust and your son. They can help protect the life of the King of England. Do not leave my side. I will have you given the chamber next to mine." He gave me a wan smile. "It will be as it was in Eltham save that my lovely wife will not be there." I knew without him naming her that he meant Anne. He waved over his page, "Have the Baron's gear brought to the room next to mine; your chamber."

The page nodded, "And we will move to Sir William's chamber. It shall be done."

By noon the change had been affected. As the King and his senior lords planned their offensive we were disturbed by a rider. He bowed, "My lord, the Duke of York sent me. The King of France has been imprisoned by the Duke of Orleans. The Duke of York begs you to return to England. He fears that this signals a change in the French policy towards England."

This was the moment when the Duke of Lancaster's advice would have been vital. Henry Bolingbroke, equally, could have advised him. The King looked confused and looked to his simpering lords. They looked unconcerned. The Duke of Exeter said, "What can Orleans do? He is not an anointed King. We finish this task, Highness, and then return home."

The King smiled. Their fawning would cost him his throne. "That is sage advice. It will be just the work of a week to defeat these barbarians."

His lords smiled and nodded and his fate was sealed.

When we left to head north it was three days later. As we had been instructed the three of us rode behind the King. For Hal and Tom this was a nerve-wracking time. They did not know who to watch for. I was more confident. I had done this every day when I had been the King's

Captain. The English lords who had come with us from England were not a threat. They had too much interest in keeping the King on his throne. It was the local knights I watched. The King, too, was wary of them. He had them watching the fore. He had brought a dozen of his guards with him and they rode ahead of him. It meant we were a ponderous and slow-moving blind worm. The King's guards were not scouts and those acting as scouts could be traitors. We were heading from The Pale into Ulster when we were attacked.

The men who rose like wraiths from folds in the ground and from the undergrowth were not knights. They were warriors armed with knives and swords. If I had had my men with me then they would not have even come close to doing us harm but my men were back in England. Their purpose soon became clear. They hacked at the horses of the King's guards and the local knights who were the van. Unhorsed they were easy targets. The lack of experience of those men cost them their lives.

I stood in my stirrups and shouted, as the first of our knights was slain, "To the King! To the King!" I drew my sword and pulled my shield around. I put my horse next to the King. Hal and Tom placed theirs on the other side of him. Any Irishman would have to get through us. His standard bearer, Sir Walter Effingham, rode behind the King. A handful of the attackers ran directly at me. I was not wearing the King's livery and, perhaps they thought to kill me quickly and capture the King. I pulled back on the reins of my horse and stood. The horse reared and his mighty hooves clattered on the group. The skulls of three of them were mashed to a pulp. I leaned forward and used my sword to despatch two more and the last was killed by the King himself.

His earls and dukes had heeded my cry and they galloped up to crash into the Irishmen. With all surprise gone and their plan exposed they began to flee. As the English knights began to pursue them, I saw the cleverness of the Irish plan. "Highness, call back your men!"

The King shouted, "Fall back! Fall back!" His words fell on deaf ears. The knights were oblivious to the orders and they hurtled after the ambushers.

I saw, from the west, horsemen. Irish knights were coming for us. We would not be able to defeat these with rearing horses. They came to capture the King and to reclaim their land. The ransom would be Ireland.

"We should head back down the road, Highness. Your archers can protect you."

He turned and I saw then the young King who had defied the peasants in London. He shook his head, "If I am to die this day it will be facing my enemies. But you are right. We need our archers. Tom, fetch our bowmen!"

My son did not hesitate, "Yes, King Richard." Most of the archers were afoot. They would not reach us quickly enough.

He turned and galloped through the handful of milling knights behind us. I shouted, "Protect the King!"

We had, perhaps, twenty knights and their squires with us. The rest were still galloping after the Irish who had attacked us. The knights and their squires placed their horses before us. The Irish knights were now within charging distance. They charged. Our knights and squires did the only thing they could do, they counter charged but their horses were barely moving when they struck. I saw eight of the King's men unhorsed but their bravery stopped the enemy. Hal and I, along with the King, were ready when the first knights approached us. Hal had never fought in such a mêlée. His father would curse me if he fell and yet none of this was of my doing. The Irish knight who tried to spear me had a lance. The end had already been shattered when he had unhorsed Sir William d'Aubigny. The balance from the weapon had gone. I took the blow from the spear on my shield. The broken head slewed alarmingly to my left and towards the King. I had taught him well and the monarch backed his horse away. The Irish knight wore plate and so I swung the flat of my sword at his right arm. As I did so I kicked upwards towards his horse's neck with my right foot. It was not a knightly act. Peter the Priest had taught it to me. His horse reared and the combination of the two caused him to fall from his horse. I heard a cry as he fell and broke his arm.

In the distance I could see the Earl of Gloucester leading our knights back from their fruitless chase. I was not certain they would reach us for already most of the knights and squires who had put themselves between the King and danger were unhorsed, wounded or dead. The King was fighting and I heard an Irish voice shout, "Surrender! You are surrounded!"

King Richard replied, "God is with me! He will not allow me to die in this ungodly land!"

I spurred my horse and it lunged at the knight. He was taken by surprise. As he turned to face me, I swung my sword at his head. He had no visor and, seeing the sword come for his eyes, he jerked his head back. His hands made his horse back off. My horse moved into the gap created by his movement. Hal had managed to disarm an Irish knight who turned his horse and fled. The departing knight stopped others from reaching us.

The King shouted, "Thank you cuz! That was bravely done!"

I saw that Hal was grinning. This was something for which he was born. The knight who had called upon the King to surrender came at us again with three more knights. Their intention was clear. They would kill me and capture the King and Hal, who also wore royal livery. I smiled as I pulled my shield around. I had felt the same when I had defended Sir John Chandos in Spain. The difference then was that the knight was dying, Here King Richard could defend himself. The joy of battle was upon me. I spurred my horse and shouted, "God, King Richard and England!" I surprised them by riding at them.

The leading knight thought he had the measure of me. As his sword swept towards my head, I lowered it and lunged. His sword flew over my head. The knight had a breast plate beneath his surcoat. My sword could not penetrate it but his swing had unbalanced him and my blow knocked him from his saddle. Raising my head, I stood in my stirrups and swung my sword at the back of the head of the knight who had been on my left. His helmet held and his arming cap afforded some protection but the blow was so hard that it rendered him unconscious. My horse took me deeper into the mass of Irish knights. My wild charge had unnerved them. They hesitated. All wanted the glory of capturing the King. There was no glory in falling foul of the blade of the mad knight with the staff on his chest.

I am not sure how long I would have lasted had not a bodkin tipped arrow suddenly struck the knight before me. He looked in surprise at the goose feathers which sprouted from his breastplate. The arrows were carefully aimed and, soon, more knights and their horses were struck. As the Earl of Gloucester led our knights back towards us the Irish fled. Their ambush had failed.

I did not turn my back on the Irish. I watched them fall back and turned my horse to walk back to the King. I saw that Hal was safe. He had a dented helmet but he lived. The King, too, looked whole and when I saw my son, grinning at me, then I was content.

The King had sheathed his sword and he held his arm out to me. I sheathed my own and took it. "Will Strongstaff, you have saved the life of your King, again! Right glad am I that my father chose you to be my guardian."

The Earl of Gloucester reined in, "Are you safe, Highness?"

The King snarled, "Aye and no thanks to you and the other lords who followed you. We ride to Carrickfergus Castle. Send a rider to the Uí Néills. Tell them I want to speak with them."

"Aye, King Richard."

As we headed towards the mighty castle on the shores of Lough Lee, the King turned to Hal. You earned your spurs this day. I shall dub you when we return to England."

"Thank you, King Richard. Can I ask you what you expect to happen next?"

"Aye, you can for this is how you learn. I daresay that one day you will be King of England. I have no children and it is unlikely now that I shall ever have them. Here it is: the Irish thought to ambush and capture me. That tells me that they have no stomach for a battle with the large numbers of men I have brought. Carrickfergus is a strong fortress. By summoning them there we show them our strength. I will threaten to burn their homes, their castles and their lands. We have brought every English noble save for the Duke of York. We captured twenty of their knights this day. I have no intention of tramping around this God forsaken isle. It is not worth it."

"Then we return to England."

"We do but we keep the army together and we will cross to France. If the Duke of Orleans has taken the throne of France then we can go and help King Charles to regain it. We will have the help of half of France. This is an opportunity to regain the lands lost by King John. God has saved my life and given me a new purpose."

The King had read the minds of the Irish correctly. They did not want a repeat of the battle which had conquered the west of Ireland. The King was in no mood for concessions. He demanded a huge amount of gold and hostages. The Irish might rebel again but, if they did, then their families would pay the price.

We returned to Dublin a month later. The King's strategy had worked. We now had more hostages to join the ones we had taken years earlier. Any celebrations, however, would have to wait. The Duke of Orleans had shown that he was a clever man. He had allowed Henry Bolingbroke to return to England. Hal's father had landed at Ravenspur. Was he back in England to claim the throne?

Chapter 20

When the King heard the news Hal and I were close by. King Richard looked at Henry of Monmouth and shook his head, "If I was the tyrant they all assume me to be, then I would have you executed here and now." My hand went to my sword. I could not allow that to happen. He smiled, "I am not and, besides, I have the nobles of England at my side."

The Duke of Exeter said, "Aye, King Richard! We will sail to England and join the Duke of York. We will quash this challenge to your authority!"

The King nodded and turned to Henry, "But first, before we leave, I shall dub you. Your father's actions are nothing to do with you for you have been at my side and as brave as any man!"

And so, Henry of Monmouth was knighted by King Richard while Henry's father sought to claim the throne of England. King Richard was nothing if not complicated.

There were not enough ships in the harbour. Thomas le Despenser pointed out that Henry Percy had not sailed with us and that Ralph Neville was also a supporter of Henry Bolingbroke. He suggested using half of the ships we had to ferry the bulk of the army to Chester while the King, his household knights and the crown jewels sail to Milford Haven. The King agreed for he did not wish to lose his treasure and it would be safe in his castles in South Wales. I thought it a mistake but I was a lowly knight. I was just a bodyguard. The fateful decision taken, we sailed for Wales.

As we sailed east the King was in ebullient mood. He teased Hal, now Sir Henry, "Your father risks death, you know? I banished him for ten years. He has been abroad but a single year. I hope he does not mean to take my throne and my crown."

Hal was nothing if not honest. "I cannot believe that he would seek the throne for himself. Perhaps he means to return in the hope that I might be named your heir."

The King laughed and clapped Hal about the shoulders, "Then he has chosen a strange way to do this."

I had kept silent long enough, "Highness, I think it is a mistake to head so far south without your army. Order the captain to sail to Conwy or Harlech. Both castles are strong enough for your treasure to be safe and we would be closer to your army when they arrive."

"I have five hundred men with me, Will. That should be enough. When my treasure is safe then I will go north and meet my army. The crown jewels must be kept secure! Remember what happened to King John in the Wash."

The voyage took two days. We had little idea of what was happening further north. Once we reached Milford Haven, we headed for William Marshal's castle at Pembroke. It was the most secure castle in this part of Wales. The huge circular donjon was the perfect place to keep the crown jewels safe. We wasted another two days there while King Richard tried to find out what was happening further north. The Earl of Rutland, Edward, the son of the Duke of York was the most senior lord with us. He approached the King. "Highness, let me ride ahead on the road to Chester. I would not have you ambushed again."

The King smiled, "A sound idea, Edward. It is good to have such loyal lords at my side."

I could not remain silent, "King Richard, is this wise?"

The King frowned, "Will, you are a soldier and as such I accept your advice. On the battlefield your advice would be sage but this idea has merit. You yourself advised me to have scouts kept ahead of me. What better scout than the Earl of Rutland and his men? Besides, my most loyal men are in Cheshire! With those at my side and my army from Ireland then we can quash any opposition to us."

Despite my warnings the Earl left with three hundred of the King's army. What remained to the King was less than two hundred men. Ten were knights but all were bachelor knights. I was the only banneret. Worse, the Earl had taken all of the mounted archers and men at arms. We moved at the pace of the men who walked with us. We tramped for ten long days. Each morning saw us wake to fewer men in our camp. They just drifted off. Desertion was rife. They were like rats leaving a sinking ship. They thought that the King was doomed. By the time we reached Criccieth Castle we had less than one hundred and twenty men. Those ten days saw King Richard fall into a deeper and deeper melancholy. Hal, Tom and I rode at his side and tried to raise his spirits. It was fruitless.

"Since my dear Anne was taken from me, I know not whom to trust. You, Will, have ever been loyal and, Sir Henry, you are made of nobler stock than your father. You could have slipped away in the night like so many of my base and false followers. I need Robert de Vere. This would not have happened if he had not been driven from England by my murderous Uncle Gloucester." He laughed and it was not a happy laugh. It was a mad almost maniacal laugh. "We did for him! I should have been as ruthless with all of them who plotted against me. I was too kind, Will, that was my trouble. Ask Dick of Craven." He shook his head, "Poor Dick is dead. Why do the good die young, Henry, why? My father died too young. My life would have been better had he not died. Perhaps he was lucky. If I was dead then I would be with my wife, would I not, Will?"

"Highness, do not speak that way. No one will take your life. This melancholy will pass. You have a young wife and you have a future."

"A future without a throne? Without a crown upon my head? Few English kings have ruled as long as I have! My grandfather Edward was one but there were few others. Even Richard, my namesake, ruled for just ten years. I know of no other life. The throne and the crown are all to me! Without the crown this life is not worth living."

He was silent for the rest of the day as we edged around the Llyn peninsula. With Snowdon to the east and Anglesey brooding to the west all of our spirits sank. The weight of the mighty Welsh mountain seemed to weigh down upon us. When we reached Conwy Castle on the twelfth of August, I was relieved. We had just over one hundred men with us but Conwy was one of the strongest Castles built by the first King Edward. We had barely entered the castle when we heard even more devastating news. We were met by the castellan, Sir John Fitzwalter and the Earl of Salisbury. All the King's hopes were dashed. The Earl of Rutland was not there and the Earl had news which sucked any hope which remained in the King's heart.

"King Richard, I have grave news. The Duke of York and the army you sent from Ireland have joined the Earl of Northumberland and the Earl of Northampton. They have taken Chester. You have no men left. I had to flee Chester with my household knights. This is the last castle which supports your rule."

The King flew into a rage, "I am surrounded by traitors and weak-minded fools. I will have the Earl of Rutland's head! He abandoned me! I made his father powerful. That was a mistake I will not make again! When I bring them to battle, I will be ruthless! I will heed your advice Will! I will use archers and men at arms. They are loyal to me! I won the common folk to my side at Mile End when Wat Tyler revolted. I will appeal to the people! They think I am beaten but I am not."

Henry of Monmouth showed his maturity and his character. "King Richard, it is over. Look around you. We have not enough men here to withstand an attack but my father and the other lords need do nothing. They will go to Parliament. Who do you think that an English Parliament will support, you or my father?"

Suddenly his high-handed treatment of his peers and commoners came back to haunt him. He had thought he did not need Parliament. Now he did.

He slumped into a chair, "Then what can I do?"

I saw that Henry had thought this through. He was acting for the country and for the King. The last thing England needed was a civil war. I know that, later, there were those who said he was seeking to have his father crowned. That was untrue. I was with him and we had no idea that Archbishop Arundel was the one who suggested that Henry Bolingbroke became King. "You could abdicate. You could relinquish the throne of your own volition."

King Richard looked at Henry. Abdication meant he would retain his lands and, perhaps, even his title. "And then what? Live as a prisoner for the rest of my life?" He shook his head, "Will, you have ever guided me and given me sage advice. Could we fight on?"

This was bizarre. I had been the son of a camp follower and now the King of England sought my advice. The crown and the throne were in my hands. I wished to be anywhere but in that room. Whatever I said I would be betraying someone. I had faced enemies in battle and never flinched but here I baulked at speaking. I realised that I had to give him an answer and so I answered from my heart, "King Richard, I would ride out with you and face all of your enemies even though we fought alone. We would slay many but we would die. I am willing to take that as my end and, I suspect, so are you but I cannot see others who would do that. My Lord Salisbury, would you don mail and ride with us to fight Sir Henry's father?" He hung his head and did not answer. "If we asked every man in this castle, we might find twenty or thirty who would be willing to ride and to die with us. All that it would mean is that thirty odd of us would die and you would still not have either your life or your throne." I sighed, "King Richard, I know you seek death. You wish a glorious death and then you will be reunited with your wife." The look he gave me told me that I had spoken true. "It is your choice. Do you wish your most loyal of men to die with you? If you say aye then I will arm and find others who wish such a death."

He said nothing but left the Great Hall and went to the royal chambers. Sir Henry of Monmouth said, "That was well said, my lord. I know you meant it. I am not sure that I would be able to ride into battle knowing that I would surely die."

"I made a promise to his father. What else can I do?"

The Earl of Salisbury said, "I will send a rider to Flint Castle. The Earl of Northumberland is there. He has sided with the Earl of Northampton." He shook his head, "I thought I would have fought alongside the King until you asked me the question. I hated you for asking it. Like Sir Henry I admire you for it but still cannot understand it."

Tom and I went to sit outside the King's chamber. We had promised to guard him and guard him we would. Tom was almost white, "I never thought it would come to this, father. How could the King have lost all and so quickly?"

"He was badly advised and made poor choices. It may be that the seeds of his self-destruction lay within him." I had a sudden memory. "Your grandfather was the same. He made poor choices and lost his friends but his comrades never deserted him. Even when he behaved appallingly, they stood by him. He destroyed himself in battle. At the end he redeemed himself and he saved me. The King will have no such opportunity. He does not have friends who are as loyal as the men of the Blue Company."

Six days later a rider came from the Earl of Northumberland. He invited the King to surrender himself at Flint Castle to himself and Ralph Neville, Earl of Westmoreland. The King looked a lost and lonely man. He nodded, "Henry of Monmouth, I release you. You could have left at any time and you showed great honour for you stayed. You are noble. Return to your father. I hope that he shows me mercy."

"King Richard, others may speak badly of you but I will not for you have shown me nothing but kindness. I swear that I will still be as Sir William here and be your protector. None shall lay a finger on you. That is my pledge."

The King nodded, "And you, Will Strongstaff, will you come with me to Flint? If you, too, abandoned me then I would not blame you."

I smiled, "King Richard, I have never abandoned a friend in my life and I shall not do so with the King of England. I shall ride at your side until you tell me to leave."

We left for Flint. Henry and the remaining men at arms and archers left us to go to Chester where his father waited.

Archbishop Arundel was with the Earl at Flint. The Archbishop had been with Henry Bolingbroke in exile. The two men were no friends of the King. Henry Percy said, "Richard Plantagenet, it is the will of all of your lords that you abdicate the crown and surrender yourself to Parliament."

The King's eyes flashed, "So that I may be dragged on a hurdle and abused by the rabble of London? I think not! Would you spill the blood of an anointed King? Would my cousin Bolingbroke? I do not think so. His own position would become parlous indeed. I want guarantees."

"Guarantees?"

"Archbishop, you will bear witness." He turned to the Earl. "Henry Percy, I would have you swear on the Holy Sacraments that no harm will come to me and I will retain both my freedom and my title."

The Earl paled for this was the most sacred of oaths. Eventually he nodded, "I so swear."

"Archbishop, you witnessed the swearing." Arundel nodded. "More importantly, someone I trust witnessed it. Sir William Strongstaff will testify if there is treachery!"

We rode to Chester. There we were greeted by the Duke of York and the other lords who had abandoned the King. He had given them all their titles and none could look him in the eye. Henry Bolingbroke was the exception.

"Well cuz, I am sorry that it came to this. You banished me when all that I did was to watch out for you. I reported treason and you banished me. I had no desire to take your crown! I would have been content had you made my son your named heir. Then I would have fought at your side. Then I would have defended you with my life."

The King sighed, "And what happens now?"

"We ride to London and there, Parliament will decide. The lords here gathered wish me to be King of England. I am ready to sit upon the throne."

The King pointed an accusing finger at Henry Percy, "The Earl of Northumberland has sworn an oath that my life will be spared and I will retain my title."

The Earl nodded, "Your life is safe. I swear that none shall take your life but as for your title and estates? That is up to Parliament."

The King turned to me. On his left hand he had a ring with a blue stone. His wife Anne had given it to him on the occasion of one of his birthdays whilst at Eltham. He took the ring from his finger. "I have little left to give you, Will Strongstaff, but I give you this for it is precious to me and it shows how much I owe to you. You are the only one, save Henry of Monmouth, who has not betrayed me." His eyes glared around the assembled lords. "I now free you from your oath. Take Tom here and return to your family. I am King in name only. He unbuckled his sword from his belt and handed it to Tom. "Here, this sword and scabbard are yours. I would not have the carrion fight over it once I am gone, I would rather it went to a true warrior with a heart which was not craven!"

Tom took it, "Thank you, Highness."

I went to the King and put my arms around him. I embraced him. There was a time when that would have resulted in my death. Now he hugged me back. I said, in his ear, "If you have need of me, for any purpose, then send word and I will be at your side. Nothing shall stop me."

When I stepped back, I saw that tears coursed down his cheeks, "My wife was right, you are the best of men and I should have aspired to be more like you. Farewell, Will."

"Farewell, lord." As I turned, I looked Henry Percy, the Earl of Northumberland, in the eye, "And know this, my lord, I was there to witness your oath. Do not break it or you shall risk my wrath!"

The room was shocked. Henry Bolingbroke said, "Sir William, let us not create animosity."

My voice was cold, "My lord, I know that you did not betray the King but in this room are others who did. I do not forget and any who makes an enemy of me had better ensure that they do not betray you or Henry of Monmouth. I am a hard man to kill! Many have tried and few have succeeded."

I dared, with my eyes, any to challenge me but they all lowered their gaze. None had the courage to face me with bared sword. I saw hatred in the eyes of Henry Percy as he looked away from me. I had made an enemy of him. I cared not.

Tom and I left Chester and headed home. I was sick of the lords of England. I wanted to be back with my men. They had more nobility than any of the lords I had just left. Tom and I rode most of the way in silence. We spoke of the King's gifts and of the way he was treated but we did not do so when others were listening. It was as we neared Weedon that my son spoke his fears out loud. "Father, we have made an enemy of the Earl of Northumberland and those other lords. Are you not afraid?"

"I am not afraid for they are cowards all. Mowbray had courage for he would have fought a duel with Henry Bolingbroke. If they had had courage and honour, they would have challenged me in Chester. They did not."

"Why?"

"They thought I would beat them. A duel is a test of skill and courage. It is not like a battlefield where accidents and fate can intervene. It is truly in God's hands."

That first week at home saw both Tom and I reluctant to talk. We had witnessed something momentous. We had seen the end of a King's rule. We told my family what we could and I spoke with my men. They had liked the King and were as saddened as I was. They could not understand how he had been abandoned. They were happy that Hal had been knighted. They liked him.

We heard, in early October, that Parliament had deposed Richard and Henry was to be crowned King. We heard it from Henry of Monmouth who rode to my manor to tell me personally. "I am also here to tell you, my lord, that you will not be invited to the coronation."

I smiled, "I did not expect an invite."

"But I did! And my father wanted you there. Without you neither of us would be in the position we are."

"I did nothing to undermine King Richard!"

"No, my lord and we know that. Had you been invited then there would have been trouble. You upset too many lords in Chester. They seek your life. There is already likely to be trouble soon after the ceremony."

"Why, my lord?"

He sighed and lowered his voice, "I can speak openly for I know you are trustworthy. My father plans to take back the titles and lands which Richard gave to Thomas le Despenser, the Earl of Huntingdon and Kent and Edward son of the Duke of York. He believes they betrayed the King."

"And King Richard?"

"Is secure in the royal apartments in the Tower. He is safe from those who would wish him harm." He paused, "All save himself. My cousin Richard is now his own worst enemy."

Now I understood. "Thank you for taking the time to tell me, my lord. Know that I will happily serve both you and your father should you need me."

"And the same goes for you. I have heard that Percy and Neville still rankle about the comments you made. My father has warned them that he will not condone duels and so they are contained but we thought you should be warned."

I nodded, "I do not worry about border raiders who live far to the north but I thank you."

When he had left, I threw myself into the task of running four manors. In the first month I rode with my men at arms and Tom to see that all was done well. Harold Four Fingers had proved himself to be an able Reeve and Sir John was more than happy. More importantly Sir John had met the daughter of one of the merchants in Dauentre, Richard of Blecheley. Blanche was a beauty and John was happy. As a bachelor knight he needed my permission to marry. I gave it to him and also the manor of Stony Stratford as a wedding present. My wife was happy for Dauentre yielded us far more riches than our first manor.

It was in late November that word came to us that Red Ralph was ill, possibly dying. His son came to tell me that he wished to speak with me. I took Ralph with us as well as Tom, six archers and my men at arms. They all liked Red Ralph and insisted upon accompanying me. The weather was atrocious and our mood sombre. I could have stayed in Middleham Castle but it was a Neville castle and they were friends of the Percy family.

When I saw him I was shocked. Red Ralph looked like a skeleton. His wife tried to be brave but I knew that she was holding back tears for the sake of her family. Outside his room she said, "He has hung on, my lord, just to speak with you. He is in great pain. I do not know why he has not died already. He has been shriven. Heaven knows he is in no condition to commit any more sins."

His eyes opened as soon as his eldest son and I walked in, "You came! I knew that you would." He tried to smile. "And your company too. I am honoured." My men, those who wished to say farewell, came in with me one by one. Each said their goodbyes and left.

When they had gone and there was just Tom and Ralph in the room I sat on his bed and took his hands in mine. They were icy despite the fact that his wife had a good fire burning. "I came as soon as you sent for me but you have been ill for some time. Why did you not send earlier?"

"I asked you to come but not to see me die. I will just slip away quietly. I have news for you. I needed to tell you that there is a price on your head. Men come here to buy horses. Some are less than honest men." He inclined his head, "I take money where I can. One knew that I knew you and he warned me that when he had been in Northumberland there were men being hired to kill the Baron of Dauentre."

"Who was hiring them?"

"He knew not. It could have been Scots. They still wish vengeance for the war you made on them but it could equally be the Percy family. The Earl has made no secret of the hatred he bears you."

I waved my hand, "That matters not. I will deal with threats later. What matters is you."

"Thank you. Those in the Blue Company all felt as though you were our son. For Peter and Tom, you still are. I now have Ralph and my own children. I pray you watch over Ralph."

"You know that I will." I saw that Ralph was already weeping. When we had ridden north his brother had told him how ill his father was but neither expected him to look as he did. He was like a corpse already. Red Ralph's eyes closed and I thought he had gone. Then he opened them and tried to smile at me. "Red Ralph, you are as true a friend as I ever had. Each year on this day we will hold a feast and my men and I will remember a great warrior. I will say farewell now for you need your family with you,"

He tried to squeeze my fingers. "Will, you are family. Farewell."

Tom and I left the chamber. His wife and the other children were waiting, "I think, Mistress Mary, that his time is almost come. I have said my farewells."

His family all went into the chamber and I joined Tom before the fire. Red Ralph's words had worried me. I was not afraid for myself but I had put his family in danger. I took Tom and went to the barn, "Roger of Chester, there are men who seek to end my life. I fear they may try something here. They are either Scots or the men of the Percy family. We had best keep watch."

"Aye lord. We will watch!"

Red Ralph died in the middle of the night. He was surrounded by his family and he appeared to be content. He was buried two days later in Middleham at the Church of Saints Mary and Alkelda. The lord of the manor sent his steward to represent the family. As a Neville he would not risk a meeting with me. As was the way in the north the death was celebrated, that evening, by drinking, eating and remembering Ralph's life. It was good. We had smiles on our faces for Red Ralph was a good man and he had loved life and his family. The world had lost someone worth mourning.

The result was that we did not leave his farm until mid-morning. My enemies found us to the south of Middleham. The twisting road we rode was a perfect place for ambush. It might have succeeded had I not had Alan of the Wood leading my archers. He had liked Red Ralph and wished to see him before he died. His senses worked quicker than any and he had his sword out and was shouting, "Ambush!" before any of us realised there were enemies. He rode towards a stand of bushes. His archers slipped from their horses and strung their bows. Roger of Chester galloped after Alan.

Drawing my sword, I looked for enemies. I heard a shout from the shrubs and then the hired men poured from cover. There were no nobles. These were men who had either been bandits or men at arms. They knew their business. Hart whinnied and I turned as eight of them sprang from cover close by and ran towards Tom, myself and Ralph. I whipped Hart's head around. I slashed at the head of one man. As my sword grated across his skull another grabbed Hart's reins and pulled my horse down. I had fallen from a horse before and, as I went down, I kicked my feet from my stirrups and rolled free. An axe came for my body as I lay on the ground. King Richard's sword split the axeman's head in twain. My son had saved my life.

As I stood, I heard Ralph shout, "Sir William is down! Rally!"

I was in a dell and there were five men coming towards me. Another two had hurled themselves at Tom and Ralph. My son and Sir John's squire, Ralph, were fighting for their lives. I was alone. I took out my ballock dagger and faced the five. None of my opponents had a long sword and that gave me my only advantage. I swept mine before me to keep them at bay. Behind me I heard a crash and a whinny as a horse was brought down. Two of the men suddenly ran to my left and right. They were trying to outflank me. I ran at the other three. I hacked with my sword at the head of one while I ripped up my dagger at a second. I felt a blade slice across the bicep of my left arm as my sword continued its swing and hacked into the skull of one of them. My dagger drove up into the groin of another. More men were coming towards me. The man who had sliced my arm shouted in triumph and I brought my knee up into his groin. I whirled, blindly, with my sword. I connected with a blade and I turned. Men still came after me. There were two and a third who was bent double. I saw that one had an axe. He was the most dangerous. I feinted with my dagger and he swung his axe. It committed him to a blow. Once started he could not undo it. My sword entered his throat.

I heard a shout, "Ware behind, lord!" Then I heard the twang of a bow and the man who had been about to slice into my back fell. In turning, the edge of my sword had hacked across the thigh of the man I had kneed in the groin. He fell to the ground. It was a deep wound. It bled heavily. I whirled around, seeking more enemies. They were dead or were trying to flee. Alan of the Wood had been wounded. The arrow which had saved me had come from Stephen the Tracker. Ralph and Tom walked towards me. They lived but I saw the body of John Bowland. The axeman I had slain had killed him first. His head lay next to his body.

I knelt next to the man who had been wounded in the thigh. He was pressing his hands against the wound to stem the flow of blood. "Who sent you?"

"Go to hell!"

His accent was a northern one. I could not differentiate between Northumberland and Scotland. "I can end your pain if you tell me the name of your paymaster."

His answer was to spit a bloody gob of phlegm at me. Then he raised his hands and blood flowed freely, "You are a dead man walking!" His head lolled to the side and he died.

I shook my head and stood. Roger of Chester had come to join me and witnessed his end. "He was a hard man, lord."

"What have you found?"

"Ralph says that their clothes could come from north or south of the border. They have, in their purses Scottish and English coins."

"It may be two men. The Earl of Fife and Northumberland might have combined. Ralph, fetch Hart. We will ride to York and tell the Sherriff. He can deal with the bodies."

Roger nodded, "We will keep watch. These men would not be cheap to hire. If it was not for Alan they would have succeeded. We can keep watch for men from the north."

I nodded, "This is not over. I thought that when King Richard was deposed then we would have peace. It seems I was wrong."

Roger nodded towards Tom and Ralph, "Aye lord but now we have two more warriors and your enemies had best watch out. They have the old fox to fight and he has two good cubs! The Black Prince chose a good bodyguard for his son!"

Epilogue

It was February when a rider came from the King. I was summoned to the Tower of London. I wondered what I had done wrong. I had kept close to home since the attack. We had heard news of the King but it seemed remote now that I was back in my manor. The plots and conspiracies seemed a lifetime away. King Henry was ruling with authority. He had, at the moment, the backing of Parliament although, from what I had heard, his enemies were circling. For once this was not my problem. Once he became King then Henry Bolingbroke was no longer my liege lord. I owed him duty as King but not landlord. I knew not who that would be. Perhaps his son.

It was his son, now titled Henry, Prince of Wales, who greeted me. The Tower had changed a great deal since I had been Captain of the Guard. There were more towers and it was better defended. That had been the legacy of Richard. I dismounted in the inner bailey. There were now more buildings and there were more sentries. King Henry was being careful.

"I am pleased you came, my lord. I was sorry to hear of the death of Ralph's father. I know you were close once."

"Prince Henry, once you have fought in a shield wall with a warrior then there is no such thing as once. You are like brothers until the day you die. It is months since I saw you but I am still pleased to see that you are well and I rejoice in that fact."

"Being with you, Sir William, has made me a better man."

"Your father wished to see me?"

"Come, he can explain better than I." The King had been informed of our arrival and he met us on the second floor where there were royal chambers. At one time the King had occupied them but there was now a whole building in the inner bailey which were the new royal apartments. They were more comfortable. His voice was hushed as he spoke, "I am pleased you came. Inside is Richard, King Richard. He is dying." My eyes darted to look into his. He held up his hands, "It was not my doing. He has refused food and is starving himself to death. He asked to speak with you. I must warn you that he rambles. Sometimes he speaks to his dead wife, Anne."

I nodded and he opened the door. I had seen the skeleton that was Red Ralph. King Richard had even less flesh on him. I walked to the bed and he opened his eyes. When he spoke it was as a croak. "You came."

"As I said I would. What is this foolishness, highness? You should eat."

He shook his head. I could see that the effort pained him, "I have a plan. I would be with my Anne once more." He looked to the side and spoke as though his Queen was in the room with us, "I am telling Will, my love. You like Will. He is loyal and does not stab his friends in the back." The effort was too much and his eyes closed. I thought he was dead. I could feel that the King, his son and Tom were, like me, afraid to breathe. His eyes opened, "I go to God with a clear conscience. I did my duty for my country. I want you as witness. I forgive Henry Bolingbroke, my cousin. Despite what others wanted he did not have me killed. I forgive him for I wanted him to kill me. I understand why he did not. As for the others? None are forgiven. I hope they rot in hell for having abandoned me." He sighed, "Prince Henry, when you are King keep this man as close to you as your armour. You will live. Listen to him and heed his words for they are sage. I did not and I pay the price. Will, farewell."

I was about to answer when I heard the sigh of death as he expired. King Richard was dead. Rumours abounded that he lived still while others were convinced that he was murdered. I knew the truth. Any foul play happened long before he starved himself to death in the Tower of London.

The King was dead! Long live the King!

The End

Glossary

Ballock dagger or knife- a blade with two swellings next to the blade
Begawan- a metal plate to protect the armpit
Chevauchée- a raid by mounted men
Cuisse- metal greaves
Danczik-Danzig/Gdańsk
Dauentre-Daventry
Galoches- Clogs
Hovel- a simple bivouac used when no tents were available
Medeltone Mowbray -Melton Mowbray
Mêlée- a medieval fight between knights
Poleyn- a metal plate to protect the knee
Pursuivant- the rank below a herald
Rondel dagger- a narrow bladed dagger with a disc at the end of the hilt to protect the hand
Sallet bascinet- medieval helmets of the simplest type: round with a neck protector
Sennight- Seven nights (a week)
The Pale- the land around Dublin. It belonged to the Kings of England.

Historical Notes

This is a work of fiction. Most of the events really happened. The duel, the parliaments, Bolingbroke's landing at Ravenspur and the King's strange decision to sail to England without his knights are all facts. I have made up other incidents to suit my story. Roger Mortimer did don Irish garb and ride alone towards the Irish. His death was inexplicable. I have given an explanation. The King did go to Ireland but, as far as I know, no attempt was made upon his life.

I have tried to make sense of King Richard II who was a complicated man. Some modern writers call him bi-polar. Certainly, his wife, Anne of Bohemia, was the greatest influence for good. However, this story is really about the ordinary folk of England. The archers and sergeants. William Strongstaff represents those people and it is his story which I tell. Queen Anne did die of the plague at Sheen Manor. It changed the King. After he returned from Ireland, he began the tyranny which Shakespeare wrote of. I think it stemmed from his wife's death. I think it induced a kind of madness. Ukmergė was destroyed in the Baltic crusade. Henry Bolingbroke did take women and children to Königsberg (now Kaliningrad, Russia).

When the King banished Henry Bolingbroke he took Henry of Monmouth as his ward. He did knight him and, even though he knew that Henry's father had landed he did nothing to harm the future Henry V. I have changed some events for the sake of my story but the key facts are historical. There were many stories as to why King Richard abdicated. I have not used those. No one knows and I have created one which sounded plausible to me.

Isabella of Valois returned to her father. She was still a child. King Richard died in Pontefract Castle. I have moved his death to London for the simple reason that Henry IVth was there and rumours abounded, for many years, that the King had killed Richard.

For the English maps, I have used the original Ordnance survey maps. Produced by the army in the 19th century they show England before modern developments and, in most cases, are pre-industrial revolution. Produced by Cassini they are a useful tool for a historian. I also discovered a good website http: orbis.stanford.edu. This allows a reader to plot any two places in the Roman world and if you input the mode of transport you wish to use and the time of year it will calculate how long it would take you to travel the route. I have used it for all of my books up to the eighteenth century as the transportation system was roughly the same. The Romans would have travelled more quickly!

Books used in the research:

- The Tower of London -Lapper and Parnell (Osprey)
- English Medieval Knight 1300-1400-Gravett
- The Castles of Edward 1 in Wales- Gravett
- Norman Stone Castles- Gravett
- The Armies of Crécy and Poitiers- Rothero
- The Armies of Agincourt- Rothero
- Henry V and the conquest of France- Knight and Turner
- Chronicles in the Age of Chivalry-Ed. Eliz Hallam
- English Longbowman 1330-1515- Bartlett
- Northumbria at War-Derek Dodds
- Henry V -Teresa Cole
- The Longbow- Mike Loades
- The Scandinavian Baltic Crusades 1100-1500
- Crusader Castles of the Teutonic Knights (1)- Turnbull and Dennis
- Crusader Castles of the Teutonic Knights (2)- Turnbull and Dennis
- Teutonic Knight 1190-1561- Nicolle and Turner

For more information on all of the books then please visit the author's web site at http://www.griffhosker.com where there is a link to contact him.

Griff Hosker
January 2019

Other books by Griff Hosker

If you enjoyed reading this book, then why not read another one by the author?

Ancient History

The Sword of Cartimandua Series (Germania and Britannia 50 A.D. – 128 A.D.)
Ulpius Felix- Roman Warrior (prequel)
Book 1 The Sword of Cartimandua
Book 2 The Horse Warriors
Book 3 Invasion Caledonia
Book 4 Roman Retreat
Book 5 Revolt of the Red Witch
Book 6 Druid's Gold
Book 7 Trajan's Hunters
Book 8 The Last Frontier
Book 9 Hero of Rome
Book 10 Roman Hawk
Book 11 Roman Treachery
Book 12 Roman Wall
Book 13 Roman Courage

The Aelfraed Series (Britain and Byzantium 1050 A.D. - 1085 A.D.
Book 1 Housecarl
Book 2 Outlaw
Book 3 Varangian

The Wolf Warrior series (Britain in the late 6th Century)
Book 1 Saxon Dawn
Book 2 Saxon Revenge
Book 3 Saxon England
Book 4 Saxon Blood
Book 5 Saxon Slayer
Book 6 Saxon Slaughter
Book 7 Saxon Bane
Book 8 Saxon Fall: Rise of the Warlord
Book 9 Saxon Throne

Book 10 Saxon Sword

The Dragon Heart Series
Book 1 Viking Slave
Book 2 Viking Warrior
Book 3 Viking Jarl
Book 4 Viking Kingdom
Book 5 Viking Wolf
Book 6 Viking War
Book 7 Viking Sword
Book 8 Viking Wrath
Book 9 Viking Raid
Book 10 Viking Legend
Book 11 Viking Vengeance
Book 12 Viking Dragon
Book 13 Viking Treasure
Book 14 Viking Enemy
Book 15 Viking Witch
Book 16 Viking Blood
Book 17 Viking Weregeld
Book 18 Viking Storm
Book 19 Viking Warband
Book 20 Viking Shadow
Book 21 Viking Legacy
Book 22 Viking Clan

The New World

Blood on the Blade
Across the Seas

The Norman Genesis Series
Hrolf the Viking
Horseman
The Battle for a Home
Revenge of the Franks
The Land of the Northmen
Ragnvald Hrolfsson
Brothers in Blood
Lord of Rouen
Drekar in the Seine
Duke of Normandy

The Anarchy Series England 1120-1180
English Knight
Knight of the Empress
Northern Knight
Baron of the North
Earl
King Henry's Champion
The King is Dead
Warlord of the North
Enemy at the Gate
The Fallen Crown
Warlord's War
Kingmaker
Henry II
Crusader
The Welsh Marches
Irish War
Poisonous Plots
The Princes' Revolt
Earl Marshal

Border Knight 1182-1300
Sword for Hire
Return of the Knight
Baron's War
Magna Carta
Welsh Wars
Henry III

Lord Edward's Archer
Lord Edward's Archer

Struggle for a Crown 1360- 1485
Blood on the Crown
To Murder A King
The Throne

Modern History

The Napoleonic Horseman Series

Book 1 Chasseur a Cheval
Book 2 Napoleon's Guard
Book 3 British Light Dragoon
Book 4 Soldier Spy
Book 5 1808: The Road to A Coruña
Waterloo

The Lucky Jack American Civil War series
Rebel Raiders
Confederate Rangers
The Road to Gettysburg

The British Ace Series
1914
1915 Fokker Scourge
1916 Angels over the Somme
1917 Eagles Fall
1918 We will remember them
From Arctic Snow to Desert Sand
Wings over Persia

Combined Operations series 1940-1945
Commando
Raider
Behind Enemy Lines
Dieppe
Toehold in Europe
Sword Beach
Breakout
The Battle for Antwerp
King Tiger
Beyond the Rhine
Korea

Other Books
Carnage at Cannes (a thriller)
Great Granny's Ghost (Aimed at 9-14-year-old young people)
Adventure at 63-Backpacking to Istanbul

For more information on all of the books then please visit the author's web site at www.griffhosker.com where there is a link to contact him.